2025

"The Guardian"

Help us not
To be deceived but
to overcome.
Sylvia Burke

S.D. Burke

PRESS

I would like to dedicate **2025** to my children—Julie, Jeff, Jodie, Janie, Jonathan & Jennifer, their spouses Barry, Eric, Laurie and Kerry and to my ten grandchildren who will live in the days of 2025. May God keep you as the apple of His eye.

To The Reader

The disciples asked Jesus to tell them about the last days and about His second coming.

In Matthew 24, Jesus assures them that no one knows the date of His return, not the Son or the angels but only Father God. He counsels them to be alert, be ready, and be engaged in the work God has assigned to them.

In Matthew 25, Jesus shares the parable of the Ten Virgins. What we learn is this: The bridegroom (Christ) does not come as soon as expected. All ten virgins fall asleep. Half the virgins run out of oil in their lamps, weary of waiting.

Today, many Christians believe they will not be present for the last seven years before Christ returns...the years of tribulation. I hope they are right, but if Jesus doesn't come as soon as expected and evil gains control, will we be prepared for difficult times? Will our personal relationship with Jesus be like fresh oil burning brightly in a lamp or will we be caught off guard, unprepared to take up the sword of the Spirit which is the Word of God, and stay the course until His return?

What will happen to those who do not recognize God, who think the Bible is outdated and who live their lives according to man's morality?

In 2025, we are thrust into the world of a family facing these questions.

The American president, a president of radical change, designs his own government. His goal is to join America to a global world government with a cashless economy and a one world religious system. Is America ready to bury its constitutional rights for personal freedom of religion and other life choices?

Are you?

Acknowledgments

A special thanks to my husband, George, a former U.S. Marine, who advised me on military customs and encouraged me in the writing of *2025: The Guardian.* Thanks also to our son, Jon, who served as a captain in the Army stationed in Bosnia, Germany and other European locations for his insight and experience in modern military techniques and who taught me about Shotokan jujitsu.

In the seven years it took me to write 2025, many friends from NY to CA urged me to keep on keeping on. A special thanks to my Three Rivers, Michigan friends Phyllis, Liz, Linda, Tabitha, and the girls in our Summer Community Bible Study. And thanks to my dear friend Carol, a writer and high school friend of fifty plus years.

Thanks also to Jewell Johnson and the Fountain Hills Christian Writers Group for their fellowship and encouragement.

And last but certainly not least, a special thank you to my editors: Jodie Burke and Donna Goodrich.

Writing is a solitary effort, but I appreciate the excellent Christian writers conferences that helped me learn the craft of writing: Jerry Jenkins "Writing for the Soul" Conference, Glorietta Writers Conferences in Glorietta, New Mexico, and the American Christian Writers conferences in Phoenix.

Special appreciation for all four of Kay Arthur's wonderful inductive studies on The Revelation, and 1 & 2 Thessalonians and to Peggy our faithful leader. Thanks, too, for Beth Moore's studies on Daniel and The Revelation. All of these studies inspired and caused me to wonder

WHAT IF JESUS DOESN'T RETURN UNTIL...

Prologue

Phoenix —Sept. 11, 2022

"Ladies and gentlemen," the guide's voice interrupted. "There seems to be a problem with the transport's cooling system. I'd like to tell you to open your windows, but they are sealed. I'm sorry for your discomfort; we are forty minutes from our destination in Sedona. Hopefully, the system will correct itself as we travel."

"Danny, how many people are in this Ascension?" Penny asked.

"I don't know, Pen." Daniel glanced at his sister whose overheated face warned of trouble.

"I don't feel so good, Danny. I can't breathe very well."

"Close your eyes, Pen, try to relax." With eighty people sharing the air, the transport would soon become a cooker. Daniel wiped the sweat from his forehead and leaned back, listening to the guide's voice drone on.

"On the east side of the transport you can see Montezuma's Well with cliff dwellings of the ancient Sinagua who disappeared in the 1400s. The Sinagua wouldn't live in Sedona because they believed the gods made their home there. Just ahead you'll see Bell Rock, the first of the red rock mountains—behind it, Courthouse Rock."

Daniel kicked the footrest on his seat. *Wake up people. This isn't a sightseeing trip. It's the Ascension, whatever that is.*

A thousand questions pelted his brain. What was the Ascension's real purpose and why were people just accepting it? Why did his mother think she was about to witness the most heroic and historic event in her lifetime and he just felt something was terribly wrong? He studied his dad slumped in his seat and staring out the window, tight-lipped and solemn.

"Why didn't we drive our own car?" Penny whined. "It's so hot. I really think I'm going to die from the heat, Danny."

"No choice, Pen. All the families of people in the Ascension ride the transports, courtesy of the president."

"It sucks," Penny's lips curved into a pout.

The transport reached the outdoor amphitheater located in a valley on the western side of Sedona. The perspiring riders stumbled into the cool mountain air.

"Sorry folks, I'll order another transport," the guide said. "Be careful now. Take my arm."

Daniel's head throbbed. "Are you all right, Pen?"

"I … I think I'm going to throw up."

Daniel steered her over to a huge trash can where his sister deposited her breakfast.

"Feel better?"

"A little."

The guide continued to shout instructions over the crowd. "The president will not be attending. He will address you, your loved ones and the nation by satellite. Come back to the loading area for a buffet reception after the Ascension before the transports return to Phoenix."

Pickets swarmed the area of the transports shouting obscenities. Signs read: Right to Live! $ for Life?, Hitler Reigns. Daniel grabbed Penny's hand, pulling her through the picketers. Trying to catch up with their parents, he led Penny down the stone steps of the amphitheater.

The melancholy notes of the Native American flute player snaked their way into Daniel's subconscious, grating on his nerves like the screeching of a coyote. He shuddered.

In the orchestra pit below the stage, members of the Phoenix Symphony—dressed in tuxedos and long black dresses—tuned their instruments. Two giant television screens, suspended like blind eyes on either side of the stage, awaited President Blackstone's first Ascension speech to the world.

Daniel looked around. *Where were his grandparents?* "Back in a minute, Pen." He wormed his way in and out of the rows and up the stairs. From the top of the amphitheater, he spotted the white-robed Ascension participants behind the stage. A row of Guardians formed a human fence, protecting the group from spectators.

Daniel walked to the end of the blockade and slipped around the last soldier surprised to see children in wheelchairs, also in white robes. A little girl about seven cried loudly, her sobs echoing through the amphitheater. As Daniel watched, a silver-haired woman leaned over and put her arms around the frightened girl. Grandma! Daniel hurried to the couple not knowing what to say. "Gramps, Gram." Grandpa gave him a hug. Grandma Jenny kissed his forehead.

"Why is the government doing this?" Daniel asked.

"I don't know, Danny," said Grandpa. "Perhaps they are trying to save our economy, too many old and sick people."

"But don't people understand or care?"

"I'm sure some do, but most are afraid. Talk to your father." Seeing the anxiety on Daniel's face, Grandpa added, "It's all right, Danny. Grandma and I enjoyed our life. We're ready to go home to God." Grandpa slipped something into Daniel's hand and whispered, "Remember,

Danny, remember." Grandpa's blue eyes showed no fear, only sadness.

Daniel looked at the worn arrowhead Grandpa had placed in his hand, then, he slid it into his jean pocket. *Remember what, Grandpa?*

A Guardian signaled Daniel to leave. As he climbed the stone steps back to his seat, he saw Guardians restrain the picketers, preventing them from entering the amphitheater. As he watched, the Guardians drew stun guns and shoved the rioters onto transports. Daniel rejoined his family. Dad sat stiffly on the edge of the stone ledge, a frown carving lines in his leathered face. Mysteriously relaxed, his mother whispered something to Penny.

The satellite hookup crackled and the television screens came to life showing President Blackstone in the Oval Office. He cleared his throat, smoothed his dark blue necktie and began,

"On this historic occasion, I would like to thank the first people of the Ascension and their families for their sacrifice. There is no greater love than to lay down your life for your country. God will bless you for your sacrifice and America will count you heroes and patriots."

Chapter One

Phoenix: 7 p.m. May 2022

Daniel Jordan turned his foot, skillfully trapped the soccer ball, blasting it through his friend Joey's legs as Joey dived to block it.

"Dude, you're killing me. And you killed the ball." Joey pointed to a zigzag tear in the soccer ball. "That had to be a 100-mile-an-hour kick. It's just me, DJ…Joey. It's practice, remember? We're trying to keep limber and stay in shape." Joey slumped onto the grass breathing hard. "Wanna talk about it?"

Daniel focused on the sun setting behind the mountains of their old high school soccer field. Newly graduated from the all-sports Desert Mountain High School, he and Joey were out of school for the summer. "You accepting the school's nomination to try for the Guardians?"

"You and I were the only two who got it." Joey lay on his back trying to catch his breath, sweat rolling down his body with the 104 degree heat.

"You didn't answer my question."

Joey rolled over. "I haven't figured it out yet. Is that what's eating you?"

"Maybe. How do you make a decision you know will change everything for the rest of your life?"

"What do you wanna do?"

Daniel squatted down, rolling the soccer ball between his hands. "I've wanted to play pro soccer my whole life." His voice trailed off. "I thought it was a good dream."

"Someone telling you it's not?"

Daniel looked down. "My mom."

Joey's eyes darkened. "What's wrong with parents, Daniel? Why can't they just let us live our own lives?"

Daniel realized Joey must be going through the same thing. "You, too?"

"Yeah, morning, noon and night…"

"Still want to be a vet?" asked Daniel.

Joey nodded.

"Got a summer job?"

"I'm working for Doc Winters. He's going to let me assist him with minor stuff."

"Cool."

"Will you be working on the ranch?"

"Yeah, tourist season's almost over. We gotta build a couple new cabins and replace some fencing."

The boys walked slowly to Joey's sun-faded Jeep. Daniel unrolled the towel around his water bottle and took a gulp, then toweled his wet hair. "Want some?"

"No, got my own." Joey took a long drink, squirting the remaining water over his face and head. He reached under his seat, pulled out the car keys and started the engine. The old Jeep coughed and sputtered but finally caught its breath and roared.

"I hope she doesn't die before we get home."

By the time Joey dropped Daniel at the ranch, it was almost 9 p.m. "See you later, Big Guy." Joey peeled out of the drive, stopped and leaned out his window, "If you need to get away from your mom, call me, we'll do something."

The light in his mom's office signaled she was working late on the books for the guest ranch, paying bills and figuring out the profit for the year.

"Daniel, is that you?"

Why hadn't he taken off his cleats? Not in the mood to get beat up in a confrontation, he held his breath hoping she'd think he'd gone to his room. He loved his mom, but in the last few weeks, she'd been a real pain.

"I'd like to talk to you."

"Not tonight, Mom. I'm tired." He walked on, hoping to get out of the range of her voice.

"Tired from what, Daniel, kicking your little soccer ball?" She stood in the hall with her hands on her hips ready for battle. A frown knit her eyebrows together. Her lips formed a tight line.

Reluctantly, Daniel followed her to the office.

"You have to file your applications." She pushed her half glasses down looking over the top. "If you don't, you'll have no opportunities for fall."

"I'm not ready to make a decision, Mom."

"Ready or not, it's time. And I'm not going to let you throw away an opportunity of a lifetime."

"The Guardian nomination? Or my opportunity to play professional soccer?"

"The Guardians could be a steppingstone to life in our new government," Judith countered. "Wouldn't you like to be part of that? Don't you want your life to have real meaning?"

"It's a paramilitary corps, Mom. They don't fight terrorists. I don't even know what they do!"

"Tonight I watched the news with your father. The president called the Guardians his arms and legs to carry out the new initiatives. Not only is the Guardian school located here in Phoenix, Daniel, but many of the president's new health initiatives will be implemented from the Center for New

Age Medicine here. Each year the states choose fifty new Guardians. And you, Danny, have a good chance to get the Arizona appointment for this year. You're an excellent student and a wonderful athlete. Think of the honor if you're chosen."

Daniel stared at his mother. How could he make her understand? He had no political ambitions. He just wanted to follow his dream of playing professional soccer. "I'll do some research on it, Mom, but three teams are scouting me. The recruiter from the San Diego College of Professional Athletes interviewed me at school and filled out a pre-acceptance for the college. He said I wouldn't have any trouble getting in. When I turn pro, I might even get a signing bonus." He took a breath. "I'd get to travel and see the world." His arguments ricocheted unheard. The look on his mother's face said it all. To her, sports were for kids.

"Have you filed a formal application for the San Diego school yet?" She waited for his answer.

"No, I've been struggling with the two options."

"Tomorrow, Danny, decide and file an application. You really don't want to stay here with Dad and me and work the ranch, do you?"

Daniel didn't answer. At this point, working the ranch sounded pretty good to him but he didn't need a third option. Feeling like a dog that'd just been whipped, he turned to leave but decided he couldn't let his mother get away with this intrusion in his life even if she was his mother. "Mom,"

"What is it now, Daniel?"

"You do realize it's... MY... life we're talking about." Not waiting for an answer, he left the office, the clattering of his cleats on the tile floor echoing all the words he hadn't been able to get out. *Why couldn't he draw his mom a line...a do-not-get-in-my-life line? How did she always manage to make him feel like he was doing something wrong?* Frustrated, he kicked his bedroom door triggering motion lights which flooded the room. He punched off the lights and stood in the moonlight. The wall of trophies earned in the high school Olympics and the life-size mural of Durhan McConnaly, his soccer hero, didn't help his mood.

Daniel threw himself on the bed, closed his eyes and remembered the final game of the U.S. High School Olympics. West was ahead by one goal but the North team's star was dribbling right toward Daniel. Blood pumping through his veins, sweat rolling down his face, every nerve stretched to breaking, he heard the whoosh of the kick before he saw it. Instinctively, Daniel threw his body lengthwise in front of the net, narrowly blocking the goal. West won the Olympics without a tiebreaking shootout. Daniel was a hero! Soccer made him feel alive. It was like home to him, a place where he knew his job and felt not only excited but comfortable. He belonged in soccer.

Daniel sighed. Mom always thought she was right and she'd manipulated him ever since he was a kid. Not this time!

A voice interrupted his thoughts. "Danny, can I come in?"

"Sure, Dad."

"I overheard you talking with Mom. Is she bugging you?"

Daniel smiled, "You could say that."

"She loves you...and she means well...but she doesn't have the right to make this decision."

"I know, but Mom doesn't seem to understand." He paused, then continued, "And I don't want to hurt her feelings."

Harry knew exactly what Daniel meant. Judith set high expectations for both Daniel and his sister. Although Penny listened to her mother's ambitions for her, she ignored her, content with helping Harry with rodeos and ranch work. Daniel wasn't so lucky. Judith wrapped her tentacles around him pushing him toward the Guardians convinced that this new government was going to save the world.

Harry wasn't so sure. He didn't like the arrogant attitude of the Harvard-educated new president who ignored the Constitution and appointed a Council of Twelve now running the country, changing America and giving the president unlimited powers. According to President Blackstone the corruption and paralysis of the Congress had nearly destroyed America.

The Council voted to eliminate the Congress, saving taxpayers the enormous salaries of the senators and representatives and their administrative assistants. The news media balked but finally supported the president when he agreed to a Board of Governors representing all the states—their job to approve the decisions of the Council of Twelve.

Was the U.S. president becoming a dictator? The America Harry loved was disappearing and he feared for Daniel to be any part of this new government. However, Harry had to follow his own advice. The decision to apply for the Guardians or follow a sports career belonged to Daniel and he wouldn't try to influence his son.

"You'll figure it out, Danny. Give yourself all the time you need. Of course, Mom will stay on your case until you do something, so you might save yourself some hassle by cutting her off at the pass." Harry patted his son on the shoulder and left the room.

Daniel rubbed his forehead. His head ached. Suddenly, he realized that he was afraid. He'd never been afraid in sports, but this was different. He was afraid of making the wrong decision. He was afraid of committing his life to a career he knew so little about. And he was afraid of letting his family down, especially his mother. What if she was right? Maybe becoming a professional athlete *was* a kid's dream. Should he give his life to his country and try for the Guardians?

He studied the brochure from his high school principal more closely. A cadet in a silver jumpsuit stared back tough and proud. "The $100,000 uniform is a technological marvel," he read. "Climate controlled, lightweight, space-aged material." The brightly-colored photos showed a computerized classroom, state-of-the-art workout facility and electronic firing range. He continued reading… "team competitions…the president's elite corps."

The future he'd hoped and planned for seemed cloudy and far away. Confused by the two choices, Daniel drifted off to sleep.

Chapter Two

Exhausted from struggling through a sleepless night, Daniel crawled out of bed aware that the tension over the decision had drained his energy. What did Dad say? Take a day off to clear his head and get away from his mom? Perhaps then he'd be able to think straight and make his decision. Eager to get out of the house, Daniel skipped his shower, grabbed a cranberry-oat bar and a vita-juice from the kitchen and headed for the stable looking for his dad. He spotted him leading the black stallion into the barn.

"Dad."

Harry turned around. "You're up kind of early…trying to escape your mom?"

"Yeah, I guess. Thought I'd call Joey and see if he wants to go waterskiing with some kids from school. Can I borrow the truck?"

Harry sensed Daniel's need to escape, "Sure Danny. You can help me pick up hay bales for the horses tomorrow."

"Thanks, Dad." Daniel spoke into his communicator. "Joey Decker."

A sleepy Joey appeared on the communicator. "What's up DJ?"

"Want to go skiing with the kids at Lake Pleasant? Dad loaned me the truck."

Joey groaned. "I think I'd rather sleep in."

"It'd get us out of the range of our moms for a day."

"True, I forgot about that. Okay, gimme me an hour."

Daniel turned off his communicator and wandered into his horse Sandy's stall. The beautiful chestnut shook his head and stamped his foot in anticipation.

"Sorry, buddy, it's a little too hot for a ride." Reaching into his pocket, Daniel broke off a piece of the oat bar and held it out for the horse to nibble.

He unlatched the stall where he stored his sports gear, grabbed his water ski, life vest and UV water goggles and headed for the truck. Anxious to avoid another confrontation with his mom, Daniel backed the truck out of the drive. Mom was a night owl working late on the books for the ranch, but sleeping in till about 9 a.m.

Arriving at Joey's, he decided not to toot the horn in case Joey's mom was still asleep. He pulled the crumpled brochure from the Guardians out of his shorts pocket, unable to let go of the question that burned inside him. What should he do? The deadline was close. Disgusted with himself for being unable to make a decision, he shoved the brochure into the glove compartment, determined to relax at least one day before filing the application.

Joey burst out of the house, his loud Hawaiian shirt unbuttoned, tennis shoes untied and his baseball cap on backwards. He stowed his ski in the back of the pickup and then unloaded his other paraphernalia behind the seat. "Big guy, any chance we could stop for a cheese and egg bagel on the way out?"

Daniel made a face. "How can you eat those things, Joey? Don't they just lay on your stomach?"

Joey ignored him. "We'll go right past the Bagel Hut."

The two boys pulled into the Lake Pleasant Marina parking lot. A group of kids from their high school were piling into two boats. Daniel dug out a $20 bill and gave it to the boy collecting money for the gas. Joey followed his lead.

"Any flea-males coming today?" Joey asked Daniel.

"I hope so...I feel like that's one area of my life that's vastly neglected."

"We got time, DJ. By the way, if we made it into the Guardians, there'd be no girls for eight months."

That fact had escaped Daniel's attention. *One more negative for the Guardians,* he thought as he and Joey climbed into Shawn's Ski Nautique, nearly tripping over some loose beer cans. Daniel wasn't a hard nose but beer and boating didn't mix. He and Joey took seats facing the back so they could spot, while Shawn waved to two of the girls on shore who climbed aboard. As soon as they found a seat, Shawn shoved the boat in gear and raced out onto the lake.

"Who wants to be my first victim?" he drawled. Daniel ignored the comment and tossed his ski into the water. He dove in, grabbed the tow line and braced himself for the thrust of the motor, knowing that Shawn would jerk him out of the lake at top speed hoping he'd fall and embarrass himself in front of the girls.

Just as he thought, Shawn floored it and the thrust of the boat ripped Daniel out of the water. He tightened his grip on the tow rope and held on as Shawn cut into the coves, changing directions and forcing Daniel to cross the wake often to avoid the cliffs. It didn't matter. He loved the excitement and danger. Sliding through the water with the spray in his face was such a high. Noting the intense look on Joey's face while he spotted, Daniel forgot everything except the sun on his body and the wind in his face. A perfect day to ski. He scanned the mountains as they drew near the cliffs, spotting a few longhorn sheep and an eagle's nest. Unable to shake Daniel, Shawn yelled, "Hey, how 'bout giving someone else a chance?"

Daniel let go of the rope and sank into the water, waiting for the boat to circle around and pick him up. Back in the boat, he noticed the empties had multiplied. With each skier Shawn grew more reckless. Joey barely survived the erratic driving and the girls still needed to ski. Daniel helped one of the girls into the water. "You ever do this before, Katy?"

"Yeah, a few times. I'll be okay if I can get up on my wakeboard."

Afraid that the alcohol was now driving the boat, Daniel yelled at Shawn, "Knock off the funny stuff, Shawn."

Shawn glared at Daniel. Revving the motor, he pulled Katy out of the water but instead of cutting his speed after Katy balanced the wakeboard, he floored the accelerator and quickly cut to the left. The severe turn tossed the board and Katy in a backward somersault. Daniel signaled Joey who leaped into the front of the boat, cutting the engine as Daniel dove into the water after the injured girl. Unconscious, Katy lay face down in the water. Daniel slipped his arm under her body, turning her face up. "Katy, can you hear me?"

Joey shoved Shawn out of the driver's seat and took the wheel. He eased the boat alongside Daniel, cut the engine and hurried to help Daniel pull Katy, still not breathing, into the boat. They laid her gently across the backseat while Daniel unbuckled her life jacket and started chest compressions. Stunned by the accident, her friend Sharon watched in tears. At first Katy didn't respond, her skin blue from lack of oxygen.

Daniel focused on administering CPR. "C'mon, Katy!" Suddenly, Katy coughed up a fountain of lake water, gasping for breath.

"Are you all right?" Daniel asked.

"I don't know. I can't remember what happened. I was up and then..."

Daniel and Joey exchanged glances. "I think we should take you home. Do you live far from here?"

"No, not far, Daniel, in Cave Creek."

"Can you walk?"

Trembling, Katy nodded, "I think so. Sharon will take me home." She clutched Daniel's hand, "I'm glad you and Joey were here."

The boys walked Katy to her friend's car and helped her into the backseat. Daniel leaned over and whispered to Sharon, "Can you take her for x-rays, make sure nothing's broken?"

Still shaking, Sharon nodded.

"You're sure you're all right, Katy? Joey and I could follow you."

"No, no, I just got the wind knocked out of me. I'm sore, but nothing feels broken. Thanks for your help. I'll be all right now."

"How old do you think Katy is?" Joey asked as they turned to leave.

"Not sure, Sharon's a year behind us but Katy is probably fifteen." Daniel stopped to watch the ski boat head into a cove.

"Two bits those idiots dive off the cliffs," Joey said.

Daniel shook his head, glad they were out of the boat.

The boys were quiet on the way home. "What *are* you going to do about the Guardians, Daniel? Your mom's right, we do need to make a decision."

"The only way I'll get my mom off my case is to file an application for the Guardians."

"But what if you make it?"

"Fifty guys are trying out—that's fifty-to-one odds, but if I do, then maybe that's the way it's supposed to be. I'll file my application for San Diego, too; then I'll have all my bases covered."

"Mind if I clone that idea?"

Daniel grinned. "You gonna apply for the San Diego College, too?"

"You know what I mean. I'll apply for the Guardians *and* vet school."

"Deal, bro."

Chapter Three

Frustrated that Daniel refused to fill out his applications for either the Guardians or the San Diego College of Professional Athletes, Judith Jordan headed for the grocery. Nothing was going her way. Normally, she ordered groceries on Mondays through the web at Arizona Natural Foods with home delivery on Wednesdays, but in all the upset over Daniel's applications, she'd forgotten. When she tried to order steaks for the dude ranch's last weekend cookout, she learned the butcher's father died and he'd closed shop to attend the funeral in New York. Now Judith had to take time out of her day to go to the supermarket, time she could be working on the ranch books.

In the meat department she picked up two boxes of Omaha steaks, then wheeled her cart down unfamiliar aisles searching for the items on her list. Feeling like she'd run a marathon, Judith pushed her cart to the checkout, only to discover none of the counters manned with a live person; she would have to scan the groceries herself. *Did it really cost that much to hire a few live checkers?* Locating the bar codes, she scanned each item as she transferred groceries from her cart to the counter. Out of the corner of her eye, she watched the assistant manager post a legal-looking notice at each checkout. Straining her eyes she read, "**As of July 27,**

2022 no cash or credit cards will be honored. Purchases must be made using your World Federation mark."

Puzzled, Judith finished her order, adding oatmeal, romaine lettuce, sweet red peppers, corn on the cob, Arizona tea and melons, placing them in the canvas bags provided by the grocery.

The woman in line behind her smiled and pointed to the sign. "Have you got your number yet?"

Judith frowned. *Just one more thing to get done.* "No, not yet."

"It's easy. I got mine at the library…no pain…no strain. They put your hand under this machine, look up your World Federation number, connect it to your bank accounts and in three minutes…zap…your invisible number is transferred to your hand. See," she finished, out of breath.

Judith looked at the hand waving in her face. She saw no mark.

The woman continued, "No more credit cards, checkbooks, no one can steal your credit identity. It's," she searched for an explanation, "it's radio waves or something! Put your hand under the scanner at the store…zap…it goes to your account and deducts the amount."

Annoyed by the word "zap," Judith turned away from the woman and finished her purchase. She placed her groceries on the mechanical walkway, typed in her license plate and joined the groceries as the moving walkway made its way to her ancient yellow Land Rover. Could the woman be right? Maybe she should stop by the library on the way home and get her number. At least one member of the family would be ready for this change and she *was* the family shopper.

She touched the keypad and the ignition turned over. Hot air blasted her in the face. Why hadn't she set the temperature control? It wasn't supposed to be 104 degrees in May.

The Palomino Library parking lot buzzed with activity. Judith sighed, *bad timing*. She cruised slowly up and down the rows of cars watching for someone to leave so she could pull into their space. She glanced at the dash—5:15 p.m. Suddenly, the red taillights on a small black hybrid signaled the chance for a space, but before Judith could pull in, a rundown Ford truck cut her off. Two cowboys climbed out waving their hats in triumph. Irritated, Judith swerved around the two teens. *Just as well*, she thought, *the steaks wouldn't survive left in the car.*

Harry pounded the dust on his jeans, pulled off his worn, leather boots and tossed his Stetson on the hall tree in the back porch—5:30 p.m. and no one was home. He pushed 11 on the kitchen butler and waited for his favorite Fat Tire beer to fill a frosted glass, then strolled into the great room.

Through the floor to ceiling windows, he viewed the ranch, purple Mazatzal Mountains silhouetted in the background. He thought back to each addition through the years—the riding stables, rodeo area, the housing for the ranch hands and the guest cabins down by the Verde River. Today the horses huddled under a cluster of paloverde trees, looking for shade from the heat.

With Judith and the kids' help, he'd created Sunset Acres to be a profitable guest ranch. Harry was content. It was a good life. He'd hoped Daniel and Penny would run it after he and Judith retired, but Daniel had other opportunities.

Harry sank into his favorite recliner. Judith didn't approve of him sitting down in his work clothes but he still needed to feed the horses and bed them down for the night. He stared at a picture of Daniel training Penny on her horse, Buffy. The picture caught Daniel's mischievous brown eyes, tan muscular body and big grin as he lassoed his thirteen-year-old sister. Unlike many teens, Daniel stayed away from drugs and partying, choosing to invest his time in soccer and the ranch. Harry was proud of the man his son was becoming. He just wished Judith would stop trying to plan Daniel's life.

He clapped twice and the media center came to life, President Blackstone's face filling the screen. What was the man up to now? The people elected Blackstone to make change and one change he'd made clear was that the Constitution, written in the 1700s, no longer served a purpose. The president appointed a Council of Twelve who virtually ran the country and made the law. The Council voted to replace the Congress with a Board of Governors, using the media to sell the new U.S. government structure while the liberal Supreme Court silently supported the changes.

Judith believed the president was saving the country but Harry had his doubts, sad to see the country he loved changed so dramatically. He listened warily as the president spoke:

"On July 27, people all over the world will join One World Finances. One member of each household will acquire the mark of the World Federation to be used for all purchases and financial dealings. This number will be attached to your family financial accounts. Citizens over the age of twenty-one will have six months to receive a number. As the president, I encourage you to embrace this new financial system which will propel America and the world into a real global economy."

The pulsing of Harry's digital wrist phone distracted him from the president's message.

"Harry?"

He recognized his dad's voice. "Dad, how's the weather in Three Rivers?"

"Lovely, in the 70s..."

"How's Mom? Everything all right?"

"Yes, son, Mom's fine... tired a lot of the time but, listen...I'm not calling about our health, Harry. Did you hear President Blackstone tonight?"

"Yeah, I have him on now...something about a new financial system...a shopping number, I guess."

It was quiet on his father's end of the line. "Yes, you've got it right, Harry, but there's something you should know... your mother and I will not be taking the World Federation mark."

The announcement came as a shock. Harry let the words sink in. "Doesn't that mean you won't be able to buy groceries or pay your bills?"

"That's what it means, but we won't be taking it. It goes against our beliefs. We just can't do it."

"But Dad—"

"I'm sorry, our decision is final. Be careful; it's very complex, but you don't want to take the mark."

"I don't understand. How in the world will you live? Have you thought this out? How will you access your bank accounts or pay your taxes?"

"I don't know how we'll live." His father hesitated, then continued, "But I do know—we can't take the mark."

What could he say? His father's beliefs ran his life. Harry remembered the Sunday rule—everyone attended church, rain or shine, blizzard or tornado. It was such a relief when he married Judith who thought Sunday was like any other day. He hadn't been in a church since he was married. Of course, the busiest times on a dude ranch were the weekends.

"Are you still there, Harry?"

"Sorry Dad, but not taking the World Federation mark has long-range implications."

"Yes, it does." His father cleared his throat. "Please don't let anyone take the mark until I can show you what I mean."

"Okay, Dad." Harry turned off the phone wishing Judith would hurry. For twenty-five years he'd relied on her to work through problems. What would she think of his parents' decision?

Harry leaned back in his recliner. He loved Judith. Time did not dim his passion. But lately, she seemed cold and untouchable, pushing him away when he tried to put his arm around her. Confused and hurt, Harry didn't know what to do about it. Perhaps this crisis with his parents would draw them closer.

He lit his old meerschaum pipe, and inhaled his favorite tobacco, Western Star. Smoking, illegal everywhere now except for home, was Harry's only vice, unhealthy but comforting.

His mind wandered back to his wife. Physically, Judith hadn't changed much, just added shadows under her eyes and a frosting of gray in her dark hair. But there were other differences: Judith always looked like she stepped off the cover of *Southwestern Woman* while he was content in T-shirts and jeans. (He gazed again at the president who was still being interviewed.) And that was another difference. Harry was not a political person, but Judith was so enamored with this president that she was pushing Daniel to try for the president's new Guardian Corps.

A sharp tap on the car horn signaled Judith's return. Harry rested his pipe in an ashtray and walked quickly to the front door where he found his wife unloading the car.

"I was hoping you were home to help with the groceries," she said as Harry joined her. "Is Daniel here yet?"

"No, but it's just as well because I need to talk to you privately about something. Dad just called while I was watching the 5:30 news. The president announced that each family had to have someone get the World Federation mark..."

Judith cut him off. "I'm way ahead of you. I stopped by the library to get mine, but it was too busy today. I'll try again tomorrow then we'll officially be in the program."

Harry frowned. "Dad and Mom refuse to take the mark. They don't want any of us to take it either. I promised Dad we'd wait for his explanation." Harry watched Judith's face flush with impatience as he helped her carry bags into the kitchen.

"Well, someone has to get it, Harry. You can't buy food or clothes without it. I thought you'd be pleased; I do all the shopping for this family anyway. I can't imagine why your parents won't take the mark, how will they—"

Harry closed his eyes. "Dad said taking the mark went against their beliefs."

Judith stopped putting away the groceries, "Harry, I don't mean to seem unsympathetic but your parents are not my priority right now. Daniel is. Where is he anyway?"

"I told him to take some time off. Relax. Make his decision."

"As far as I'm concerned, there is no decision. He needs to stop playing and become a man."

Harry felt his jaw clench. "He has the right to decide his own future."

"Not if he's making a bad decision. I want his life to have meaning. I want him to do something important. The Guardians—"

"I *want*, Judith, I *want*? What about what Daniel wants? You've forgotten something important. It's his life...*not* yours."

Chapter Four

C aught between sleep and reality, Daniel stretched and rolled onto the side of his bed watching the blue light from the video intercom fill his room. Someone was monitoring him. He leaned up on one elbow waiting for the signal to rise. "Mom, are you spying on me?" The communication wall glowed, followed by the life-sized figure of his mother.

"No, just wondering how long you'd sleep. Take a shower and when you're finished I'll have burritos and juice."

"Spying and bribing?"

Judith ignored Daniel. "You need to make a decision and file your applications."

"Whoa, Mom, let me wake up."

"Either application should have been sent in March, Daniel."

He swung his legs over the edge of the bed enjoying the cool sensation of the Spanish tile floor on the bottoms of his feet. Although he'd sent his applications by Internet last night after coming home, he decided a little "mom torture" was deserved. Entering the shower, Daniel set the shower-head to pulse letting the rhythm of the pings shock him back to life. The warm water soothed his muscles still sore from his adventure at Lake Pleasant.

The intercom squawked and he heard his name. Reluctantly, he turned off the shower, shaking the water from his eyes like his golden retriever Molly after a swim in the Verde River. Wrapping a bath towel around his waist, Daniel leaned over the sink to brush his teeth, flexing his biceps as he lay down his toothbrush. His fingers slid through his short, blond crew cut. He felt naked without the tattoos most kids sported but his high school Olympic coach didn't allow them. Pro athletes wore tattoos like an undershirt. Guys in high school tattooed their sport or the girls they'd slept with but Daniel wasn't into that. At eighteen, he'd never slept with a girl. He was waiting for that one special girl, one special relationship like his dad had with his mom. Anyway, girls treated him like a big brother.

His image stared back as he leaned closer to check his overnight beard. Was it coming in red? Cool. He fingered a razor then put it back on the shelf. Maybe he'd grow a beard for a few weeks. Mom would love that!

He dropped his towel in the laundry recycler, watched it pass through an ultraviolet light, get folded by two metal arms and, sterilized, slide down the chute to the towel shelf.

Meanwhile, Daniel threw on an old Diamondback shirt, shorts and his Nikes and hurried into the kitchen. "Boy, do those puppies smell good," he said inhaling the spicy odor of the Mexican burritos. He polished off two, rinsing them down with grape drink laced with ginseng and Vitamin C, his mom's answer to good health.

She watched him like a cougar waiting to pounce. Should he put her out of her misery? No, he'd let her have her moment. The burritos were a good bribe. "Sorry about yesterday, Mom. I just didn't want you making my decision." He looked down, "But I'd like to hear your ideas."

His mother cleared her throat and Daniel knew she'd rehearsed the reasons he should apply to be a Guardian, "Danny, we live in an exciting time. Our president is a problem solver with new ideas for changing America."

"Like when he bypassed the Congress and selected the Council of Twelve?"

"Exactly. He isn't afraid to try new ideas. I don't want to influence you, but I think our nation needs bright young people like you interested in creating a better world."

Daniel weighed her words. She did want to influence him, but maybe she had a right. She was his mom—and she was smart. She handled all the publicity and finances for the dude ranch while his dad ran the physical ranch, equal partners.

"And you think I can do more for my country by being a Guardian, Mom?"

"Perhaps. It's a first step."

He played along with her letting her think her arguments convinced him. "Thanks Mom, I appreciate your point of view." Halfway out the kitchen door, Daniel turned, "By the way, I submitted my applications on the Internet last night. Now it's up to the fates."

A look of surprise spread across his mother's face. "Daniel, you let me—"

"The burritos were a nice touch." Daniel smiled. "It's okay, Mom, you're a little pushy but I love you."

Chapter Five

"**I** told my parents they could visit, Judith. You are with me on this, aren't you?"

"I love your parents, Harry. It's just such a busy time with Daniel putting in his applications and summer coming. You know I set up our whole fall and winter schedule during the summer, besides posting ads on a hundred commercial websites." Judith hesitated. "A visit, Harry….a short visit." She frowned. "You realize your parents won't be able to access their money, or buy medicine. What if they need hospitalization and can't use their health card?"

Harry nodded. "I haven't thought that far ahead. Dad's upset, Judith. He sounded firm. Practical or impractical, they won't take the World Federation mark unless we change their minds."

Judith caught the look on Harry's face and backed down. "Of course, they're welcome. Find out when they want to fly and I'll help them with their reservations."

Relieved, Harry decided to wait until morning to call his parents. The reality of their decision not to take the mark weighed heavily on him. *What could be behind it?*

Judith walked down the hall and entered her office leaving Harry to stare at the coffee in his mug. Summer was supposed to be slower paced but this one already defied that image.

His thoughts drifted back to his parents. *When was the last time he'd seen them? Had it really been two years?* He'd taught Daniel to waterski on the lake where his parents had lived for over fifty years. But after graduating college, like so many of his friends, Harry didn't return to Three Rivers. He hungered for excitement and a new adventure so despite his love for his parents, his dream of running a dude ranch drew him west. At this point in his life, however, Harry felt protective of his parents who were now close to eighty. The past winter both of his parents spent months battling bronchitis and pneumonia, leaving his mom frail and his dad with a hacking cough that refused to go away.

Harry set his coffee cup down and reached for his pipe. *Odd what you remember.* His mother always dressed fashionably but never wanted to stand out. The last time the family visited the lake, her soft, brown hair was nearly overcome with white. On Mother's Day, she planted summer flowers around the cottage, a different color scheme each year—red geraniums, hot pink and purple petunias, or blue ageratum and yellow marigolds. *Did you plant Dad's favorite red geraniums this year, Mom?*

He took another drag on his pipe. And Dad...straight and tall even at eighty, thick white hair combed and parted just so. His dad always carried a nail clipper and a small black comb in his pocket. Every day he read his Bible while he drank his morning coffee. Harry had never read the Bible and only remembered stories from Sunday school of David and Goliath, Noah and the ark and Daniel and the lion's den—Christian fairy tales. Yet, his parents' lives shone with a gentle power...a kindness...an honesty. He blew a final cloud of smoke before getting up. Despite the circumstances, it would be good to see his mom and dad. Judith's concerns were valid. Perhaps together they could help his parents see the reality of the situation.

The atmosphere at supper was quiet. "Kids," Harry cleared his throat, "something's happened and Grandpa George and Grandma Jenny are coming for a visit."

"Great," Penny and Daniel chorused.

"Is something wrong, Dad?" Daniel asked. "Phoenix isn't exactly a summer getaway."

Caught off guard by Daniel's question, Harry stuttered, "Not wrong exactly...it's complicated."

Judith interrupted. "The president is joining the United States to a world financial system. Everyone receives a number on their right hand connected to the World Federation—a mark to buy and sell. Your grandparents refuse to take the World Federation mark. They're coming to visit until we sort it out."

Harry shot her a look that would stop a stampede.

"Why won't they take the mark, Dad? What's the problem?"

"That's what we'll try to find out, Danny."

Harry dialed the familiar number, relieved when his dad answered the phone. "Dad, Judith would like to help with your plane reservations. Would you like that?"

"That's fine, Harry, the sooner the better. Let us know and we'll transfer some funds into your account." The old man paused, "No one should take the World Federation mark, Harry. No one. Please don't let Judith take it until we show you..."

"I promise, Dad, we won't take the mark until we hear your reasons."

George hung up the phone. "I know you just bought your flowers and tomato plants, Jenny, but if we can convince them not to take the mark."

"You're right, of course, dear. The children are much more important. We'll ask the Bradley's to water my plants till we get back."

"The president is only giving families till July 27. We won't be able to buy food after that...or pay our bills," said George.

"When we get back we can stock up on canned food, put in a bigger garden. I'm thankful you can fish, that'll help," Jenny added.

George looked thoughtful. "We have enough money in our savings to prepay our taxes and perhaps even our electric and heating bills but we have to do it before the 27th.

Harry relaxed, hopeful that he and Judith could make his parents see the seriousness of not taking the World Federation mark. Judith interrupted his thoughts.

"If they continue to refuse to take the mark, perhaps we can become their guardians or at least transfer their financial accounts into ours in case of medical emergencies." Judith was on a roll. "I think I'll get my number today so that—"

"Dad asked us not to take the mark until he can explain." He watched Judith deflate.

"I'm not to do anything? Why are you tying my hands, Harry, when there's so much to do?"

"Judith, are you listening? It's important to Dad, and I want you to promise not to get the mark until he's presented his point of view. I know you think you're right but they're coming a long way so just wait. We need to hear them out. Please do as I ask."

"All right, Harry, don't make such an issue out of it," she mumbled under her breath. "But it makes no sense to me."

Chapter Six

3300—The Tower.

D r. Greg Hart punched in the code that opened the door to his twenty-third floor suite. Removing his sunglasses, he placed a filter in his ancient drip coffee machine, filled the machine with difficult-to-find Seattle's Best coffee and waited for it to brew—totally ignoring the advice of the latest health czar that coffee was linked to....whatever. As a doctor, it should be his choice what he put into his body.

The doctor timed his arrival to view the sunrise. Rose and fuchsia clouds flamed across the early dawn sky. He watched as the colors faded and the sun came up—his favorite seven minutes of the day. He continued to scan the horizon. The Bank One ballpark (what was its name now?) brought back memories of the once-a-year baseball game with his dad: singing the Star Spangled Banner, the catsup, mustard and pickle relish race, and the trip to the Diamondback's gift shop where he tried on every hat until he found just the right one. The park now held only memories for him since his dad passed away.

The aroma of the fragrant coffee pulled him back to reality as he filled a mug of the steaming brew. He dropped his 6'4" body into his black leather office chair and, teetering on the two back wheels, reviewed the day's agenda.

"In that mood again?"

Greg glanced up at the door. His nurse, Nan, smiled at him as she came over to inhale the rich-bodied aroma.

"A harmless rebellion, Nan. You can have a cup, if you promise to cover for me."

"I'll spray the anti-germicidal soon as we're done." Nan laughed.

Greg thought back to the day that President Blackstone called his small desert medical practice. Nan, had answered the phone.

"Doctor," Nan pushed the hold button, "it's the president calling, President Blackstone?" She stared at Greg in shock.

"Put him on, Nan."

Paralyzed with astonishment, Nan connected the president with her boss, unable to believe the president asked for him by name.

Greg gently pushed her out of his office and closed the door on her inquisitive face. "Hello, Mr. President, what can I do for you?"

"Greg, I need someone I can trust to organize and head a center for New Age medicine in Phoenix. Are you interested?"

Greg didn't hesitate, "Of course, sir. I've always dreamed of being part of a research center."

"Well, you'll have plenty of opportunity to work on your research, Greg. I'll see that those doors open for you." The president paused. "But your main job will be to set up the center and implement the health initiatives that the Council and I pass. Think you can do that?"

"Yes, Mr. President, I'd be honored."

He hadn't thought of Alex Blackstone since college when he and Alex pledged the same fraternity, Beta Omicron. All fraternities hazed and challenged pledges with activities that bordered on getting them expelled; it was part of the danger—

part of the bonding. Were you worthy? Adventurous? Did you have more loyalty to the brothers than to the outside world?

Greg's desire to be a doctor and his study workload won over his desire to pledge a fraternity and he quit midway through rush. Nights without sleep, plus the unending drinking, didn't allow time to study and he didn't dare risk losing the scholarships he depended on. Entrance into a good medical school demanded straight A's; Greg couldn't afford to slack off. Alex Blackstone, a charismatic leader, became president of Beta Omicron.

Later, a scandal occurred while Alex was president of the fraternity…a young freshman girl was found dead, dressed in a white gauze dress with a wreath of daisies in her hair. Was Alex involved?

Looking back, Greg wondered why Alex asked him, an unknown desert doctor, to set up the new research center. Did he expect less trouble from Greg over the initiatives because of their history together?

Following the president's directive, Greg organized CNAM, the Center for New Age Medicine, according to the specific plans sent by the Council of Twelve. The plans included a research wing, surgical units, high tech labs and doctor's suites.

Three years ago, Greg could not have predicted the radical and sweeping health initiatives the Council would pass. He glanced, disapprovingly, at the latest initiative:

Initiative to Relieve Financial Health Debt No. A1

The Ascension

On September 11, 2022, the initiative referred to as the Ascension will take place at 5:30 p.m. in Sedona, Arizona. The Center for New Age Medicine (CNAM) will handle all preparations and prepare all candidates. These candidates, heroes of the new millennium, will offer their lives for the service of their country. "That one might give his life for the many."

Dr. Greg Hart and the Center for New Age Medicine will select participants according to the guidelines provided. The Guardian Corps will physically prepare the site.

The first Ascension...September 11...Greg felt like a fly trapped in a spider web, hating his role in executing the initiatives but unable to free himself. His dream turned into a nightmare and now he carried out medical initiatives, so questionable he wrestled daily with his medical oath "to do no harm." Was he so naïve that he assumed CNAM would only extend life and conquer disease? He'd yearned to be on the cutting edge of medicine. Well, he was on the cutting edge!

The first edict Greg received prohibited lifesaving surgeries for those over seventy-five. He'd denied people extra years of life to save health care dollars. *But an Ascension?* By September 11, Greg needed to select one hundred people to participate in the most heinous elimination of people since the Nazis exterminated the Jews in World War II. Phoenix would be the pilot program. If the public accepted the Ascension—and no doubt the administration would present it as a heroic event—next year other cities would be ordered to duplicate it. The madness would spread!

He looked over the guidelines for selecting candidates: over eighty, suffering from terminal conditions or genetic anomalies. Greg shook his head. Just being over eighty made you a possible candidate? The old people fought in wars, paid their taxes, worked hard to earn a living, many existing solely on Social Security. Asking them to surrender their lives for their country to save the economy was heartless and unethical. How could Greg do this? How could any doctor? Did he have a choice? To oppose the president would be dangerous. Rumors circulated that journalists had actually disappeared for criticizing the initiatives. *Wait till they saw this one.*

He scanned the new initiative again, pained that he—Greg Hart—would decide life or death for many people. He wiped beads of perspiration from his forehead, *My God, I feel so helpless.* He filed the initiative in a drawer. Tomorrow he'd send to the hospital for patient files. Perhaps he could at least find some who were destined to die anyway. He'd discuss it with Nan later.

"Doctor, are you all right?" Nan asked.

Greg emptied his cold coffee into the sink. "I'm okay, Nan, really...I'm okay. Bring me the files of the young men we're interviewing tomorrow." He'd interviewed twenty-five Guardian prospects last week and was a little surprised there were no young women candidates. This week he'd interview another twenty-five.

Dr. Hart's instructions emphasized three areas: a personality evaluation, DNA testing and an interview. On the candidate's arrival Nan administered a personality profile, which became part of the candidate's record. Two personality types were not acceptable: namely, the sensitive, deep thinker—the melancholy; and the gentle, indecisive type—the phlegmatic.

Next Dr. Hart drew blood and took a buccal smear in order to make a DNA genome blueprint. The blueprint recorded the candidate's vital organs and alerted the doctor to any genetic mutations. The blood chemistry analyzed the current state of health. Any genetic mutations disqualified the candidate. Finally, Dr. Hart conducted an interview using the criteria provided by the Council.

- Did the candidate appear confident?
- Did he seem overly-independent?

- Was he able to take orders?
- Was there any sign of hostility toward the government or its policies?
- The doctor read over the interview questions puzzled that independent thinking was a negative. What was the regime trying to do, build a corps of mindless robots?

He glanced down the list of Guardian candidates for this week's testing and pulled out the first file—Daniel Jordan, eighteen years old, a graduate of Desert Mountain Academics and Sports program. *Interesting.* This young man considered spending his life as a professional athlete. He read further, "Winner of a gold medal for participating on the high school Olympic soccer team, winner of a silver medal in the triathlon."

"Nan, please call and remind these candidates of their appointments."

Chapter Seven

G enevieve Jordan brushed a strand of white hair from her eyes as she looked out at the geese parading across the placid lakefront. "It's my favorite time of year," she sighed.

"I know," said George, "but I think it's important to try to convince our family not to take the mark. Hurry dear, we have a two hour drive to the Detroit airport. The neighbors will be picking us up any minute."

"Did you tell them where we're going?"

"Yes, but not why. I don't know where they stand on the issue of taking the World Federation mark. Better to have them think it's just a vacation, don't you think?"

"I suppose. I'm glad they're taking care of things for us while we're gone." Jenny reached down and pinched off a red tulip.

When had Jenny gotten so thin and pale? George wondered.

"Are you watching me, George?"

He cleared his throat caught in the act. "Are you well enough to fly, Jen?"

"Of course, I'm just saying goodbye to the lake."

"We won't miss the Fourth of July boat parade or the lake breakfast, I promise."

Jenny smiled. "We should go. I hear the Bradley's' car."

Arriving at the airport, George thanked their neighbors, instructing them not to stay at the airport. "You folks run along. The parking garage is too far from the Western Airlines terminal. We'll be fine."

"Are you sure, George? It's really no trouble," said Letty.

"No, no we'll be fine. Thanks again. Sorry for the long drive."

Letty hugged Jenny. "Now don't you worry about your pretty flowers. I'll treat them just like my own."

The old couple stepped on the moving walkway relieved not to drag their suitcases through the airport. George looked for the self-check in longing for the days when you could check your bags outside the terminal with a person. He remembered Judith's instructions. Slide the credit card in... look for their name in the machine's window, but nothing happened. George's hands trembled.

"Trouble, dear?" Jenny asked.

"I can't get it to work."

A Western Airlines attendant saw their distress. "Can I help you?"

"I'm sorry, Ma'am, but my name doesn't come up when I put my credit card in. Our daughter-in-law made the reservation. She said it'd be simple."

The woman stepped up and tried the card, immediately discovering the couple was tagged for special security. "I'm sorry, you've been randomly selected to be security scanned. Step over here. Bring your bags, too."

George lifted his bag and then helped Jenny with hers. They followed the woman to a secure area where a machine performed a full body scan.

"Take off your shoes, please. Put your carry-ons, purse, wallet, watches, and contents of your pockets in this tray. Do you have any liquids in your carry-on?"

George reached over and steadied Jenny while she slipped off her tennis shoes.

"Walk through the scanner one at a time. That's right. Now gather your belongings. Let me take your bags… Phoenix wasn't it?" She checked their boarding passes noting their gate. "Gate 19 is something of a walk. Would you like me to find you a tram?"

George nodded. "Perhaps it would help."

The couple climbed on board the tram. "Oh, I've dropped my book, George," Jenny said, grabbing George's arm as she leaned over to retrieve it.

"Let me get it Jenny, I don't want you to fall." George got off the tram and walked to the other side noting the impatient look on the driver's face. "Sorry to hold you up," George said.

The man didn't respond but shifted and drove off in a hurry. They passed shops and restaurants finally ending at Gate 19. George turned to help Jenny. "Be careful, hon."

"I'm a little dizzy."

"Take your time."

They made their way to a chair to wait for their flight.

A robotic voice announced, "Flight 1034 is ready to board. Children and those in wheelchairs may board now."

George wished he'd requested a wheelchair for Jenny. When their rows were called, they got in line. As they made their way down the aisle to Row 14A and B, he was thankful Judith had booked them in the two-seat aisle so they'd have privacy if they wanted to talk or sleep.

"Sweetheart, you take the window seat," George said.

Always the gentleman, Jenny thought. George liked to stretch his long legs into the aisle once in awhile and she loved looking at the clouds. As the plane lifted off, she saw the clouds looked like pink-tinted pillows. She imagined herself sitting on one playing a violin, her idea of heaven when she was young. Turning to her husband, she asked, "What did you think heaven would be like when you were a child?"

"Oh, I never gave it much thought—giving it a little more these days though." He winked at her, reading her mind about the clouds.

"George, I know we'll be all right living on the lake... having a garden...but how will people live if they don't take this buying and selling mark?"

"God will be with His people. I don't know if He'll provide food miraculously like He did in the wilderness but His promise is always to be with us. Maybe He'll start an underground movement. Pastor Bauer tells me he's heard about some Christians who are buying farms and ranches to grow their own food. None of this time is a mystery to God, Jenny. He knows the end from the beginning."

"I hope we can convince the children," said Jenny.

George looked away.

"George, you do think we can convince them..."

"We can try..."

"But the Bible says..."

"We'll show them, Jenny, but they don't live their lives by the Bible."

"You don't think Judith will..."

"Judith doesn't know God or believe in Him. It won't seem important to her," said George.

An awkward silence fell between them. "What about Harry and the children?" Jenny asked.

"We taught Harry about God..."

"But he hasn't gone to church since he married Judith."

Jenny was right. Judith would think their stand illogical but they had to try. He turned to Jenny. "The busiest times on the ranch are weekends."

"I'm so afraid for them," said Jenny.

George reached over and took her delicate hand in his. "Let's trust God to give us the right words."

They settled back into their seats, closing their eyes to rest.

Western Airlines Flight 1034—Detroit to Phoenix—landed on time. Daniel saw his grandparents first. "C'mon, Dad, they're at the Western carousel." Running up to his grandparents, he grabbed his grandma.

"Put me down, Danny."

"I've got to give my favorite Gram a hug, don't I? You look beautiful, Gram," he said, dropping her gently.

She turned to hug Harry. "He takes after you, Harry. Full of charm. It's so good to see you."

"Mom, you sure made it easy to spot these cases with your yellow ribbons." Harry lifted the last of the bags onto the moving walkway. "Everybody ready? Let's roll," he called cheerfully. "We're anxious to get you home."

Daniel watched Grandpa George wipe the perspiration from his brow as they loaded the green ranch van they used to pick up guests. He'd forgotten how old and fragile his grandparents were. Grandpa was almost eighty and Grandma Jenny looked as though a good breeze would knock her off her feet. He exchanged glances with his dad. Daniel wasn't sure why his grandparents had come, but he loved having them visit. He climbed behind the wheel.

"Are you going to be our chauffeur, Danny?" Grandpa asked.

"Yeah, Gramps, you scared?"

"No, he's not, but I am," chirped Grandma Jenny. They all laughed and settled in for the forty minute ride to the ranch.

George turned to Harry. "Harry, Judith didn't…"

"No, Dad, she didn't take the mark but she seems very determined. She's waiting to hear what you have to say."

"I'm not sure she can understand the importance of this decision, Harry."

"Neither of us understands your decision, Dad. I know it has to do with your religion but…neither of us is religious. The only time I even hear about God is when you visit. Judith is a good mother. We've tried to teach Daniel and Penny to respect authority and to be good citizens." He paused, not wanting to hurt his father's feelings. "Judith thinks refusing the World Federation mark defies our government. It will be the law."

"Son, there's a higher power than our government. You don't realize it yet, but this is a life-and-death issue."

"Dad, should I take the 202?" interrupted Daniel.

"Yes, let's go the back way and take AZ87 to the Indian reservation and then through the Verdes. There'll be a lot less traffic at this time of day."

"I think this is our first ride on the 87," Grandpa said. "It's nice to see more scenery. We've never seen the saguaros in bloom."

"They call it the Beeline Highway, Gramps," said Daniel.

When they reached Trails End, Daniel parked the van on the drive and began to unload. "Grandpa, Dad and I'll get this. Why don't you and Grandma go in and see if Mom's in the kitchen. We'll take these bags to your rooms."

The door chime interrupted Judith's thoughts. She opened the door and welcomed the older couple. "Come in, can I get you a glass of lemonade before dinner?"

"We never turn down a glass of lemonade," said Jenny. "C'mon Dad, let's sit in the kitchen where it's nice and cool."

Sunlight streaked through the heavy wooden blinds lighting up the rosy Saltillo tile floor. The high, dark-beamed ceiling contrasted with the soft gold stucco walls. Cactus and aloe plants dotted the Mexican tile countertops. Copper pots hung over the kitchen island which was surrounded by comfortable wicker bar stools.

Jenny sat down, feeling a little breathless. "We'll have to get used to this temperature, I'm afraid, or stay indoors all the time."

"Perhaps you'd like to rest before dinner? Your rooms are ready and I've made one into a sitting room, so you can have a little privacy."

"Thank you, Judith," Jenny said as she finished her drink. "I'd like to rest. The time change is a little hard. I tried to doze off but the clouds were especially beautiful today."

Chapter Eight

D rawn to the kitchen by the odor of the cheese and garlic loaves baking in the solar oven, Daniel watched his mother add cilantro, peppers and pea pods to the chicken stir-fry.

"Mom, I don't get what this number thing is all about. It must be serious or the Grands wouldn't have come all this way, especially in the summer."

"I really don't understand myself, Daniel. They don't want to take the mark they'll need to buy and sell. Maybe Grandpa will explain his mysterious position after dinner. Can you help me carry the food in?"

When everyone was seated, Daniel watched his mom lift her fork, a signal to begin eating, only to be interrupted by his dad. "Would you give us a blessing, Dad?"

Embarrassed, Judith put down her fork.

Grandpa bowed his head, "Dear heavenly Father, we thank you for your care, your blessings and this dear family. Give us wisdom in the days ahead and bless this food to our bodies' use. Amen."

"Amen."

The family finished eating and Judith invited them to take their dessert into the family room. Daniel and Penny stayed behind to help serve. The old couple sat down on the comfortable leather couch facing the fieldstone fireplace where a basket of bright orange Mexican Bird of Paradise replaced the logs used in winter. Harry joined them and soon the children and Judith served Key Lime pie and glasses of iced tea.

"We love having you here," Judith said quietly.

"Thank you, dear." Grandpa George looked thoughtful. "It's odd to be visiting Phoenix in the summer but the president's announcement about taking the mark to buy and sell—"

"Tell us how you came to your decision not to take the World Federation mark. We're all curious," Judith interrupted.

Grandpa opened a worn leather book. "Grandma and I follow the old ways—the ways dictated by the Bible. We've tried to live our lives according to its words. This book speaks of a time when we will have to accept a mark or number in order to buy or sell. Revelation—the book Jesus gave to His friend John—chapter 13, verses 16 and 17, say, *'And he causes all, the small and the great, and the rich and the poor, and the free men and the slaves, to be given a mark on their right hand; or on their forehead, and he provides that no one should be able to buy or to sell, except the one who has the mark' (NAS).*

"I hesitate to read this," he said turning the page, "but you must know what God says will happen to those who take this mark. Chapter 4, verses 9 to 11, read, *"If anyone receives a mark on his forehead or upon his hand, he also will drink of the wine of the wrath of God, which is mixed in full strength in the cup of His anger; and he will be tormented with fire and brimstone in the presence of the holy angels and in the presence of the Lamb. And the smoke of their torment goes up forever and ever; and they have no rest day and night, those who...receive the mark...'*

"Grandma and I believe we are living in that time and we can't accept the mark to buy and sell."

Judith fidgeted in her chair, her face a mask. How could they live their lives based on a book written thousands of years ago, totally outdated and impractical for life in the twenty-first century? She didn't want to hurt their feelings but she found their beliefs ridiculous. Not wishing to offend them, she held her head high and said simply, "I know you believe what you read, but what you say seems mystical and unbelievable. My mind tells me we can't live without taking this mark. I almost got my number last week but Harry asked me to wait to hear your explanation." She cleared her throat. "I'm sorry, but you haven't changed my mind."

A strange quietness took over the room each person lost in his own thoughts, their faces wearing a question mark. Harry wondered where they would live if they couldn't pay the ranch mortgage; Daniel and Penny wondered what kind of world it would be for them if Grandpa and Gram were right and George and Jenny wondered whether their family would listen to the warning.

Judith slid her chair back, straightened her shoulders and stood up. "As an American, I must obey my president and his council." With that said, she left the room. A moment later, they heard the sound of a car drive away.

Trying to ease the tension, Daniel got up and walked over to his crestfallen grandparents. "Are you too tired to sit on the porch with Penny and me? We haven't seen you for such a long time."

"Not tonight, Danny. Grandma and I are very tired. It was a long plane trip." George helped Jenny to her feet and they walked slowly to their rooms.

The last words Daniel heard were, "Judith can't hear, Jenny, we've tried to warn her. We can pray for her but she doesn't know God and she doesn't want to know Him."

"I just wished we could have been in their lives more, George, maybe—"

"Jenny...enough. We've lived our lives by the Bible, Harry saw this. We took him to church every Sunday. He must make his own choice now and we'll pray that God will help him and the children not take the mark. That's all we can do."

Daniel was puzzled. He loved his mom. She was smart. Something important was happening, something he didn't understand. He returned to the family room where Dad sat with his arms around Penny who was crying softly.

"Do you believe Grandpa and Grandma, Dad?" asked Daniel. "They came a long way to warn us."

"I don't know, Danny. I don't know."

Penny looked up, drying her tears, "Maybe Mom is right. She's usually right..."

"But if she's wrong," Daniel stopped, "if Grandpa and Grandma are right..."

Daniel wanted to ask Grandpa more about the strange warning in the old Bible, but decided to wait until the two were alone. It sounded to Daniel like whoever took this buying and selling mark was doomed.

Chapter Nine

Judith tossed all night. Questions bombarded her mind like bombs in a war zone. It made no sense. You had to be able to buy groceries. If you didn't pay your taxes, the IRS could take your home. The more she wrestled with her doubts, the more questions exploded in her mind.

Did Harry's parents expect them to lose everything they'd worked so hard for? Was this their way to get them to return to the lake? It was a nightmare. And why didn't Harry stand up for her? They'd made a pact to try to convince his parents, yet she saw him considering their stand. And all because of a few lines in an ancient book. Religion!

Well, depending on Harry was out of the question. One thought returned between every question. Their wonderful life on the ranch ended if no one took the mark and, despite the hurt looks, Judith planned to save them all. She planned to take the number to help the family live. Didn't anyone understand that?

Judith knew nothing of the old ways. Her parents, both college professors, valued education and progress. They taught her values and ethics and she did her best to pass these along to Daniel and Penny. Yes, she'd gone along with the Christmas and Easter traditions of the old ways because she liked tradition—a Christmas tree, Easter egg hunt. Religion took away your freedom. She wanted Daniel and Penny to experience life. Finally, tired of the mental struggle, Judith crawled out of bed, showered and dressed for the day.

Remnants of Harry's breakfast stared at her from the sink. It was just as well, she really didn't want to discuss the issue of the number with him this morning. She hated his inability to take a hard position, always more concerned with not hurting anyone's feelings. Well, she'd help him out. There could be no more argument or discussion if she just— got the number. The words of the scatterbrained woman in the grocery came to mind…"It's easy…no pain…put your hand under the machine and zap!"

Entering the barn she unplugged the SUV from the battery energizer. Then she heard it…sssssssss. Her stomach turned over. A rattlesnake. Fear traveled down her body like an electric current. Sssssssssss…where was it? She looked up to see a diamondback coiled and hissing on the hood of the car. Judith panicked, backing up. Afraid to take her eyes off the snake, she reached behind her and grabbed a pitchfork. Thrusting it under the snake, she shoved with all her might. The snake went flying out of the barn and landed directly in back of the SUV. Quickly, Judith climbed into the car, shifted into reverse and backed out hoping to hit the snake. Its diamond scales reflected in her rearview mirror and she watched it crawl back into the garage as if waiting for another chance to attack. She knew little about the Bible but a snake seemed like an omen, a really bad omen.

"Daniel." She spoke into her car phone.

"I'm here, Mom."

"There's a diamondback in the garage, be careful."

"Whoa, Mom, are you okay?"

"Yes, I've some shopping to do. I'll be back later. Will you take care of the snake?"

"You got it." Daniel hesitated. "You're not going to get the number are you?"

Judith hung up pretending not to hear Daniel's question. She hated to deceive her family but she intended to get the World Federation mark and she didn't want anyone talking her out of it. Her mind drifted to last night's discussion. *Did George really think if she took the number she would burn in hell?* She brushed a strand of hair from her eyes, glad she didn't believe in heaven or hell or a God who would judge everyone on the last day. Maybe stupid people would blow each other off the face of the earth but....a day of judgment?

She increased her speed, watching the dust cloud form behind her vehicle. As she approached the library, the line of people surrounding it surprised her. The president's news conference had its effect and the parking lot overflowed with cars. She pulled out of the lot searching for a space on the street. Two blocks away she found one, set the climate control to eighty-four degrees and jumped out of the car, hoping the lines moved fast before she was missed—two hours to accomplish the deed.

She took a deep breath and let it out as she got in line.

"Judith."

She turned to see Ruby, one of Daniel's soccer moms. "Hi, Ruby."

"Taking the number for your family? Where's Harry?"

"Home. His parents are visiting. I had a little time...I do all the purchasing for the ranch," she stammered.

"Of course. We had no idea so many people would show up." She turned to her husband. "It's all right, Charlie, you go ahead to work. You can get your number later. I'll stay another half hour then I have an appointment. This could take all morning."

Irritated, Judith sighed. The lines hardly moved.

"What's Daniel going to do this fall?" Ruby asked.

"He has an appointment for a physical this week for the Guardian interview."

"Oh, Todd thought he'd go pro—soccer. Weren't a couple of teams scouting him?"

The line moved a few feet. "I guess." Judith shifted her shoulder bag, upset that Ruby intruded into their family business.

Unable to wait any longer to get her mark, Ruby gave up. "I've got to go…a doctor appointment…good luck, Judith."

Judith watched Ruby leave. She didn't feel like small talk. Her head ached. Her life felt as heavy as her old purse. Harry's father's concern and sincerity made her uneasy. *Why was the line moving so slowly?* Only six people had gone through the library doors. She counted the people in front of her—twenty-seven.

At this rate it would take hours for her to reach the head of the line. She hated lines. She hated crowds. And she hated to give up, but her nerves would not let her wait in the line for hours. She turned, bumping into an older man. Apologizing, she almost ran for the car. What was wrong with her? She felt claustrophobic, nauseated, and the words "you'll burn in the lake of fire" kept running through her mind like a fragment of song on a warped CD. She shoved the key in the ignition, the car roared and she drove out Hwy 17 to the old wholesale mall. Shopping soothed her better than a tranquilizer.

Harry unsaddled Lad, wiping the sweat off his back. Each day he tried to get up early enough to ride out to check on the cattle and give Lad a workout. Summer was hard on the horses and the cattle.

"Harry?"

"In here, Dad. It's pretty hot out here for you."

"I know but I wanted to talk to you privately. I thought while Jenny had her nap…"

Harry sat down on a bale of hay motioning his dad to another. "Sorry, Dad, no chairs."

George lowered himself to the hay bale. "Never mind, I don't want to hassle you, son, but have you given any more thought to taking the mark?"

Harry stalled. "No, not really. I can't see how I'd run the ranch without access to money."

"I know, son but you wouldn't have to do it forever." George hesitated. "Maybe only three and a half years."

"I don't think I can avoid taking it, Dad."

George looked grave but determined to make Harry understand. "At your age you don't think about death but the longest people live is around one hundred years, if that long. The body dies—dust to dust—but you can't kill the soul. It lives forever. The question is, after you die, where does it go? If you've believed in God and in Christ, your soul returns to God. If you haven't believed, your soul can only go to Hades to wait for the final judgment."

Something stirred in Harry. His father's words lit a fire that had nearly gone out. He listened in respect. "You say if we take the number we lose that right...to go to heaven, I mean."

"True, the mark isn't just for buying and selling. It means you belong to the system. You belong to evil and receiving the mark changes you. You're deceived. You see everything through the government's eyes. Aren't you worried about this government?"

Harry was worried, the strange and terrible initiatives... the president who made his own laws. He agreed with his father. Unlike Judith who idolized the president, he definitely felt evil coming from this man. "But Dad, even if I convinced Judith, how would we live?"

"Do you know God's name, Harry? It's Emmanuel, God with us. I can't answer you but I know He will be with His people. Maybe your life wouldn't be the same but you could go to the lake. Your mom and I plan to prepay our bills, plant a big garden, fish...try to stay alive until..."

"Until what, Dad?"

"Until Jesus comes again."

"He's coming again?"

"Yes, to take those who believe in Him to be with Him forever."

Harry raised his hand to stop his father. If he had to cram another religious idea into his brain, he'd disintegrate. "I'm sorry, Dad; it's a lot to digest."

George patted Harry's shoulder, "Think it over, son, it's your eternal soul. It will live one of two places—in heaven with God or in the lake of fire."

Chapter Ten

Daniel pulled the covers over his head trying to shut out the shrill beeping. The emergency alarm? Covering his ears, he stumbled to the wall unit pressing the alarm off. It had to be Mom. Then he remembered, today was his interview with the Center for New Age Medicine. Dreading the Guardian interview, Daniel trudged to the shower.

Why was his mother still pressuring him about the Guardians? Her constant questions and reminders about the interview and physical were driving him crazy and he was nervous enough. He took a deep breath, *Relax, Daniel, the odds are on your side fifty-to-one, remember.*

Last night he reviewed the Guardian material, finding it much cooler than he'd expected. The recruits pictured in the brochure looked like guys he'd hang out with. If something went wrong and they chose him as a Guardian, he could deal. The stakes were high and he wouldn't know his fate until the last card was played.

Daniel stepped out of the shower to discover his navy sports coat, slacks and a tie lying on the bed. He rejected the tie and the dress shirt and selected a light blue golf shirt. *What was she thinking? No one wore a tie at 104 degrees.* He shaved, ran a comb through his hair and patted on some aftershave.

"Daniel, are you dressed yet? Remember, you can't eat anything. You're having blood work. And don't swallow the toothpaste."

Daniel sighed, slipped on his black leather loafers and threw his jacket over his arm. He met Penny in the hallway.

"Good luck on your interview, Danny. I'll be thinking about you."

"Thanks. What are you up to?"

"Taking the new guests horseback riding and tonight I promised to play the guitar at the campfire. We even invited Gram and Grandpa."

Daniel smiled. Penny was such a cowgirl. She loved working with Dad on the ranch. "Sounds great to me, Pen."

Daniel walked into the kitchen just as Grandpa George and Grandma Jenny sat down to eat breakfast.

Grandpa whistled. "My Daniel, you look impressive. Big day, eh? Pull up a chair and join us."

"I can't, Gramps. Joey's picking me up any minute. What are you guys doing today?"

"Just taking it easy. Gram's a little under the weather. Good luck on your interview, son, if that's what you want."

"My life is in the hands of the gods," Daniel joked.

Grandpa looked up from his coffee with a sudden, serious expression on his face. "It's in the hands of God, Daniel. God created you and he has good plans for your life."

"Right."

Daniel didn't know much about God except for what Grandpa taught him through the years. Grandpa believed the night sky was a star map of God's creation—sort of his signature in the night sky—a different view from the theory of evolution that Daniel learned in school. Gramps was old, and he stuck to the old ways. But one thing for sure, the old ways hadn't hurt his grandparents. They were kind and helpful to everyone and he'd never heard them say a mean word. Outside in the driveway, a horn tooted.

"Mom, you around here somewhere?" Daniel called.

Judith poked her head out of her small office. "In here, honey, are you leaving now?" She came into the kitchen to give her son a final onceover. "You look handsome, Daniel. Remember, be respectful, a gentleman and a scholar. No jokes, and good English."

"Mom, I'm not in kindergarten. Give me a break." Daniel gave her a hug and waved good-bye to his grandparents. "See you later, alligators."

Behind the wheel of his sun-scorched Jeep, Joey reached a leg out and kicked the passenger door open for Daniel. "Sorry, door's jammed."

"Dude, you look sharp. Did your mom pick out your tie?"

"Yeah, how'd you get away without one? Your mom off duty today?"

Daniel punched him, "No, she tried. Laid out all my clothes."

Joey hit the horn. "They're all alike, DJ." He set the satellite radio to Top 20 and backed out of the drive. "You nervous?"

Daniel shrugged his shoulders, "A little. You?"

"I guess."

They drove to the Tower in silence, listening to the music. Joey pulled into the underground parking garage. He slipped the metallic parking pass into the robot greeter and it flashed B106. "Slick," Joey said. They parked the old car in B106 and headed for the elevator.

Daniel glanced at his friend. "Race you up the stairs..."

"It's on the twenty-third floor...." Joey scowled at Daniel. "So."

Daniel threw back the metal door that led to the fire stairs. The boys took the stairs two at a time. Daniel's triathlon training kicked in and near the twelfth floor he edged ahead of Joey. He stopped at fifteen to catch his breath and Joey sailed past him.

"Remember the turtle and the hare?"

"No turtle's gonna beat me, " Daniel laughed, and with a burst of energy passed Joey. At the twenty-third floor he pushed open the heavy steel door and found himself standing outside a glass door, which read *Center for New Age Medicine*, Dr. Gregory Hart.

Daniel slipped on his sport coat while he waited for Joey to catch up. He peered through the door. The waiting room was empty.

"We must have the first appointments," Daniel said.

"Excellent." They went up to the receiving desk.

"Can I help you, boys?" The receptionist glanced up from her computer screen.

"Yeah... I mean yes, you can. My name is Daniel Jordan. This is Joey Decker. We're here for the Guardian tests."

The receptionist smiled politely as she sized them up. "Sign in, boys. You have to take this personality profile first. Take a seat at the tables, read the instructions and try to answer the questions carefully and completely. Feel free to ask me anything you don't understand. When you finish, the doctor will see you."

"Thanks for your help, Ma'am."

Daniel turned away from the reception desk with his arms full of paper. He glanced over at Joey already studying the questionnaire. Joey glanced up at him. "They got some weird questions here."

"No talking, boys."

A half hour later, Daniel entered the examining room where he found Dr. Hart looking over the applications.

"Good morning, Daniel."

"Sir, I mean, hello."

Greg smiled at Daniel, kindly. "Is it getting hot out there yet?"

"Not too bad."

"That's good. So, did the nurse tell you what I'm going to do?"

"Yes sir, draw blood and take samples."

"That's right. May I have your arm?"

The doctor took Daniel's arm noticing that he had none of the usual tattoos. "No tattoos?"

"No sir, I'm an athlete. Coach didn't allow our high school Olympic team to have tattoos."

"You're lucky. Even with laser treatment, they're hard to get off. And...somehow what seems cool when you're eighteen doesn't seem to fit when you're my age."

The doctor filled five test tubes with Daniel's blood. "We'll run a chemical analysis on the blood samples. Now I need to swab the inside of your cheek for the DNA genome blueprint. Open your mouth, please." The doctor placed the swab in a sterile bag and sealed it, adding a sticker with Daniel's name. "The DNA blueprint is the part of the test you can't control—you inherit your genetics." The doctor put away his implements and spoke softly. "Come over to my desk and let's talk."

Daniel watched the doctor as he leafed through the chart and glanced at some of Daniel's answers. Then he set Daniel's chart down on the counter. "Good...so you can relax now. Think of this as just a casual conversation."

Daniel knew that the conversation would not be casual, that the doctor would weigh each answer Daniel gave. He'd try to give the answers the military wanted to hear.

"What would be your attitude toward your superiors, Daniel?" The doctor rubbed his eyes, and then pushed up his glasses, waiting for a response.

"Sir, I would do my best to carry out my orders and to follow the directions of my superiors."

"Tell me why you want to be a Guardian, Daniel."

Daniel thought for a moment, *Should he tell the truth that this was all his mother's idea and in truth he didn't want to be a Guardian?* Then discarding that idea, he chose his words carefully. "I like being part of a team. I don't think there is a more important team I could be on, sir."

Dr. Hart nodded, and made a note in Daniel's chart. "One last question, what if the Guardians asked you to do something you didn't approve of?"

"Sir, I'm confident anything the Guardian Corps asked me to do was thought out and carefully considered by wiser people than I. I mean, than me."

Dr. Hart closed Daniel's file. "Thank you, Daniel. You'll receive our decision in the mail. Have a good day."

Daniel hopped off the table. "How long before I know, sir?"

"As soon as the genome blueprints come back, and I've reviewed all the qualified candidates, about three weeks."

"Thanks for your consideration, Doctor. And thank you for your time today." Impulsively, Daniel reached out and shook the doctor's hand, surprising them both. Embarrassed, he hurried out to the crowded waiting room and leaned against the door to wait for Joey. It looked like about nineteen guys his age were filling out personality profiles, a few from the high school Olympics.

"How'd it go, Joey?" he asked as Joey returned to the room.

"Okay, I guess…but Daniel, I don't think I'm the type they're looking for."

"Like I am?"

"Yeah, maybe you are. How'd you do with the interview?"

"Just gave them what they wanted to hear. Played the game."

Joey looked at Daniel, "Why would you do that, Daniel? Why didn't you just tell the truth, then you'd be home free."

Daniel's face reddened. Joey was right. It wasn't very smart on his part to give the doctor what he wanted to hear. If he'd told him he really wanted to play pro ball…Daniel dropped his head. So dumb…why hadn't he thought it out?

Joey saw that he'd struck bone marrow and said, "It's okay, Big Guy, like you said fifty-to-one."

After dinner, Grandpa George invited Daniel to come into the woodshop. Daniel loved the smell of the mesquite and pine in the shop. What was Grandpa working on? "Tying a few fishing flies, Danny, thought you might like them for your fishing trips."

"Caught a nice trout with the last one you made, Grandpa, remember it?"

"Green fly…one of my favorites."

Daniel dropped down on a stool to watch his grandfather work.

"So how did the interview go?"

"Fine."

" For a while there I thought you were going to be our next world soccer star."

"Maybe I still will. Fifty guys tried out for the Guardians. I don't know what my chances are. It's a tough decision, Gramps. Joey's confused, too. He always wanted to be a vet. I love the athlete's life, but…I don't know." Daniel paused. "Mom wants something more for me. She wants me to *be* somebody, I guess."

"No matter what you do with your life, you'll be somebody, Danny."

"Yeah, I guess. But you know how she is. She's really excited about the new president and all the changes. She thinks if I become a Guardian I'd be on the right track to becoming a legislator or something."

Grandpa didn't look up. "So it's really your mom's idea?"

"I guess. I figured I could try. Chances are I won't make it anyway, and taking the interviews gets her off my back. I mean, it would be cool to be a Guardian but if I don't make it, I'll go to the San Diego College for Professional Athletes."

Grandpa looked up at Daniel, impressed. "You've been invited to that?"

"Yeah, I sent my application in yesterday."

"Daniel, we are going into some dangerous years. I hope your life works out the way you want it, but be careful, son."

"Is this about the mark?"

"Yes, partly. Have you ever read the Bible?"

" No, sir. I don't have one."

"Its words are full of hope and power. It's never let Grandma and me down and neither has the Author."

"The author? Do you know who actually wrote it? I mean, it's so old."

"Well, we believe it is the inspired Word of God spoken through the ages to certain men and women whom God chose."

"You believe God talks to people?"

"Yes."

"Even today?"

"God can do anything He wants. And His book might seem ancient to you, but the part I read to you is right on target for today. Amazing that someone two thousand years ago could write about today, don't you think?"

"You don't want me to take the mark, do you, Grandpa?"

"I don't want anyone to take it, Daniel. But when you turn twenty-one, you will have to wrestle with that question yourself. I can't make that decision for you. Just remember the stakes are high. I don't know if you believe there is life after we leave this world, but the Bible teaches that there is and we will either spend it with those who love God or be cast into darkness and fire with those who reject Him."

"My parents don't talk about God much."

"I know, but that doesn't make Him unreal, only in their world. I'm praying for you. I hope someday you'll meet God and come to know Him."

Grandpa picked up the fly he was working on, "We'll make its head a brilliant blue and its body yellow." He turned to Daniel, "Let me know what you catch with this fella, huh Danny."

The two worked silently on the flies: Past and future, sitting side by side.

Chapter Eleven

P enny opened the refrigerator door on a sweet-tooth safari. She needed sugar. Her eyes searched each shelf... carrot juice, avocadoes, asparagus, tofu, cheese...there must be something a thirteen-year-old could eat. Where were the colas, something with chocolate, even a smoothie. *I'll starve to death,* Penny thought. Hearing footsteps behind her, she turned to find Grandma Jenny.

"Getting a snack, Penny?"

"I wish, Gram. Nothing here but carrot juice and alfalfa sprouts."

Gram winked. "I know just what you need." She opened the pantry, took out a large tin and pulled off the lid.

"Chocolate chip cookies!! Thanks, Gram."

"I made them this morning while your mom was out."

"I love having you here, Gram...it's just better."

Jenny nodded. "We're both glad for this special time with you, Penny. Life is short. Seems like we've only seen you once or twice a year."

Penny noticed that Gram looked sad. Her skin looked funny, too, kind of gray. "Are you feeling all right, Gram?"

"I'm fine. Just feeling my age, I guess. Oh listen, do you hear that quail call? The poor little thing sounds lost."

"You should see them when they have babies. They parade across the top of the garden wall so proud."

"They're a family, Penny. I'm sure they're very proud and protective of their young. It's God's way, even with birds."

Penny finished her cookies, leaned over and gave Gram a hug. "Got to run, Gram. Hope you feel like coming to the campfire." She picked up her guitar, placed a bright red felt cowboy hat on her head and grabbed her sunglasses.

Grandma watched Penny walk to the stables. From the kitchen window, she could see the stalls for the horses, the rodeo ring and the line of cottonwood trees that lined the bank of the Verde River. A few winters ago, she and George stayed in one of the guesthouses, but at 104 degrees, Jenny appreciated the ranch with its air conditioning.

Her mind wandered, remembering the day Harry graduated from the University of Michigan. George asked him what he planned to do with his business degree and he surprised them by sharing his dream of going out west to work on a dude ranch. Later, after he married Judith, they purchased Sunset Acres and built a dude ranch now written up in travel guides worldwide.

Jenny was proud of him, but very concerned. She'd seen Judith taking more and more control both in the business and in the family while Harry grew further and further from his roots. She felt strongly that Judith would take the mark to buy and sell but... she prayed, "*Lord, give our son the strength and wisdom to resist it.*"

Jenny cleaned up the kitchen and set the table for four. Unaccustomed to the food butler, she waited for Judith to program the evening meal. Her mind didn't comprehend how a meal appeared in the butler within fifteen minutes.

As Jenny bent down to close a cupboard door, a stabbing pain exploded across the top of her shoulders. Astonished and frightened, she grasped her chest unable to breathe. Then everything went black and she slipped to the floor.

George finished carving the lid of the wooden box he was making for Daniel and leaned back to examine his work, pleased that his first horse carving actually looked like one. He traced the shape with his finger and was blowing out the chips when a feeling of anxiety washed over him. Something was wrong. He dropped the box and went to look for Jenny. Was she resting? The bed was undisturbed. His heart drummed a warning. The kitchen…he smelled chocolate chip cookies but there was no sign of Jenny.

"Jenny?" Puzzled, he stepped around the kitchen island to find his wife lying crumpled on the floor. He knelt beside her.

"Jenny, are you all right?" He cradled her head on his arm. Her breathing was shallow. He held her for a second, then stood up and rushed over to the intercom unit. He pressed a large red button labeled "Emergency" and addressed the security system. "Medical alert." The security system automatically dialed the emergency response team—911.

"May I help you, sir?"

"It's my wife. She's collapsed."

"Is she breathing?"

"Yes … barely."

"Can you get a pulse?"

Moving his fingers from wrist to neck, George tried to find Jenny's pulse. "I'm having difficulty finding one...a beat now and then."

The computer shows you are at 25821 Trails End, Scottsdale, off Dynamite. We'll send a medivac.

"We're in the kitchen."

Tears made paths down the lines on his cheeks. Dearest Jenny. He spoke softly, "It's all right, Jenny, help is coming. I'm here. You'll be all right. Please, don't give up." George felt a light touch on his hand.

He was terrified. What if she died before help arrived? What would he do without her? He looked at his beautiful wife of fifty years and his throat tightened. Swallowing the tears he couldn't control, he whispered, "Don't leave me, Jenny, not yet."

In a few minutes, he heard the whirr of the medical helicopter, but he stayed next to Jenny afraid to leave her side.

The hurried clicking of shoes on the foyer tile told him the paramedics had arrived. Three men entered the kitchen dressed in green scrubs and wearing masks. They spotted Jenny and lifted her onto a stretcher. "She'll be better when we get her aboard," one of the paramedics told George. "The transport has oxygen vents, and we'll hook her to the heart monitoring equipment."

George rose to his feet following Jenny and the paramedics out of the kitchen. Unable to keep up, he tried to follow the men to the plane. One of the paramedics saw him and yelled, "We can't take you along, sir." George could hardly hear him over the noise of the propellers.

A hand pressed his shoulder and he turned to find Judith. "It's all right, George, I'll take you to the hospital." She tried to make her voice heard over the engines, "What hospital?" she yelled.

"Phoenix Heart Institute, folks."

The helicopter lifted leaving them in a cloud of dust. George followed Judith's hand motion and climbed into the SUV. Neither spoke.

Chapter Twelve

George held his breath while Judith weaved in and out of traffic on Dynamite Road finally connecting with the Piestewa Freeway off the 101. He watched her verbally set the GPS for the Phoenix Heart Institute. Twenty-five minutes later Judith dropped George at the emergency entrance to the hospital instructing him to go to the business office to give his insurance information while she parked the car. George followed the yellow line painted on the floor. He waited his turn, handed the admissions clerk stationed behind the bulletproof glass his Senior Services card and watched her swipe the card, inserting Jenny's information automatically into the system.

"Is this your present address?" questioned the woman.

"No, we're staying with our son and daughter-in-law."

"Their address?"

George's mind went blank. The woman tapped her fingernails on the counter.

"25821 Trails End, Scottsdale," Judith announced putting a hand on his shoulder.

George's legs felt like Jell-O. He steadied himself holding on to the window ledge. "Where do we find my wife?" he asked.

The woman took a moment to trace Jenny's location. "She's on the third floor in the west wing. Judith put her arm around George's shoulders and helped him to the bank of elevators, pushing the call button for the third floor. The elevator door slid open and they stepped on in silence.

"I'm sure she'll be all right." Judith said trying to comfort George. The doors to the elevator opened and they stepped off, intercepted by an aide who directed them to the waiting area.

"You're here for?"

"My wife, Jenny Jordan." George said.

"Your wife is with the doctor, sir. They're running a 405 series on her."

"A 405 series?"

"It's the series for emergency heart admissions."

George followed Judith into the empty waiting area. Blue lights and a glass wall of tropical fish greeted them. Judith helped him into a seat across from the tank. He sat quietly hypnotized by the movement and colors of the beautiful salt water fish. A pair of striped angelfish caught his eye. They swam side by side in perfect rhythm, turning simultaneously, stopping at precisely the same moment as if they were one, long accustomed to the dance, *a little like Jenny and me,* George thought—*tuned to one another.*

The vibration of Harry's digital wrist phone startled him. He glanced at the number, Judith?

"Harry, something's happened. Your mother collapsed in the kitchen and George found her unconscious. He called the emergency care system and they sent a helicopter to take her to the Phoenix Heart Institute."

Stunned by the news, Harry found himself at a loss for words. "Is she okay?"

"She's still unconscious—maybe a heart attack. We're both here. They're running tests. I'll keep you posted. If things get worse, I'll call. I promise. I'll call, okay?"

Harry sighed as he switched the phone off and turned to the group of visitors. "Folks, I have an emergency. Lester will finish grilling your steaks. Just eat up and enjoy your dinner."

Penny galloped up from the rear. "What happened, Dad?"

"Grandma collapsed. I need to go to the hospital."

"I want to go, too."

"No, I need you to lead the sing-along."

"But—"

"Please, Pen. Can you do that for me? I'll call as soon as I know anything. Here, take my phone. If Daniel's at the ranch, I'll send him down."

He galloped back to the ranch letting Dusty have his head. As he dismounted, he was relieved to see Daniel coming out of the barn to greet him.

"Dad, what's up? Nobody's home, is something wrong?"

"Grandma had a heart attack. They took her to the Heart Institute. Can you take Sandy and ride out to the northeast acreage? I'd like you to help Lester and Penny with the tourists while I go to the hospital. I want to be there for Grandpa, but I need you here son, understand?"

Daniel nodded. "Sure, Dad, you can count on me."

Harry entered the waiting room where his dad sat quietly, mesmerized by the tropical fish. Judith sat beside him, reading. Harry strode over, put his arm around the old man's shoulders, not knowing what to say. George nodded in recognition. "Any news?"

Judith put down the magazine she was reading. "Not yet. They said it would take three hours and we've one to go. I'm fading away, Harry, I think I'll go to the hospital emporium and get a latte. Can I bring you anything? What about you, George?"

Both shook their heads.

A few minutes after Judith left, the doctor appeared in the doorway. "Jordan," he called out. George and Harry got up. "Mrs. Jordan has suffered a major heart attack."

George started to sway, but Harry reached out to steady him as the doctor continued. "We no longer perform heart procedures on anyone over seventy-five." He paused to let them digest the news.

George and Harry stared at the doctor, shaken.

"But she just turned seventy-five," George appealed to the young doctor.

"I'm sorry. I really am, but the Council of Twelve's new guidelines prohibit anything but vitamins and pain meds. I'll give you a prescription. We'll let her rest here tonight and you can take her home in the morning."

Dumfounded, Harry and George digested the incredible information. "Can I stay with her?" George asked.

"Of course, the nurse will take you to her room." With that, the doctor fled through the swinging doors into the medical zone, safe from any further questions.

"Harry, you and Judith go on home. No reason for all of us to stay," said George.

"Will you be okay, Dad?"

"Yes, I'll just see if they'll let me sleep in Jenny's room. I don't want her to wake up alone. You go along. I'll call when we're ready to come home tomorrow."

Harry waited until he and Judith were on the elevator. "I can't believe they won't do anything for my mother because of her age. Another initiative to save money on the backs of old, defenseless people."

Judith kept silent, afraid anything she said would make things worse.

The next day when Harry returned, he expected to see his mother in bed; however, Jenny greeted him fully dressed and ready to go home.

"Come in, Harry. We're nearly ready to go. Can you believe George slept in that chair all night?"

Harry relaxed. *Maybe it wasn't as bad as they'd thought.* He watched his father pat his mother's hand, a resigned look on his face.

"Ring for the nurse, Harry," George said. "She'll bring a wheelchair." Harry pushed the contact button and the nurse came scurrying in.

"Ready to go? I've sent for a wheelchair." She bent down speaking softly to Jenny. "Now, don't you go getting in trouble again, Ms. Jenny. Not a whole lot we can do for you here." Then lowering her voice, she whispered, "Just stay at home and let your loved ones take care of you next time."

Harry listened, upset that the hospital personnel offered his mother no bypass, stent or laser treatment for her heart. When did this change take place? There'd been nothing on the news. Then he understood, the president and his Council made the decision, leaving the hospital personnel powerless to do anything. Sadness mixed with outrage filled his heart. How evil!

George addressed the nurse. "Thank you for your good care," he said generously.

The nurse's face reddened. Embarrassed she looked away, frustrated that the hospital was unable to help these sweet old people.

A young man in a white jacket wheeled in a chair and the nurse continued. "Here are her home care instructions. She's scheduled for an appointment in a week with the Center for New Age Medicine, her neighborhood center. You take care now, Ms. Jenny, hear?" The orderly pushed the wheelchair and the group moved off. Only Harry hung behind.

Harry looked at the name on the badge. "Ms. ... Ms. Monroe, could I speak with you a moment?"

The nurse stopped, a worried look on her face. "Yes?"

"I don't understand. Are you saying the next time my mother has a heart attack she will die because you aren't allowed to give her any heart procedures?"

"I'm sorry sir, but those are our instructions. In fact, just so you know, we can't even do tests on her, so next time you're better off making her as comfortable as possible... at home."

"But that's inhumane...she'll die without surgery...I'll sue the hospital..." Harry sputtered.

"It won't help," the nurse said quietly. "The order came from the president. It's a new health initiative. The government is trying to save our national health care system. I won't make excuses. None of us understand." She turned and walked slowly away. Harry caught up with his family.

"What were you talking about, son?"

"I'll tell you later, Dad. Let's get this pretty girl home. Ready to go, Mom?"

Jenny gave him a thumbs-up. No one spoke on the way home. Finally, Harry broke the silence. "I don't understand, Dad, we live in a scientific age."

George struggled for words. "It's going to be a difficult age, Harry. Things will get worse. Think of the millions of dollars the government saves if no one over seventy-five has life-saving surgeries." What he didn't add was if these were the last years, worse things lie ahead. George felt like weeping. His lovely wife would die needlessly. George put his arm around Jenny's shoulder trying to comfort her. "Jenny and I had a full life. We're ready to be with the Lord whenever he calls us."

The Old Ways again. Harry kept silent although he wanted to bash something or someone.

"Harry," Judith said, "watch where you're going. You're scaring us. Do you want me to drive?"

Harry snapped back to reality, realizing he'd been driving 70 in a 25-mile-an-hour zone. He tried to calm down but why was his father accepting this when they needed to fight? Did his religion prevent him from protesting an injustice? So they were ready for heaven, but who even knew if there was a real heaven? Maybe this life was all there was. He forced himself to be quiet, not wanting to upset his mother but in his eyes the battle wasn't over. If his dad wouldn't fight, maybe he'd have to.

The gas indicator turned red indicating an empty tank. Unless he got the mark soon, he'd be unable to service the car. "Dad, if I don't get the mark I won't even be able to gas my cars."

George closed his eyes, took a deep breath and then said, "I told you, Harry, according to the Bible, anyone who takes the mark will be deceived and lose his chance for eternal life."

"Which means what in English, Dad?"

"It means when people with the mark die, they will not go to heaven. They will be sent to the lake of fire."

Harry slammed the car door…the lake of fire?

Chapter Thirteen

J udith bustled around the kitchen preparing a favorite meal for her family, glad the tourist season had ended. For now the attention centered on Jenny not her. *What will become of these old people,* she thought. It saddened her to think the hospital would do nothing further for her mother-in-law.

Phoenix drew old people like moths to the light; Judith saw them everywhere—mostly snowbirds trying to live longer, spending their winters in the sunshine. Sometimes their driving annoyed her because they pulled out without looking, drove too slowly and acted like they were the only ones on the road, but she couldn't imagine how denying them life-saving surgeries would impact them. She found it hard to think of them as a group costing the government millions of dollars. They were, after all, someone's parents and grandparents.

Judith pulled out her cookbook and located the recipes for chicken quesadilla and peach cobbler. "*Carpe diem,*" she said to herself. "At least we have today."

After preparing the dinner, Judith made a centerpiece for the table. She filled a bowl with water and floated a handful of orange poppies in it, then added Mexican candlesticks on each side, finally placing dark blue napkins next to each plate. She stepped back to survey her work. *Festive,* she thought. She glanced at the clock, 4:30 p.m. Harry finished work around 5:30 and dinner at 6:30 gave him a chance to clean up and catch the news.

Jenny scuffed into the kitchen seeing Judith's preparations for dinner. "Oh, Judith, why didn't you let me set the table for you?" Disappointed she sat down on a kitchen stool. "It looks very pretty. I…just feel so useless."

Judith glanced over her shoulder reading the sadness in her mother-in-law's face. She hadn't included Jenny in the housework lately. Penny and Daniel cleaned up the kitchen each night and Judith prepared the meals. Reaching up into the cupboard, Judith took down the salt and pepper shakers that matched her Mexican candlesticks. "Would you fill these for me, Jenny? They're almost empty."

Jenny beamed.

"How are you feeling today? You haven't been home from the hospital that long, Jenny. I'm trying to take good care of you."

"I know, dear but I'm so used to doing things, the stress of doing nothing is worse. You can only rest so much. And George tells me we'll stay until I'm on my feet, whatever that means. To be honest, I'd just like to go home."

Judith understood why Jenny missed the cottage. Michigan was beautiful in summer, especially the lake, but they couldn't let the old couple go home until they convinced them to get the World Federation mark. Without it, they wouldn't survive. But for now, she needed to find a few things to keep Jenny busy. "Do you quilt? I inherited a quilt from my mother and I have no idea what to do with it."

Jenny nodded. "I'd love to quilt it while we're here. I hope we can go home soon but the nurse said not to travel for a few weeks. Thanks, Judith, I need a project."

Maybe if Jenny had her own project, Judith could get back to scheduling next season's clientele. The heart of their business came from families who wanted to get away from their lives and spend quality time on a family adventure. The corporate leadership camps for business executives were getting more popular, probably as a result of people living their lives in cubicles. And through her Internet ads she'd drawn a faithful foreign clientele of Germans, Russians and Japanese fascinated with the American cowboy scene.

Scout troops and Boys and Girls Clubs also contacted her from time to time. Judith squeezed them in between bigger groups trying to keep the costs low. She searched hard to find companies to sponsor scholarships so the urban children might get out of the city, and have an opportunity to ride horses, camp under the stars and even fish in the Verde River.

She reminded herself to call a few editors she'd befriended at the travel magazines and lobby them to feature the ranch in their Best of the West editions. Then she wrote herself a note to pick up the new brochures from the printers. She'd ask Penny and Grandma Jenny to help her send them out next week to encourage repeat customers. So much to do!

Daniel slipped into the kitchen, sweeping his mom off her feet, literally.

"Put me down, Daniel! What's that in your hand? Your letter from the Center for New Age Medicine? I knew this was a special occasion. Did you open it?"

"No, Mom, I thought I'd give you the honor. Break the news to me after dinner."

"With dessert." Judith smiled. *Could Daniel have made the Guardians?*

The family drifted in taking their seats at the rustic dining table.

"Mom, something special tonight?" asked Penny. "You really outdid yourself."

"You never know," Judith replied, winking at Daniel. Her appetite gone, she picked at her food waiting for the others to finish their meal.

After serving the cobbler, Judith took the envelope, scanning the lengthy legal document. Her face burst into a smile as she read aloud: "Daniel Jordan has been appointed as a Guardian for the state of Arizona. The candidate will report to Luke Air Force Base on 1 October, 2022, for enrollment in the U.S. Guardian Corps." She stopped to catch her breath. "Oh, Daniel, I'm so proud of you."

Penny clapped her hands. "Oh, Danny, wait till I tell my friends. They'll think you're so cool!"

Harry cleared his throat, "Congratulations, son."

George reached over the table and shook Daniel's hand. "They're lucky to have you, Danny."

Daniel accepted their good wishes, feeling like someone had ripped his heart out and buried his dreams for the future. He batted tears away. *Why did he try for the Guardians? Was it just to pacify his mother and get her off his case? Why hadn't he been honest and followed his lifelong dream. The doors to a pro soccer career had been open.* He pasted a smile on his face but had nothing to say. The best thing to do now was to act like a man, change his dream and become the best Guardian Arizona had ever sent. He gambled and lost.

Jenny sat quietly taking it all in. She whispered to George, "Shall we tell them our news, George?"

"No, dear, tonight is Daniel's night. Let's just be happy for him."

As Judith cleared the table, the family moved out to the verandah to enjoy the evening. George and Jenny sat on their favorite glider while the rest of the family chose the old Mexican rockers.

Grandpa George pulled out his harmonica, "Penny will you play something on your guitar? You lead, I'll follow."

Penny strummed the notes of Shenandoah and Grandpa added his soft harmonica accompaniment. The moment seemed perfect and everyone listened as the two played in harmony. Finally, George played "Taps." The old clock on the mantelpiece struck eleven o'clock.

"My, it's late," said Jenny. "I need to put my old bones to bed."

"You go ahead, dear," George said. "I think I'll watch the eleven o'clock news with Harry."

The family departed and Harry and George moved inside where they sat companionably watching the news. A World News reporter, the wind whipping his hair, stood with the red rock mountains of Sedona looming majestically behind him.

"Dad, have we ever taken you to Sedona?"

"No, son, I don't think so. Looks like a beautiful spot."

"Wait. Listen a second. What's he saying?" Harry turned the volume up.

"On September 11, the first Ascension will be held here in Sedona, Arizona. The new initiative passed by the Council is part of the president's plan to enable America to become financially solvent again. The Ascension will provide an opportunity for America's seniors to give service to their country..."

George reached a weathered hand into his pocket and fished out a crumpled envelope. He handed it to Harry. "Looks like we'll all be seeing Sedona," he said.

Harry unfolded the crumpled letter and read it silently. He looked up from the paper and regarded his father solemnly. "I don't understand. What does this mean, Dad?"

"The Center for New Age Medicine selected Jenny and me for the first Ascension. This letter says the Guardian Corps will escort us to Sedona."

"They can't do that, Dad. You and Mom aren't even residents of Arizona."

"True, Harry, but we are citizens of the US and this program is evidently a national program."

"I don't understand. What exactly is the Ascension?"

"The letter said it was our opportunity to give our lives for our country."

"But Dad…"

"I'm 80 and…Jenny's heart. When we went to the hospital…I don't know… they must have turned our information over to the Center for New Age Medicine. We each got a letter. They came before Daniel's did, but we didn't want to spoil his big moment."

Speechless, Harry stared at the fire. Who did this government think it was? What happened to the individual's right-to-life and the pursuit of happiness? The initiative to withhold life-saving surgery was terrible, but this? Condemning his parents to death and telling them they were giving service to their country—it was outrageous! Harry lowered his eyes so his father couldn't see the anger or the tears.

"It's out of our hands, Harry. We'll talk about this later. Maybe, if we hadn't come to Phoenix. But we did. We came because we love you and it seemed important to try to make you understand not to take the mark. I don't regret it. I think perhaps it's time for your mother and me to go to heaven. It's not a world we can live in anymore."

George's words were like a knife in his heart, "perhaps if they hadn't come to Phoenix…" It was Harry's fault. He'd begged them to come.

Chapter Fourteen

Needing to escape the ranch, Harry decided to brand the cattle before he and Penny drove them to Colorado. He was disappointed that Daniel wasn't going to San Diego for the sports college. He was dumfounded when the hospital refused to take care of his mother, and now the Ascension? Was he supposed to take this heinous new initiative in stride, an initiative that would kill their only living parents?

Harry wiped his forehead which dripped with sweat. But the worst part to him was the fact that somewhere along the line, he'd lost Judith who praised everything the president did, even the Ascension. How could she think the Ascension was a wonderful American event making heroes of the old and disabled? *I can't think about it anymore,* thought Harry. He lifted the branding iron and put the Sunshine Acre sun brand on the steer in front of him. The smell of burning flesh nauseated him but he patted the steer on the rear sending it back into the herd.

A cloud of dust rose and Harry saw Judith wheel the Jeep to a stop. Surprised that she'd drive out to the branding, Harry left the herd and headed her way. "Something wrong?"

"No, I needed to talk to you without your parents around."

Harry led her into the shade under the mesquite trees. "So what's on your mind?"

" It's close to the twenty-seventh…time's running out, Harry. Someone has to get the number for our family. I've decided to go. Will you go with me?"

Harry looked down. "Can't today. Branding."

Judith drew in her breath, "Harry, you do plan to get the mark, don't you?"

"I'm thinking about it but I can't do it with Dad here. He's…"

"Forget your dad, think about us. You need the number to buy horses in the fall. You don't expect me to ride to the sale, do you? Am I supposed to take over putting gas in all the vehicles, too? Be practical, Harry."

Harry studied his wife. The determined look on her face told him she meant business. "I haven't decided whether to take the mark. My parents…think the president is an evil man."

Judith gasped. "Our president, an evil man? Now I've heard everything. He's the first president to solve any problems in ages." She stared at Harry in bewilderment. "I can't believe you, Harry. You're really ready to give up all we've worked for because of your parents' paranoia?" Angrily, she turned and walked away, slamming the car door as she got in. Without looking back, she headed for the library determined to stay if it took all day.

Thankful no line wound around the outside of the building, Judith parked, setting her temperature control to 84 degrees. She grabbed her shoulder bag and made her way in between the cars. When she reached the lobby, she saw book shelves had been removed and replaced with chairs. Tables lined the walls. She got in the JKL line observing the people getting their number, most were women like herself, a few couples, very few children—but at some point, everyone would have a number.

She reached the head of the line and a stern-looking woman greeted her too busy to look up. The woman shoved a packet of papers at her, "Take these over to the chairs and fill them out," she snapped. "Your number is 256. Try to have your papers finished by the time your number is called."

Judith took the papers, found a seat and started filling them out. She listed her bank accounts and account numbers, glad she'd remembered to bring her bankbooks. *How many people in her family yet to receive the number*? Three. She wrote rapidly hoping to finish before the woman called her number.

"Excuse me," a young woman interrupted. "Do you have an extra pen? I seem to have forgotten mine."

Judith finished and handed her a pen. "Here, keep it. Are you taking the number for your family?"

"Yes, it's only my daughter and me but, yes, I am. I'm told those who don't take the number by a certain time will be considered dissidents and will suffer the consequences. I don't know what those are," she paused, "but I'm all my little girl has."

The news troubled Judith. What would happen to Harry and the children if they didn't get the number?

"Number 256."

Judith got up. She studied the simple machine. Although she didn't understand how it worked, the woman in the grocery said it didn't hurt and didn't take long.

"Give me your name and your paperwork," stated a ruddy-faced, balding man. Repulsed by the odor of stale garlic, Judith stepped back, at the same time handing him her paperwork. She watched him type *J-u-d-i-t-h J-o-r-d-a-n* into the computer which apparently was connected to the world financial network adding her financial accounts. A number appeared.

"Hold out your hand, please." Without looking up, the man strapped a small metal machine on the top of her hand. He pushed a lever and the number appeared in the window of the little machine. Judith felt an electrical sensation as radio waves copied the invisible number onto her hand. For an instant, she felt like one of Harry's steers receiving its brand.

"Welcome to the World Federation."

"Thank you," she told the surly state employee eager to get out of the library.

Outside a hot, dry wind blew sand in her eyes before she could put on her sunglasses. She squared her shoulders and walked determinedly toward her car. With each step a plan formed in her mind. As long as Harry's parents lived with them, she'd avoid a discussion about the World Federation number. When they were gone, she hoped Harry would come to his senses. Still, anxiety crowded out any feeling of accomplishment and the words "lake of fire" drifted in and out of her mind. The deed was done; no turning back.

Judith decided to soothe her conscience by trying out the new financial system. Dillard's was less than a mile from the library. Pulling out her 20 percent off coupon, she entered the store to buy the green leather Kate Spade satchel she'd been wanting to replace her old shoulder bag.

Comforted by shopping, Judith brushed a tear away, reassuring herself that she was not a traitor…taking the mark would save her ranch and her family!

Chapter Fifteen

T he news of George and Jenny's participation in the Ascension upset the family. Alone, Judith and Harry discussed the solemn news.

"I hate to say it, Harry, but this does solve some difficult problems with your parents. I love having them here, but by not taking the number, they were going to face so many problems ahead."

Astonished, Harry looked at Judith. "How can you say such a thing? They're no trouble at all. I think the government has gone way out on a limb with this policy."

"It's really no different than sending eighteen-year-olds to fight for our country—their lives are still in front of them. At least George and Jenny have had a long, lovely life. And...they will be honored for their sacrifice. The pres—"

"The president..." Harry muttered under his breath... "I don't see the president sending his parents for the big sacrifice."

"It's going to happen, Harry, whether we like it or not. We need to put the best face on this situation for the children's sake and for George and Jenny's, too. I, personally, am going to treat them like heroes just like the president asked us to."

"I can't discuss this with you, Judith. I have an entirely different perspective. You're right about one thing though...

it will happen." Harry turned away. There was no talking to Judith these days. She was different, always defending and siding with the government, never questioning any of the strange new policies. Harry banged out the kitchen door and headed for the stables to work off his anger and frustration.

Daniel entered the kitchen. He poured some cereal into a bowl, sensing the tension. "What's wrong with Dad?"

"He's upset about the Ascension. I tried to tell him that we need to stress how proud we are, but he won't listen. The government is trying their best to save our country from economic disaster. The Ascension may seem cruel, but I don't find it any more cruel than sending you or Penny to fight in a war. At least your grandparents…"

"I know, Mom." He understood his mom's point of view, but he felt like his dad about the Ascension and he didn't want to discuss it anymore. Why didn't she understand? It was okay to sacrifice Grandpa and Gram and a bunch of other people—to save the economy? It made him want to throw up.

"Did you know the Guardians are helping with the Ascension?" Judith asked.

"Yeah, I noticed that, Mom." And it scared him that the Guardians were involved. Is that what the brochure meant about carrying out the president's initiatives? Daniel changed the subject. "Speaking of the Guardians, Mom, starting Monday my conditioning starts at Arizona State. The Guardian school arranged for me to work with a trainer, a guy named Chad Riley.

"Is he from the Guardian school?"

"No, the school's paying him; he's a physical trainer for the university. And, oh by the way, they sent a special diet. Hope it won't be too much trouble. They pretty much just want to take the sugar out so no pop, doughnuts, dessert… that sort of stuff. No more of Gram's chocolate chip cookies, no ice cream." Daniel pretended to faint…I'll fade away."

Judith made a face. "You'll live, just put your diet on my desk and I'll work out your meals.

Daniel grabbed a sweet roll, rolled his eyes and said, "We can start tomorrow. I better go out and help Dad and tell him about my new training schedule. We have a lot of projects this summer. We're cleaning out the stables today."

Still shoveling cereal into his mouth, Daniel walked over to the barn. "Sorry I'm late, Dad. Let me help with that." Setting his empty bowl down near a saddle, he grabbed a pitchfork and started to chuck new hay into the stalls. They worked side-by-side saying nothing but Daniel sensed his dad was really tense. Finally, they'd cleaned twenty-five horse stalls putting new hay in each. Daniel helped his dad lead the horses out of the sun and back into the stable. It was 9:30 a.m. and the temperature was starting to climb.

"Thanks, Danny. Thanks for the help."

"No problem, Dad. I wanted to tell you that I got a notification from the Guardian school that conditioning begins next week. I'll be able to help with the ranch from 5 till 9 a.m. mornings, then I have to report for training to ASU. It's a pretty rigorous routine."

"What's your schedule?"

"Monday through Friday, I do an hour of strength training, run five miles around the indoor track followed by a fifty-lap swim. I'm supposed to meet the trainer tomorrow to go over stuff."

"Well, it's beginning."

"Yeah, I also have to report to the Phoenix police target range to learn how to handle small arms, a rifle and a stun gun. Good thing you taught me how to hunt, huh?"

"When do you practice at the rifle range?"

"Target practice? Anytime, once I've had the introductory session."

Harry stopped working, leaned against his pitchfork and regarded his son. "Don't let the Guardians change you, Daniel."

Daniel looked puzzled.

Harry wiped his brow and sighed. "You have a good heart, son. Don't let the military change you."

Was his dad trying to warn him? He hadn't been excited about Daniel's selection into the Guardians but somehow Daniel attributed his silence to what was happening with his grandparents. He was certain his dad had doubts about the new government, did he have doubts about the Guardians, too?

"I hope this conditioning won't keep me from helping you. We have a lot of projects to do this summer."

"It'll be fine, DJ. If you can get the rail fencing done before you go, that would be a big help. The boys and I can handle most of the other stuff. Penny wants to help this year and she's a good worker."

Daniel watched as his father put his tools away. Then he started towards the house.

"Daniel?"

Daniel turned, slowing down.

"If you ever need someone to talk to, I'm here."

George kept a close eye on Jenny who seemed quiet and resigned. "Do you think much about the lake, hon?"

"I'd rather not talk about it, dear. It makes me feel sad."

George watched her quilt. "What's the pattern called?"

"It's an Irish Chain with appliquéd irises in the open spaces. I'm quilting one-quarter inch from each seam. I think it will be very pretty. I've asked Judith to give it to Penny when I'm through. Penny's made such a fuss over it."

"Penny's spending a lot of time with you."

"She's sweet. I love swinging with her on the porch. We're reading *Little Women.* She found it in some old box in the attic and we decided to read it together." Jenny ran out of thread and reached for a new length.

"Daniel's doing the same thing with me," George said. "He shows up every night in the woodshop. We're tying some flies for his fishing. I made him a treasure box but he doesn't know about it."

Jenny smiled. "Like when he was little and you two went on your camping trips? I can't remember, what did you used to put in it?"

"Well, different things, sometimes an arrowhead or a bird's nest. Once I even found a dead tarantula and put it in the box. I think he took it for Show'n'Tell."

"What are you going to put in this time? He's kind of old for those things."

George pulled out the beautiful wooden box that he'd carved the horse on. "I'm going to put in my Bible and a few other things. He's not ready for it yet. But someday, I hope he'll remember and dig it up. I'll bury it under the old cottonwood tree at the cave just like I used to."

"But how will he know it's there?"

"I guess I'll leave that up to God."

"Are you afraid, George?"

"Of the Ascension? Yes, I'm afraid." He looked over at Jenny. "How 'bout you, Jen?"

"I'm terrified. But I'll be all right as long as you're beside me."

George felt helpless. He'd always tried to protect Jenny, take care of her but...the Ascension was out of his control. "It won't be hard to leave this world but it will be hard to leave our family." George got a serious look on his face. "Jenny, I called the lawyer in Michigan today and told him to update our will. The house will be left to Harry and Judith. They can sell it or keep it. If they sell it, I've asked that the lawyer instruct them to give the pontoon to the neighbors. They've never owned one and they enjoy riding on it so much. I don't think the kids will mind, just one less thing for them to worry about. "

Jenny frowned. "Do what you want, George...if only I hadn't got sick."

"Now Jenny, I could say the same thing, 'If only I hadn't pushed you to come out to Phoenix'."

"I can't bear to think about it, to know we'll never see our lovely lake again."

"He'll send a copy for us to sign...I just wanted you to know." George had stopped being angry. He wasn't going to waste his energy or the last months before the Ascension. They needed to squeeze out every moment with the children. Even so, he couldn't stop worrying about what his family would face after they were gone. What would they do about the number? He shifted gears, "*Dear heavenly Father, forgive me for doubting. Watch over this precious family when we are gone. We've done our best to make them understand. Now, it's up to You.*"

Chapter Sixteen

Two months of summer left. George winced as he got up from his seat in the workshop. At 4:30 p.m. he woke Jenny from her nap. Rubbing his knee, he walked quietly to their room hating to disturb Jenny from her rest. From the beginning of monsoon season, he and Jenny sat in the rockers on the verandah and watched the sky. The monsoon was a chameleon changing each day. Sometimes the air cooled down. Occasionally a gentle rain fell on the desert or the wind whipped up blowing clouds of dust. But the most dramatic monsoons lit the ski with zigzags of lightning. He touched Jenny's arm. "Time for the monsoon, dear. Do you feel like watching tonight?"

Jenny opened her eyes, taking a minute to remember where she was, wishing she were home at the lake. "Yes, let's get an iced tea and go watch it." She stretched, sat a minute on the edge of the bed then stood up taking George's arm. They stopped by the kitchen, punched in a 77 for iced tea and sauntered out to the porch.

George caught sight of Daniel climbing out of the ranch truck. "He's moving slower than we do," George said to Jenny. "They must be working him pretty hard in that Guardian program. Hey, Danny."

Daniel smiled as he saw the sweet old couple on the porch. "What are you old sweeties doing out here?"

"The usual, watching the monsoon," said Jenny.

"I could hardly see to get home, the dust's so thick. Sure glad I wasn't out with the herd. You end up with sand in your teeth, your hair—it's nasty." He sat down in one of the porch rockers stretching out his long sore limbs. "Man, I feel a hundred years old...no offense."

"None taken. You need a cold drink, let me get you one," George offered.

"Thanks, Gramps but it feels good just to sit. How was your day?"

"The usual, I guess." Jenny thought how young and manly Daniel looked with no shirt and his hair wet from the pool. "Do you have a girlfriend, Danny?"

"No, no girl's been lucky enough to snag me yet, Gram. If I'd met you first, Grandpa wouldn't have stood a chance."

Jenny beamed.

"It sure would feel good to have a pretty girl give me a backrub though. Every muscle in my body hurts. I didn't think I was so out of shape. Do you miss the lake?" Daniel asked.

"Yes," replied Jenny. "Sometimes we fished off the pier at night, didn't we, Dad?"

George nodded. "Caught some nice bass in that lake. Nothing big, but real tasty."

"I remember taking out your sailboat," said Daniel. "What a great feeling catching a breeze and flying across the waves."

They smiled, remembering how Daniel had run the sailboat up on shore not sure how to turn it around. "You were pretty brave at ten to go out by yourself," said Grandpa.

"Not sure it was brave...maybe dumb. If you hadn't rowed the fish boat out when I turtled it..."

"Oh, you'd have figured it out," said Gramps.

The dinner bell clanged and they took a last look at the lightning display before moving inside.

After dinner the group moved into the family room. Harry slipped a DVD into the TV. "How bout a few movies?" Everyone clapped and soon pictures of Penny at baby gymnastics and Daniel riding his first pony filled the screen. It was a fine evening, but as George and Jenny made their way to their rooms, Jenny leaned over and whispered, "It's the end of August."

George took her hand and held it tightly. "I know, Jenny. I know."

"I know I'm obsessing, George but I can't stop thinking if I hadn't had that heart attack, we wouldn't have gone to the hospital and neither of us would be on the Ascension list. It makes me feel so bad, George, you're perfectly healthy. You could have lived twenty more years."

George stopped and took her face in his hands. "You aren't to blame, Jenny. Remember, God knows just where we are and what is happening to us. His promise is not that we won't have bad things happen to us but that He'll be with us. He'll give us the strength. Let's not look back anymore." He dried the tears that were running down his wife's face and kissed her lightly. "I love you, Jen."

Jenny wasn't the guilty one. It was this terrible new government. His beautiful wife had done nothing wrong. It was hard not to think about September 11, to know that one particular day would be your last. They'd both tried to be involved with projects and with the family but as the time grew closer, neither of them could think about much else. George prayed for strength every day and hoped they would not bring disgrace on their family or the Lord. He wanted to die honorably.

Jenny slid under the covers. "George, we need to focus on where we are going. We're going to heaven to be with the Lord."

"Yes, let's focus on that, Jen."

The next day Daniel returned home early instead of driving downtown for target practice. No sign of life. Gram must be sleeping, Mom shopping. Where was Grandpa? Daniel was dying for a Coke but resisted. He grabbed a Fruit$_2$O and headed to the woodshop.

"Gramps, you in there?"

"Come in, Daniel. What's up?"

"Not much. I'm a little dehydrated." He held out his drink.

Grandpa looked up from his project. "Training getting to you?"

"They're working me hard, Grandpa, my muscles are hard as a rock after my hour on the machines. The trainer keeps cranking it up." He took a long drag on his water and wiped his mouth. "I can hardly make my legs go for the five-mile run and now he's put a time on each mile—four minutes."

"Times five?"

"Times five." Daniel wiped his forehead. "Swimming saves me every day."

"Fifty laps are a lot."

"But I'm used to swimming, Gramps. It takes all the pain and stiffness out." He looked down quiet now.

"Something bothering you, Danny?"

Daniel nodded. He wanted to talk to his grandfather, but didn't know how to begin. Uncomfortable, he looked at his hands. Grandpa waited.

"Gramps, you had a good life?"

"Yes, I have. "

"Are you scared about…the Ascension?"

"Not scared exactly…just hoping your grandma will be all right."

"You take good care of her, Gramps."

"I try." George looked up from his project. "Something else on your mind, son?"

"I'm mixed up, Gramps. I wanted to be a pro soccer player but now I'm going to be a Guardian. I guess I never thought I'd get chosen — but I did. I want to do something that ...makes a difference. I don't think Dad is happy about me going into the Guardians but I can't look back now. I just want to have a good life."

"Are you asking me for advice, Daniel?" Leaning back, George looked thoughtful. "The way I see it, each man has two paths he can follow. On one path, he'll search for truth and wisdom eventually finding God. On the second path, the man decides to work out his life by his own ideas without regard to God. The first path leads to life with God in heaven. The second finds only what is here on earth. Both men will live forever, but only one will live with God. It's a choice each person makes, so you will have this choice. It's not really about being a pro athlete or a Guardian."

"What about my parents, Grandpa?"

"Your dad knew God when he was young. I hope he'll return to Him someday. He tries to be a good man. Your mom, I'm afraid, thinks talk of God is foolishness. She chooses to live by her own logic and insight." Grandpa sighed. He knew Daniel had lots of questions. "Do you believe in God, Danny?"

Daniel looked down, "I don't know much about Him, Grandpa. I just know about science and stuff. We learned about evolution in school but you talk about God creating the world."

"Do you really think that cells colliding with one another could create a human being with a nervous system, circulatory system, a digestive system, an endocrine system, etc., all working in harmony with one another inside us? Think about it, Danny. Doesn't believing in evolution take more faith than believing that a power bigger than we are designed us? I think many of the secrets of the spiritual world are tucked into nature for us to find, if we only open our eyes and the eyes of our heart."

Daniel looked at his grandfather. "My heart has eyes?" He smiled at the old man.

"Oh, but it does. When you're ready, Daniel, ask God to make Himself real to you."

Daniel couldn't stand for Grandpa to talk about dying. He loved the old man and it felt like a piece of Daniel was dying, too. "Tell me about heaven, Gramps. What do you think it's like?"

"The Bible tells us it's a place where there's no pain, illness or tears. Grandma's heart won't be sick there. A river flows out of the throne of God and beside it are the trees of life bearing fruit. I know there are angels there and special creatures called cherubim. God is there and His Son Jesus. All the good people who have died believing in Him are in heaven, too. It's a very beautiful place—a dimension filled with love, joy and peace.

"So you're not afraid to go to heaven?"

"No, Daniel, we're not afraid of heaven."

Chapter Seventeen

September 11, 2022

F aint streams of light spread across the horizon signaling sunrise. Awake every hour since two a.m., George dragged himself out of bed trying not to disturb Jenny who'd struggled with falling asleep, too. *Dear Jenny.*

Mechanically, George pulled on a pair of khakis and a sweatshirt, glancing at the white robes laying on the chair—one last thing to do. If he hurried, he'd have time to ride out to the cave and bury the treasure. Entering the wood shop, he found the hand-carved box, added his Bible and the map and white stone Pastor Bauer had sent him from Michigan, then carefully wrapped the box in plastic.

He slipped out the kitchen door into the new morning. The sun peeked over the horizon and the soft morning air felt gentle on his face. He took a deep breath. Unhappy that he'd forgotten to leave a note, George decided not to return to the house, hoping to get back from the cave before the family awoke.

Making his way down the line of stalls in the stable, he chose Lad, a palomino he'd ridden a few times, and saddled him adding the box and some water to the saddlebags. Finally, George attached a camping shovel to the harness, and led Lad out of the stall.

The temperature was still in the high 60s as he mounted the horse for the thirty-minute ride. "Take me to the cave, boy." As if the horse understood, Lad picked his way east through the desert. The sun rose above the Four Peaks mountain range painting the sky pale yellow and orange. *My last sunrise*, George thought. He remembered the times he'd camped with Daniel at the caves. Good memories.

On arrival, he tethered Lad to the limb of a mesquite tree next to the Verde River. He lifted the carved box out of the saddlebag, unfastened the camping shovel and walked purposefully to the base of the old cottonwood. *Lord,* he prayed, *bring Daniel back here when he's ready.* After digging a hole in the caked earth, he placed the plastic-wrapped box in the hole covered it with loose dirt and tamped it down. Deed done. *Now it's in your keeping, Lord.*

He stopped to watch the river make its way over rocks and dead limbs yet continue on its way. George understood that like the river somehow life would continue on its mysterious and unknown way, even after death. *Perhaps,* he thought, *it's like being born. We feel safe and secure in our mother's womb never realizing what a wonderful world awaits us.* And deep inside his spirit George knew that indeed another world awaited him and Jenny. *Time to get back.* Catching sight of a worn arrowhead, he bent down and picked it up out of the shallow water shoving it into his pocket.

Harry met George at the stables. "Dad, you were riding?"

"Yes ... couldn't sleep...thought I'd have a last ride. Hope you don't mind, but I rode Lad."

Harry smiled, taking the reins from his dad. "It's fine, Dad, but Mom's a little worried. No one knew where you were."

George entered the bedroom where he found Jenny dressed in a white robe sitting in the old rocker, her hands trembling.

"I rode to the cave, Jenny, to bury Daniel's box. I'm sorry. I didn't mean to upset you." He donned the other white robe and tenderly took her hands to pull her out of the chair. They made their way to the verandah where Judith was setting up an outdoor buffet.

"I don't think I can eat, dear," Jenny whispered.

"Try, it'll be our last time with the children," George said.

The family was quiet and sad. George wanted to say something comforting, but no words came. As they finished the brunch, the door chime interrupted.

"It's the van, Dad. Let me help you, Mom." Harry took his mother's arm, gently helping her from the table.

The family gathered to say good-bye and watched while the two young Guardians loaded the old couple into the van, saluting the family as they closed the door.

It was time for the Ascension.

Chapter Eighteen

Unshaven and barely awake, Dr. Greg Hart climbed into his black SUV. Why was he driving to Sedona? What purpose would it achieve? He couldn't answer those questions. All he knew was he had to see the Ascension. He paid no attention to his speed, taking the mountain curves as fast as his car allowed, his mind racing even faster than the car. *The Ascension...the Council's diabolical remedy to the economic problems bankrupting America...and he was part of it...responsible for a hundred lives or should he say deaths?* If the government could get away with this, if no outcry occurred, other Ascensions would follow throughout the country.

Mindlessly, he drove through the 179 corridor to 89A catching the end of the yellow light and making a sharp left-hand turn. Since he'd attended Jazz on the Rocks at the amphitheater, he knew exactly where to go in West Sedona. Pulling into the parking lot, he noted brightly colored tents set up and staffed with formally dressed caterers. *Were they insane?* He sat down at the back of the amphitheater, disgusted by the theatrical staging and waited as the cameras came alive. Alex Blackstone delivered his address ending with "America will count you heroes and patriots. Your self-less act of Ascension will save America."

By the end of the speech, Greg was shaking. There must be five hundred white-robed people in line. Who selected the other four hundred, the CNAM doctors? And why were children and young people in the Ascension? On closer look, he realized the children had Down's syndrome or cleft palates and he guessed the wheelchairs must contain people with chronic diseases like multiple sclerosis, or AIDS.

Two Guardians lifted a frail, dark-haired young woman out of her wheelchair. Dazed by the bright lights, she bowed her head making the sign of the cross. Lightning flashed; a billow of white vapor enveloped her and she disappeared from view. A neon sign blinked its grotesque message, "That One Might Die for the Many." Greg stumbled out of the amphitheater wanting to outrun the panic that filled his soul.

Daniel watched the line of white-robed participants move forward, each taking their turn. Not all were calm and he noticed that the Guardians assisted those resisting or having trouble. When his grandparents turn came, Grandpa—like an old soldier on his last mission—held Grandma's arm and helped her up the stairs. They mounted the stage, looked out toward their family and then turned and faced one another. A look of gentle love passed between them.

"George and Genevieve Jordan—Scottsdale, Arizona." A flash of lightning, a billow of clouds and like those before them, the Jordans disappeared.

"Where did Grandma and Grandpa go?" Penny asked. "Danny, where did they go?"

His mother turned around. "Shhhh—not now, Penny. We'll explain it to you later. Wasn't it a beautiful and moving service?"

Unthinking, Daniel reached into his pocket; his fingers tightened around the arrowhead Grandpa had placed in his hand. *What did you mean Grandpa? Remember what?*

Seated in the Oval Office President Blackstone watched the Ascension unfold. He stroked his chin searching the television screen, then addressed the vice president, "The networks shouldn't have shown the Guardians removing the protestors."

"I'll take care of it," said the vice president.

"See that the networks are instructed to…"

"I'll do my best, but we must keep the illusion that freedom of speech is still allowed. Perhaps I can help the networks *understand* the point-of-view we expect."

"You mean the need their networks have for our support."

"Exactly."

The president turned the media screen off. "It went well?"

"A new American heritage, I'd say. There'll be little resistance from the old. It's their families who may cause trouble."

"See that American flags are sent to each family along with the Medal of Honor. Stress the hero aspect. It's not what their country is doing *to* them; it's what they are doing *for* their country."

Chapter Nineteen

N an Coleman, Dr. Hart's nurse, and the seven members of the Good Shepherd Bible study gathered in Pastor Neal's den, eyes focused on the television. Tears slid down Nan's cheeks as she watched the Guardians lift the young woman from the wheelchair and stand her alone in the middle of the large stage. The lightning looked authentic and so did the clouds of vapor that covered the girl.

"It's just so sickening. They've counterfeited the real ascension of Jesus only these poor people are dying not rising into heaven," said Nan.

"Let's think about that," interrupted the pastor. "Their spirits *are* rising into heaven. God will be waiting for them."

"Still…" Nan sniffed.

"Still," the pastor continued," it looks like our job is even bigger than we imagined. It's imperative that we pray and plan. There must be other churches concerned with building a Christian underground."

Adam, the church tech guru, broke in, "I'd like to volunteer to do a web search to see if any other Christians are starting a movement. If I don't find any, perhaps we can design a site ourselves."

"Good idea, Adam, let us know what you find by next week. Grace, you work in the library. Will you help Adam do a computer search?"

"I'll be glad to, Pastor. I'll check Twitter and see what the country's response is to the Ascension."

"Good idea. Meantime, I'll contact other pastors and see what I can find. A lot of the president's initiatives have to do with health. Nan, you work for the Center for New Age Medicine. How do you assess Dr. Hart?"

"It's breaking his spirit to refer people to the Ascension. He's moody and anxious; I think his medical ethics are upset."

"What do you mean?"

"I mean, he got his job through the president who's an old college acquaintance, but he thought he'd be doing good—not remedying the health care system by eliminating people."

"I see. He has no idea that the president could be... evil?"

"I don't know, Pastor."

"Robert, you work with the schools. Keep your ears open. Listen to the children. They often mirror their parents. See what they say about the Ascension or the president.

"Charlotte, we need you to investigate food sources— perhaps food co-ops or warehouses for food storage. Soon, people not taking the mark will need food.

"Kit, it's rumored that some Fox journalists have been removed from their broadcasts. Be careful, but try to find out what's happened to them.

"Dick, what's the police perspective on the Guardians?"

"They're trained in hand-to-hand combat and have state-of-the-art equipment. So far, the government uses them only as escorts, but I sense that only touches their potential. They're highly trained in weaponry and crowd control."

"Pastor?"

"Yes, Nan."

"We just interviewed for the Arizona Guardian appointment."

"What can you tell us about the candidates?"

"They must have unquestioned loyalty to the government. The government chooses only outgoing, aggressive young men. Daniel Jordan was chosen this year to represent Arizona."

"What do you know about him?"

"Not much, a happy kid, bright and charming...smart as a whip, athletic. But there is one interesting fact. I'm pretty sure we just saw his grandparents in the first Ascension."

"Whoa, that must have rocked him," said Adam.

"Keep an eye on him, Nan." Pastor Neal suggested.

"His training starts in October," said Nan "but he may be assigned to CNAM when his training is over,"

"It's all about people, folks. We need key people to build an underground and we need people we can trust. Your young Guardian could be an asset. Pray...be cautious. Remember God promises He will be with us and He's always kept a remnant."

"I don't understand, Pastor" said Kit. "What's a remnant?"

"It's the people who never desert God no matter how hard times get. Now let's brainstorm a little. What do we know so far?"

"Well, we know Christians can't take the number but somehow they'll have to have food and shelter," said Charlotte.

"We need safe houses where people can go and grow their own food, and take care of one another," Grace added.

Other ideas came from around the room.

"If we shared clothing..."

"We'd need milk—maybe cows, pigs, chickens, sheep..."

"Good...Good...You've got good ideas. And we need to try to provide for people like Nan so she can continue her job as long as possible."

"What we need is a whole chain of safe houses so we can move people from one to another if they are under suspicion," Adam added.

"What else do we know?" interrupted the pastor.

"We know the old people won't get any medical attention and will be sent to the Ascension," said Nan.

"Okay, enough for tonight. Let's end with prayer." The group joined hands and bowed their heads while the pastor prayed, "*Lord, Your people are in danger. We ask You to guide and protect us. Create safe places like You did in the past when You created cities of refuge. Help us to be wise and discerning in this time of evil. We ask it in Jesus' name.*"

"Pastor, what about the people in our church who've taken the mark," asked Grace.

"I warned them several Sundays not to take the mark. I'm afraid the ones who took it are lost. I'll make it clear on Sunday." Pastor Neal looked down. "But we have those in our church who do not know God's Word. They attend church because their community image benefits. Deceived when they take the mark, they'll become dangerous to us."

"Pastor, I think some people thought taking the mark saved their families," said Anna. "I feel sorry for them."

"Yes, Anna, but when they take the number it opens their mind to evil. The mark is an invitation to join Satan in his great end-times deception. Influenced by evil, they'll agree with everything the government does. And I think the Ascension is only the beginning."

"Are we talking government or Antichrist?" asked Robert.

"At the moment government, but if these are the times predicted by Christ, we may wake up to find our president in league with the Antichrist. The time before Jesus returns will be difficult."

"Explain, Pastor, said Kit."

"Wars, earthquakes, increased terror attacks, weather and planet changes, epidemics and persecution of all who believe in Jesus. By joining the World Federation and One World Finances, America is on a dangerous path."

Chapter Twenty

The Jordan family reached the mall relieved to get into their SUV. Judith tried to put a good face on the Ascension, but everyone ignored her, lost in their own thoughts, sad they would never see Grandma and Grandpa again.

Part of Harry died when his parents died or should he say were killed in the Ascension. He felt alone. Not only had he lost the parents he loved, but he'd lost Judith to the new system. Taking the number put them on opposite sides. Convinced the president was evil, Harry made a decision. In tribute to his father, Harry would *not* take the mark. He'd do his best to protect the children although Daniel joining the Guardians made that almost impossible.

He was convinced his dad was right about the president. This was an evil administration. Alone, he couldn't stand up against a government who didn't value life, but he wouldn't be part of it either. Judith chose to take the mark; she could be their financial person, but he had also made his choice.

No number! I love you, Dad.

He pulled into the ranch he'd worked so hard to make a success, a thousand questions bombarding his mind: What would happen to the ranch now? What did the future hold for his children? And especially, what would Daniel's life be like as a Guardian? He couldn't imagine Daniel escorting people to die in an Ascension. Why didn't he back his son's desire to attend the sports college? He was as guilty for not supporting Daniel as Judith for pushing him into the Guardians. Had her "I'm-always-right attitude" killed his ability to stand up for what he thought was best?

"Harry, are you all right? You look so angry," Judith chided.

Surprised at how well Judith still read him, he said, "I am angry. Angry with myself. Well, we're home. C'mon kids. Everyone out." He turned off the motor and headed for the stables. "I'll be in later. I need some time to myself."

Judith's thoughts battled like a tug-of-war. On a logical level she thought the plan to save America's health system was brilliant and practical. Old people had lived their lives. Money for health care should go to the young and middle-aged. On the other hand, did these sweet old people who'd supported their government, paid taxes, fought in wars, lived through terrorist attacks and difficult economic times deserve to be rewarded with...the Ascension? It was a dilemma.

She'd give Harry some space to work through his feelings about his parents. At least something good had happened to the family—Daniel's appointment. She remembered how helpful the Guardians had been at the Ascension. Perhaps they could focus on Daniel's wonderful new life.

Daniel said goodnight and went to his room. So... one of the Guardian's jobs was the Ascension—helping people through the event. He hoped there was more to this elite corps than that. He lay down on his bed and closed his eyes. The image of his grandparents haunted him, even with his eyes closed. What kind of government solved its problems by eliminating its people?

No turning back, Daniel thought. *I'm in the corps for five years—a Guardian... but what exactly will I be guarding?*

Chapter Twenty-one

D r. Hart stared at the overnight letter stamped with the presidential seal afraid to open it. He overcame a desire to throw the letter in the trash unopened. Every initiative caused Greg to put patients in harm's way. The question he had to answer was—could he use his position to help the innocent or should he find a way to leave the Center for New Age Medicine?

Grabbing a letter opener, he sliced the envelope only to find a new initiative marked "for your eyes only."

Health Initiative 4A—The Lamb's Project
President Blackstone, with the Council of Twelve's approval, has passed an addendum to develop an experiment known as the Lamb's Project to produce a genetically pure race. The president will donate sperm to be implanted in young women screened for genetic flaws. The sixteen-year-old virgins will be sent to Med Care South, a newly acquired facility located in the mountains near Tucson where they will continue their sophomore year of high school while they contribute to science.

The infants produced will become "children of the nation" and will be taken to an appropriate facility for nurture and education. The girls' parents and school will provide a sabbatical for a year. Each girl participating will receive credit to study at the Arizona university of her choice. The year will be referred to by school authorities as The Year Away Program.

The Center for New Age Medicine will work in conjunction with Phoenix school nurses for selection and orientation of this program.

Dr. Greg Hart will run the genetic testing and perform the implantation of sperm. Classified as top secret—there will be no media announcement.

The program will begin immediately. OMEGA I.

Greg closed his eyes feeling totally defeated. Another heinous initiative. Why couldn't he work on life-saving strategies? He looked at his schedule for the afternoon. "Nan, cancel my three o'clock and stick around and run the office for me, okay?"

Greg's nurse came into the doctor's office. "Sure Doc, everything all right?"

Greg sighed. "Thought I'd drive out to Saguaro Lake. I need to get away. And... oh, Nan, 'for your eyes only' read this newest initiative and put it in the safe." Greg put on his sunglasses and walked slowly to the elevator.

Why did Dr. Hart leave? In fifteen years he'd never left early. Nan slid into Doc's chair opening the initiative with the presidential seal on the envelope. *What now?* she thought. She read silently, shocked at the content of the letter. "So that's why he left," she said to herself. She laid the letter down and folded her hands in prayer, something she rarely did at work. *"Dear Lord, please be with Greg. He's a good man caught in the middle of terrible changes. Stay close to him and let him know You. He needs You, Lord."*

She locked the initiative in the safe, picked up the phone and dialed her pastor.

He answered on the third ring. "Pastor, this is Nan, something important, can I stop by for a few minutes after work?"

"Of course, I'll wait for you."

Hoping that no one would call or come into the office, she hung up the phone.

Dr. Hart drove the back streets of Phoenix until he reached Shea Boulevard. Turning east, he headed toward the lake. When he reached Fountain Hills, he checked his watch and exited on Saguaro Boulevard. The world-renowned fountain was set to go off on the hour and it was five till.

As he pulled his car into the parking lot, the fountain shot 540 feet into the air cascading into the small lake at its base. The roar of the water drowned his thoughts. Greg sat down at a picnic table aware that part of his fascination was the raw power so opposite his feeling of powerlessness. Caught by the sunlight, a rainbow appeared in the spray. For fifteen minutes, hypnotized by the fountain of water, Greg stared lost in the beauty.

When the fountain shut down, he again climbed into his SUV and headed for Highway 87. At the end of Shea Boulevard, he turned north increasing his speed to seventy-five miles an hour for the fifteen-mile drive to Saguaro Lake. It had been several years since Greg visited the beautiful canyon lake.

After parking in the shade, he trudged down the hill to the boat rental. The abused and neglected rental boats awaited a pilot. He paid for two hours, assured by the rental agent that the engine was filled with gas.

Only one sailboat and a couple of pontoons drifted in the distance. He turned the key starting the motor and carefully backed away from the dock, guiding the boat close to the tall gray cliffs which surrounded the lake. The sky was clear and a deep blue. A bald eagle lifted off the cliff catching a gust of wind and soaring into the sky to rest on a dead tree containing a sprawling nest. The moment was pure. He pointed the boat into an alcove and cut the engine.

Overwhelmed with life, Greg wanted to cry out to the nature that surrounded him ordered and peaceful. He felt like a racecar driver who'd lost control of his car and was hurtling into a brick wall. Why had he become a doctor? The answer was simple—to save lives. He'd never cared about the money, wanting only to do something he loved and felt passionately about. Medicine was a perfect match.

Overcome with a flood of dismal thoughts, he closed his eyes. What should he do? Who could he talk to? His wife divorced him ten years ago and he'd decided to remain single dedicating his life to medicine. To be honest, life was simpler without a family. He worked as late as he needed, ate when he felt like it and didn't have to deal with birthdays, anniversaries and so on. It had been good to be alone, to be free, but now he wished he had someone, some wise person to help him understand his life. He needed wisdom...God... he needed God.

Greg hadn't thought about God since college. *How do I connect with you, God? You seem so far away. I need You close—in my head, in my heart. I need Your wisdom; tell me how to live.* And suddenly, faces of the people he'd sentenced to the Ascension swam before him. *O God, can you ever forgive me?* The dam inside him broke and he wept until he was empty the tears washing away the terrible guilt he felt. He sat still, feeling the warm breeze and the peace, not wanting the moment to pass. Tomorrow he'd go back to work, but somehow he knew that he would not be alone.

Nan continued to sit and pray for Greg. Something was happening she was sure.

She prayed that he would not lose hope. *"Lord, meet Greg and help him understand what to do."* She wasn't bothered with any more phone calls and left the office early to meet with Pastor Neal who was waiting for her.

"Hello, Nan. Come in and close the door behind you. What's going on? I haven't been able to get our conversation off my mind so I've been sitting here praying and waiting for you."

"First, Pastor, what I have to say can go no further. Is that all right?"

"I'll do my best to keep your confidence."

"Today we received a letter telling us to choose twenty sixteen-year-old virgins for a pilot program called the Lamb's Project. We are to take live sperm shipped to us by Bethesda and implant them into these young girl's wombs to make them pregnant. Those whose implantation succeeds will go by order of the president and under his care to a rest resort to be taken care of for a year."

"Young virgins, you say? Whose sperm will be used?"

"President Blackstone—Omega I's."

Pastor Neal shook his head. "And so it truly begins. He's mimicking the virgin birth of Christ, only instead of the seed of the Holy Spirit it will be his seed."

"Yes."

"I'm curious. What response did your doctor have?"

"For the first time I can ever remember, he took the afternoon off."

"What do you think he'll do?"

"I don't know. He seems so despondent. I think he's actually thought of quitting but he's afraid they won't let him go. And...if he goes and someone in line with their philosophy becomes head of CNAM, I can only guess."

"You'd leave?"

"I'd have to."

"Well, God is aware of what's going on. Let's keep praying and see what your good doctor does. By the way, I've got some encouraging news for the committee. I've found a website called remnant.net which is making itself available to believers. There's a chat room and, interestingly, a map with safe houses has appeared on the website—six so far but none close to us yet."

"Through the Council of Churches?"

"No, an underground arm of a women's group—Women of Courage."

"Let's hope God keeps this website from the wrong eyes." Nan got up to leave. "Pastor, I can't believe we could be living in the years of Jesus' return."

"Maranatha."

Nan looked puzzled.

"It means, come Lord Jesus."

Chapter Twenty-two

"Only three weeks till you leave, Danny. Aren't you getting excited?" asked Penny.

"Sure kid, I'm excited." Daniel smiled.

"You don't look it, Danny. You seem so quiet since…"

"Since the Ascension? Yeah, I know, Pen. I just can't seem to get Grandma and Grandpa off my mind." That was only half the truth. In reality, Daniel couldn't stop thinking about how the Guardians had pushed the protesters into the bus, how they'd formed a cordon to keep the Ascension people imprisoned and separate from the onlookers, and how sooner than he wished his job would be the same. Helping with the Ascensions was not what he'd signed up for and he wondered what other initiatives the Guardians would be asked to implement.

"I don't know what to think, Danny. I miss them so much. Grandma gave me the beautiful Iris quilt which just matches my lavender walls. It's so pretty. Do you think they were heroes, Danny, or did something bad happen?"

"I'm going to think of them as heroes, Pen. They were the best grandparents anyone could ask for. But…yeah, something bad happened. The government killed our grandparents and a lot of other people. I don't know how you spin that into anything good." He'd said too much and decided to change the subject. Talking about the Ascension wasn't going to bring his grandparents back. "You ready for your cheerleading tryouts?"

Penny brushed a tear away and forced a smile. "Would you tell me what you think of the cheer I made up?"

Daniel watched Penny move rhythmically through her cheer. She was a natural; her timing was perfect.

"What do you think?"

"Well, it's got good rhythm, lots of tumbling, and it's short," Daniel stammered.

"Oh, Danny, you're hopeless. I just hope I make the team."

Daniel wished he could be around to watch over her as she got into high school. Guys were always looking for one-night stands. Penny's dark brown eyes, dimples and long eyelashes plus her athletic body would draw them like bears to a honeypot. "How many girls are going out?"

"About seventy-five."

"Tough competition...how many do they take?"

"Two teams of eight—one gymnastic, the other with more dance moves."

"Which one are you going out for?"

"I'm not sure. Tammy and I are making up a cheer in both categories. We'll try out together and either one would be fine with us. They all have the same uniforms."

"You'll make a good cheerleader, Pen. I'm a fan!"

Penny smiled. She loved Danny and she'd miss him. He was a special guy. Sometimes, when Mom and Dad had a fight, Danny would burst in, sit on Dad's lap and whisker him making everyone laugh. Penny was a little scared of a home without Danny around. "Hey, what's that in your hand?"

"A list of classes I'll be taking at the Guardian school."

"Let me see it. Wow, lots of military classes. I didn't know the Guardians were part of the military. I thought they were...Guardians...you know...special."

Daniel frowned. "They're a military arm of the government, Pen."

"I hope you like it, Danny."

"Me, too. Well, I'm off to my last training session. Then they're giving us a couple of weeks off."

Dad's disappearing act after dinner each night worried Daniel. Dad never smiled anymore and he and Mom rarely talked to each other. Was he grieving over his parents' death or angry? A light filtered from the wood shop in the barn. "Dad, are you in there?" he called.

"Yeah, Danny, come in."

"Working on something?"

"No, just putting Grandpa's tools away. Looks like he was working on a project before..." Harry's eyes filled with tears; embarrassed, he brushed them on his sleeve.

Daniel didn't know what to say. He'd never seen his dad cry. "I miss him, too, Dad. I can't stop thinking about them either. Five hundred people died. I didn't know the Guardians would be involved with something like that."

Harry sighed. "I know, Danny."

"I've got to stop obsessing about their death, Dad. I need to get away by myself for a few days."

"After I came home from the Ascension, I wanted to get on a horse, ride forever and feel the wind in my face until..."

"Until everything was normal?"

His father nodded. "What do you need to do?"

"I think I need to go camping."

"Where you and Grandpa camped up at the caves?"

"Yeah, I need to get my head on straight before I go to school."

Harry got up. "I'll tell your mom you need some time. I'd go with you but I think you need the time by yourself."

Daniel did need time by himself. He needed the quiet of the desert to think things out.

"Camping? I don't understand," said Daniel's mom. "You need to pack, get your supplies for school. Why camping, Danny? Does this have anything to do with the Ascension?"

Daniel's face reddened and he turned away from his mother, determined not to let her change his plans. "I need to be by myself for a little while, Mom, kick back, no agenda." He stared at her, "You'll do fine, Mom, just follow the list the school sent. I'm leaving tomorrow for the caves."

"Does your father know about this?"

Angry now, and not wanting to blow up, Danny managed a "Yeah, he knows," as he walked away

Chapter Twenty-three

Daniel checked his gear: sleeping bag, rifle, hunting knife, fishing rod, camping shovel, frying pan and rations. Had he forgotten anything? The flies...He walked to Dad's workshop where he found the fishing flies Grandpa had been tying. Daniel gathered up the flies shoving them into his saddlebag... *Will you be there waiting for me, Grandpa?*

He placed each piece of equipment on his horse, Sandy. "I know it's heavy, boy, but we're just going up to the caves." Finally, he fastened Sandy's feedbag around his neck, climbed on the horse and headed northeast hoping he'd have enough daylight to set up camp.

Like Dad, Daniel just wanted to ride until things were normal...to get away from his mother's constant reminders about the Guardians. He let Sandy choose his pace absorbed in the passing of the desert. The saguaros stood guard like ancient soldiers their arms spread out to welcome him. The horse's loping gait rocked him as the sun beat down on his back relaxing his tense muscles. Daniel let the quiet of the desert seep into his soul until like the Indians he felt one with the desert, in perfect harmony.

He checked the sky. Small trailing clouds signaled the passing of a jet. In the distance a line of trees told him the river was nearby. He reached down and patted Sandy's head. "Not long now, boy."

Ten years ago on a ride on National Forest land adjacent to the ranch, he and Grandpa discovered the caves. Every time Grandpa visited, the two camped there for a couple of days. It was the perfect camping spot. The trees along the Verde River provided shade for the horses while the caves sheltered them from coyotes, wolves and mountain lions. He tethered Sandy to the branch of a mesquite tree, unloaded his gear and stashed his sleeping bag and supplies in the nearest cave. Daniel waited to roll out his sleeping bag so as not to be surprised later by a snake or tarantula.

Next, he gathered pieces of dead saguaro to build a campfire in the mouth of the cave. Later, he'd cook the hot dogs he'd brought from home but first, he wanted to take care of Sandy. "Come here, boy," he said. He took out a towel, soaked it in the river and wiped the little horse down before letting him take a long drink. Daniel filled Sandy's feedbag with oats, then he snapped off a couple of green twigs from the mesquite and threaded two giant hot dogs to roast. The sun dipped below the horizon and Daniel guessed it must be about seven p.m.

After checking the caves for vermin, he rolled out his sleeping bag and lay gazing at the night sky. He picked out Venus, Mars, Orion and the Pleiades. Grandpa's voice seemed to drift through the years, "You can sail a ship by this star map, Danny—God's wonderful creation. Isn't it amazing?" It was amazing.

The next morning sunlight penetrated his eyelids, making it impossible to sleep. He stretched. The campfire still glowed so he added another chunk of wood bringing the fire instantly to life. He grabbed his fishing pole and hurried to the river. The river, although low, moved well at this point and Daniel's chances of catching a fish were best early in the morning or at dusk. All he needed was one nice one.

He threaded the sapphire fly on the end of his line and cast into the shallows. Before long, a tug on the line signaled a bite. He reeled the fish in slowly, aware that he'd caught a good-sized one, maybe a catfish. Taking out his hunting knife, Daniel filleted the fish, dropping it into his frying pan. The pungent odor made his mouth water. Grandpa would be proud. After breakfast, he'd ride Sandy into the hills before the temperature rose.

Daniel covered his campfire with loose dirt. As he walked over to get Sandy, he noticed something odd. The dirt under the old cottonwood was hard and baked except for one area which appeared recently dug up. A good tracker, Daniel bent down to examine the soil noticing hardened footprints. Although this was Indian land, he doubted anyone from the reservation had been to the campsite. Not wanting to lose the cool of the day, he promised himself he'd look into it more closely after he returned from his ride. Who would have been to the campsite?

The two rode along the river for a couple of hours, then retraced their way. Daniel watched sunlight dart across the waves causing dancing diamonds to skitter across the water. Both he and Sandy were sweating. At the caves, Daniel took Sandy's lead and coaxed him into the river. Sandy whinnied and backed away as Daniel poured water over his head and shoulders but soon the little horse came back for more. Leaving him to enjoy the water, Daniel dove into a pocket of deeper water he'd found on another trip letting the cold spring revive him.

As he waded to shore, he remembered the odd footprints and took his camping shovel to explore. The dirt under the tree *had* been loosened. Daniel shoveled until he hit something hard. A rock? He slid his shovel under the object and lifted out a box covered with a plastic bag. A horse's head was carved into the lid. Inhaling the aroma of the mesquite wood, he traced the carving with his finger. So this is what Grandpa was working on. But when did he bury it?

Daniel smiled…so like Grandpa to bury a last treasure. He lifted the lid to find Grandpa's worn Bible. Inside the Bible, he discovered a small handmade map and in the corner of the box a white stone with a dove etched on it. On closer look, numbered slips of paper marked places in the book. Was Grandpa trying to tell him something? Could this be what he meant when he said, "Remember, Daniel"?

Chapter Twenty-four

D aniel carried the box into the cave curious to see what the slips of paper revealed. Grandpa *was* here waiting for him. A treasure hunt! He opened the Bible to the first marker at the Gospel of John.

In the beginning was the Word, and the Word was with God, and the Word was God. He was in the beginning with God. All things came into being through him, and without him not one thing came into being. What has come into being in him was life, and the life was the light of all people. The light shines in the darkness, and the darkness cannot overcome it.

Ancient poetry, Daniel thought, beautiful but mysterious. Was the Word a person? He decided the writer attempted to describe the creation of the world. *I don't know what you're trying to tell me, Grandpa, but I'll do my best to go through your markers. I hope I can understand.* He read the poetic words over and over and then fell asleep listening to the sound of the river.

Daniel awoke later, his stomach growling, and decided to open a can of beans and eat some of the beef jerky. Sandy was still asleep. He reopened the Bible and continued reading about Jesus. Daniel knew little about Jesus except that He was the one around whom Christians based their belief. The kids at school used His name as an exclamation point, more like swearing. Who was Jesus really?

Daniel followed Grandpa's marker and continued to read. At dusk, he closed the Bible and thought about what he'd read—magical healings, blind people seeing, deaf hearing, even people brought back to life. He knew it was foolish, but he wondered if Jesus would have healed Grandma.

Daniel lay back on his bedroll. He didn't miss television or traffic or the nightly news with its stories about abused children, wives killed by their husbands or terrorists bombing innocent people somewhere. *I don't think Jesus would feel very comfortable in the twenty-first century,* Daniel thought.

The next morning, the temperature dropped into the sixties and a gentle breeze was blowing. "C'mon, Sandy, let's take a ride." He saddled the horse and this time headed into the desert letting Sandy gallop. They rode for a long time. How long, Daniel didn't know. He'd left his communicator at home wanting to feel the rhythms of the sunrise and sunset. Tired from the ride, Daniel returned to camp. He opened his last can of beans aware that tonight he'd have to hunt rabbits. Thanks to Grandpa, he knew how to roast rabbit over a campfire.

Resting in the cave from the heat, Daniel opened the Bible surprised at the urgency he felt to read the pages Grandpa had marked. He finished John's story, sad to learn the holy man was beaten and killed by His enemies and hung on a wooden cross to die. He guessed there was violence in those days, too, just a different kind. The amazing thing to Daniel was that although Jesus was buried, a few days later His body came up missing and people reported seeing Him alive. Later He *ascended* on the clouds into heaven.

Déjà vu! Ascended on clouds to heaven? A chill ran down his spine. Was his grandparents' Ascension patterned after this ancient holy man's? And was that why Grandpa and Gram weren't scared, because they believed they were going where Jesus went? Daniel closed the book, slipping it into his sleeping bag. The sun was setting and he needed to hunt his supper. He loaded shells into his rifle and climbed the rocks to the spot where he'd seen rabbit tracks. Ahead of him a jackrabbit sat motionless. Daniel took a clean shot, amazed the rabbit only perked up its ears and then sat without moving. Lucky for him. He carried the rabbit down to the river and washed it before taking it back to the campfire. Tomorrow he'd fish again. And…tomorrow he'd see where Grandpa placed the second marker.

Daniel fed Sandy, then sat in the caves listening to the soft hooting of an owl. The night animals and predators were out. He added wood to his campfire and fell asleep listening to the chatter of crickets by the river.

About five a.m. the sun broke through his sleep. His teeth were coated and he realized he'd forgotten his toothbrush. He grinned, doubting the Indians worried about brushing their teeth. Reaching for his fishing rod, he fastened the lucky blue dragonfly on his fishing pole and waded into the river to catch his breakfast.

Marker two was placed on a page called 2 Thessalonians, chapter 2. This writer, a man named Paul, was talking about Jesus coming to earth again. Startled, Daniel stopped reading. Could Jesus be coming again in this age? As he continued, Paul assured the readers that this coming would not happen until the man of lawlessness had been revealed. This powerful man would not pay attention to present law but would make his own law and times. Paul said that those who did not believe in the real God would be deceived by the magical signs he worked.

Paul's writing confused Daniel. Was he saying that a powerful, evil man would come into the world like Hitler, Stalin, Mao? He went on to marker three. This marker also spoke about the lawless man, calling him a beast with a prophet. Whoa! The letter referred to the mark of the beast, saying the mark was a number received on the hand or forehead without which you couldn't buy or sell.

A chill ran up Daniel's spine. This was just like the mark the World Federation demanded for entrance into the global economy. Grandpa said no rulers until now demanded a mark to buy and sell. That was the clue that something was happening today.

As Daniel put the old book back in its box, his peace was broken by what he'd read. After feeding and bedding down Sandy, Daniel spread out his sleeping bag and drifted off to sleep. About two a.m., the baying of a pack of coyotes woke him. He glanced over at Sandy still sleeping on the ground under a pine tree and decided to stay awake to discover how far away the coyotes might be. The night was quiet and he didn't hear any more howling.

Daniel fell back asleep. When he awoke, he thought of his family. What would happen to them and to the ranch? He didn't want to think this evil man might even now be living and beginning to control the world. He didn't follow world news much but he knew Muslim terrorist groups like Al-Qaida and Hezbollah were making inroads even in America. A couple of kids from his school had joined the American Taliban taking Muslim names and wearing weird turbans. Did they really think strapping a bomb on their bodies and blowing up malls, killing innocent people made them worthy of heaven? Not the heaven Grandpa and Grandma were in. What a sick way to lose your life. Since 9-11 no one in America felt safe but this religion was spreading all over the world, his world.

The words from Grandpa's Bible mirrored what was happening today. Daniel was a little sorry he'd discovered the book and the box because if the Bible was correct, Daniel might find himself on the wrong side. He checked out the map. An "R" appeared over several cities. Neither the map nor the white stone meant anything to him, but he placed them back in the box and reburied them under the old cottonwood tree, along with his questions.

Daniel was entering the Guardians Corps created especially to help the president with his new initiatives. He'd been honored and to refuse this appointment would bring shame on his family.

Chapter Twenty-five

October 1, 2022

"**G**uardians will bring the personal items listed. Communication with family and friends will resume at graduation in May."

Daniel checked the packing list making sure he had all the required items. No digital communicators allowed. Wow. They really wanted to cut them off from the world. He zipped his duffel bag, and sat down on the bed to look over the class schedule from the school.

"Are you ready, Danny? It takes forty-five minutes to get to the school."

"Just trying to figure how I'm gonna get along without you, Mom," he joked.

"No jokes. I really don't see why they're so strict about calls and visits."

"I've got a whole new family, Mom…the Guardians."

Judith frowned. "Not funny."

"Joey's picking me up in a few minutes."

"I thought I was taking you."

"No, Mom. Joey came all the way home from U of A to take me. I can't show up with a mother. You do understand?"

"But the letter we received said your parents could bring you. They're having a banquet for families. With Dad and Penny on the cattle drive, I assumed..."

"No, Mom. I'm not going to prison. I'll only be an hour away."

He would only be an hour away but somehow he didn't have the good feeling he'd had helping Joey move into his apartment at the University of Arizona.

Joey's horn broke the tension. Daniel hugged his mom and climbed into the seat next to Joey. "I'll miss you, Mom. Don't take in any wooden nickels while I'm gone."

Judith blinked back tears. She was going to miss Daniel and his corny jokes. He was one of the two best things that had come out of her marriage. "At least I won't have to keep reminding you to get up in the morning."

"No, but if it's any comfort, I'm sure the military has a system to see that happens and it'll be a whole lot earlier than you've been trying to get me up."

Joey revved his motor and the two took off in a cloud of dust. They drove in silence. "Wish you were headed for San Diego, Big Guy?"

Daniel nodded. He must have wished that a dozen times in the past few months.

"You could have followed your dream, DJ."

"I know. Bad gamble. Well, they have me for five years."

"Think the soccer school will take you back?"

"No, I guess I don't. I made a bad bargain but now I've got to step up and hope my mom was right."

Luke Air Force Base came into view. "Does the president still fly into Luke?"

"Yeah, that's what the packet said. High security." They turned into the entrance of the school stopping at the guard house to be identified.

"Guardian training?" challenged the guard.

"Yes, sir," Daniel replied.

"Step out of the car please."

Both Daniel and Joey got out of the car.

"Just the cadet, guys."

Daniel followed him to the guardhouse where security scanned his iris, matching it to his computer file. Satisfied with Daniel's identity, the guard allowed him back into the car and directed them to the school. A discreet sign read—Guardian Training School—est. 2020.

The Guardian school's red-roofed, stucco buildings were a startling contrast to the original air force base whose stark, weathered buildings lay in disrepair.

"Let's drive around and see what's here," Danny said.

Buildings surrounded a court with a desert garden featuring a copper statue of a Guardian in uniform. Each building was numbered: Administration G-1, Auditorium G-2, Classroom Building G-3, Health Center G-4, Mess Hall G-5, Barracks G-6 and Recreation Facility G-7. Behind the complex, they saw targets and what appeared to be a training area. Joey parked in the lot closest to the barracks. "Cool, huh, Joey. Kind of like a little city."

Two Guardians rolled up in an old-style Hummer. "Hey, buddy, welcome to the Village. Give us your duffel and we'll deliver it to the barracks. They've got you scheduled for orientation in the auditorium followed by a tour and dinner in the mess hall."

Daniel unlocked the trunk and lifted out his duffel which was marked with his Guardian tags. "Thanks, name's Daniel Jordan—this is my friend, Joey."

"Good to have you Joey. Afraid you'll have to leave your friend here." Noticing the license plate the Guardian added, "You the Arizona Guardian?"

"Yeah."

"The auditorium is in G-2. There's a map by the administration building that tells you where everything is. See you around."

At the auditorium Daniel found his ID badge. He was impressed that fifty guys from all over the country would be his classmates. That was cool. He studied a few badges: Jerry Adams, Kansas; Dominic Sebastian, N.Y.; Hal Kimmel, Alabama. He took a seat halfway down the auditorium. The captain signaled for their attention.

"Welcome to the Guardian Training School. Tonight you will begin a new life, a life of responsibility, order and duty. The president is unable to be with us on this occasion but we've set up a teleconference with him in Washington."

The familiar face of the president appeared. "You fifty new cadets were chosen because you are the best. You are now part of an elite corps, an important arm of my government. Work hard, respect your officers and meet the goals set before you. Experts designed your training. Your job is to master each task. I know all of you will make fine Guardians."

Daniel listened to the president's words.

The captain then continued, "My job is to see that all of you qualify. The training is intense and covers mental, physical and spiritual conditioning. In eight months you will be a Guardian. You will not be allowed to contact your family until graduation. They will survive—you will survive.

"After dinner tour the compound with your Guardian instructors. At 2100 report to your quarters in G-6. Your duffel bag will identify your rack and your sergeant will be waiting for you."

Daniel joined some cadets in the dining room. Dinner was served family style—roast chicken, steak, green beans, salad, baked potatoes and apple pie. At least he wouldn't starve here.

After dinner he joined the tour walking around the small campus and into the buildings. In the recreation center Daniel discovered an Olympic swimming pool and strength training machines. The education building was equipped with state-of–the-art computers and the Guardian instructors told them that much of their military training would be computerized simulations testing their mental and physical reactions.

Shortly before 2100, Daniel walked back to G-6. As he looked down the row of cots for his duffel bag, he noted that the Guardians were placed alphabetically by states. Alabama, Alaska, Arizona…third bunk. The sergeant entered and blew his whistle.

"When I blow this whistle, you move to the end of your rack and stand at attention. It is my unfortunate duty to turn you socialites into Guardians. You will respond to me as Sir or Sergeant. Yes, Sergeant, No, Sergeant; Yes, Sir, No, Sir. Do you understand?" He paused. **"Do you understand?"** Silence. **"DO YOU UNDERSTAND?"**

"Yes, sir." (In unison.)

The sergeant frowned at their slowness to respond. He continued, "You will do what I tell you, when I tell you, no questions asked. Now…Alaska, you have a question?"

"Yes, sir."

"No, Alaska, you have no questions. Now let's try that again. Alaska, you have a question?"

"No, sir."

"Very good. You have thirty minutes for a shower and use of the head. Lights out at 2200. Do you understand?"

"Yes, sir."

"I can't hear you."

"Yes, sir, Sergeant, sir."

Harry and Penny finished the cattle run and returned to Phoenix. Judith was relieved to have them back. The ranch felt wrong after Daniel left. Judith's feelings were hurt that Daniel wouldn't let her drive him to Luke.

"Well, did you deliver Daniel to Luke?"

Judith teared up. "No, Joey took him. I guess moms are for kindergarten not military schools. We can't see him or talk to him till graduation in May. I really don't understand why they are doing that."

Harry did. "He's not going to beauty school, Judith. He's in a high-powered military program." Harry sat down, tired of the heat and the cattle. He needed a shower, his mouth and throat felt like sandpaper.

"Where's Penny?" Judith asked.

"Out with her friends, I guess." He poured a beer and turned on the evening news. The president was being interviewed. "Omega I, tell us what your next initiative will be?"

The president straightened his tie, "Well, there are several in the works. One involves youth. That's all I have to say for now. More later."

Harry turned off the T.V. "Why are they calling him Omega I?" Harry snapped.

"Oh, it happened while you were gone, Harry. One of the newscasters got an email from the president, seems that's his Internet name. The media love it and now they're all calling him Omega I. It seems like the right name for a futuristic president, don't you think?"

"And what are they calling the vice president?"

"Jack Prophet? The Prophet, I think." Judith turned to leave, "Oh Harry, now that you're back maybe you can get your number...I got mine before..."

Harry froze, his heart turned to ice. He reached for his pipe. "I'm not getting the number, Judith." He waited for her to digest his words. "Not tomorrow...not ever."

Chapter Twenty-six

2 October: 0200

"When you hear this whistle, gentlemen, you are on your feet day or night. Do you understand?"

The fifty young Guardians leaped out of bed and stood at attention.

"I didn't hear your response."

"YES, SIR."

"Again."

"YES SIR."

"Follow me."

The sleepy troop marched behind the sergeant to the health center. Each soldier received a series of shots, and then returned to his rack. At 0500 the irritating whistle blew three times to signal morning.

"Wake up, daisies, time to rise and shine."

"Yes, sir."

"Hit the head and fall in for chow."

Daniel dragged himself into the head following Alaska and Alabama. No one talked. He showered and shaved, made his rack, stowed his gear and put on the Guardian issue uniform noting even the tennis shoes bore a "G."

At mess, the sergeant left them alone. Daniel loaded his tray with steak, scrambled eggs, hash browns and a large glass of orange juice hoping to regain some of his energy. He already missed the congeniality of his high school buddies finding it hard to start over with no friends. And you sure didn't want to make the wrong ones.

"Hey Arizona, over here."

Daniel followed the voice to a long table of cadets where Illinois slapped him on the back.

"How do you like the military?"

Daniel slid into a seat ignoring the question and concentrated on eating. Jokes and wisecracks felt inappropriate in this environment. He doubted the sergeant had much sense of humor and was proved right when the sergeant stood at the end of their table addressing the Illinois Guardian.

"So...do *you* like the military, Illinois?"

"Yes, sir, I do, sir."

"That's good, soldier. Maybe you'll like it even more after you run four miles." The Illinois Guardian followed the sergeant, leaving his tray on the table.

"Expecting a clean-up committee, Illinois? *You* are the clean- up committee."

Red-faced Illinois grabbed his tray and headed for the tray return. Then he followed the sergeant while the other cadets finished eating in silence and returned to G-6.

At 0615 Daniel grabbed his backpack and made his way to the auditorium. He heard a voice behind him say, "Wonder if our..."

"We do not wonder...we do not ask questions," mimicked Rick, the New Jersey Guardian. "Well, look who's here...a real Arizonan...a cowboy. Hey, cowboy, you own a horse?"

Daniel ignored Rick, reminding himself to steer clear of the New Jersey cadet. He didn't want trouble and some guys were like a trouble magnet. At the door of the auditorium a Guardian trainer handed him a packet. Daniel opened it to find his class schedule. While he studied the courses, the captain addressed them.

"In your packet you will find a schedule of classes. Your training will be thorough—physical, mental and scientific. The courses are short, but high-powered and in depth. Study hard. Do well. Your future depends on how well you assimilate the next eight months' training. The first twelve weeks of basic training, you will learn to be soldiers, to respond to authority. We'll bust your butts, but you'll get tough. The last five months you'll learn officer skills specific to the Guardian Corps. At graduation, you will be assigned a partner who will be your conscience. You will watch each other's backs and serve together wherever you are assigned." The captain paused. "Have you met your sergeant?"

"Yes, sir."

"He will tell you when, where and what to do. Follow his commands."

"Yes, sir."

"After mess you will spend the mornings in basic training. In the afternoon, follow your personal schedule. The sergeant is in charge of your free time. He may train you as he sees fit. You are dismissed to your sergeant."

The sergeant took the microphone. "You have been divided into three training cells by states: A-G=Cell 1, H-O=Cell 2, P-Z= Cell 3. A Guardian trainer is in charge of each cell. I am in charge of everyone. Cell 1 report to the outdoor target range; Cell 2 go with your Guardian trainer for a five mile march; Cell 3 report to the recreation center."

Relieved, Daniel caught up with his rack mates. "You guys ever fired rifles other than our summer training?"

Alaska nodded. "Guess I'm more familiar with a bow and arrow, but yeah, I've fired rifles."

"How bout you, Hal?"

Hal shrugged his shoulders. "We live on a lake in Alabama. I'm pretty good with a fishing pole."

The boys caught up to Max, their cell leader who was explaining,

"We'll begin with a rifle. Later you'll learn to handle a stun gun, a taser and tank missile weaponry. We will prepare you for terrorist attacks and national emergencies, but your assigned duty will be to carry out the president's initiatives."

He picked up the electro-rifle. "Unlike weapons of old, these weapons do not need taking apart and putting together. A microchip flashes a red light if the battery runs low. That's your cue to recharge. These weapons are precise. Any movement on your part triggers them. You miss the target, flags will fly. We call them Maggie's Drawers. Line up before a target. Hit as many bull's-eyes as possible. They will record automatically."

Daniel took the rifle in his hands. He aimed and fired missing only once. Others in his cell, not as experienced, struggled to hit the target setting off the delicate mechanism unintentionally. Bright yellow flags waved wildly. Max moved from soldier to soldier encouraging each one. When he came to Daniel he said, "Arizona, your cowboy training's kickin' in," and then he moved on.

An hour passed. Finally, Max told them to take a break, informing them that some of the weapons training would actually be computer-simulated. Later, the simulations turned out to be mock national disturbances: terrorist attacks on the dams, forest fires, crowd hysteria. The Guardians learned their role—attack the perpetrator and control the people.

Daniel got used to the tempo of basic training: five to ten mile runs, hiking, mountain climbing, camping in the desert, weapons training, conditioning in the work out area, classes in Shotokan karate. The cadets also attended classes in yoga and visualization. The only routines he didn't adjust to were the sergeant's extemporaneous midnight excursions and his relentless whistle. He could hear the sergeant even in his sleep saying "Do you understand? **Do you understand? No questions, is that understood?**"

In high school, he'd been taught to analyze everything, but the Guardian philosophy was unquestioned obedience and loyalty. "Don't confuse your action with thinking. Thinking paralyzes—obedience gets results."

One evening Daniel walked to mess with Hal, the cadet from Alabama. Rick Hathaway entered a cleaning closet outside the mess hall. "Where's he going?" asked Daniel.

"You don't wanna know." Hal paused. "He's calling his girl in New Jersey."

"Whoa… punishable by death."

"He'll get caught one of these days. He's sure got an attitude."

"Rules are for everybody but him?"

"You got it."

After mess, the sergeant blew his whistle. Daniel had a bad feeling in his gut. The cadets stood at attention. The sergeant held up a communicator. "Do you see this?"

"Yes, sir."

"What is it, soldiers?"

"A communicator, sir."

"No, it is restricted trash."

"Yes, sir."

"Now this restricted trash was found in a cleaning closet by a janitor. The question is, who does it belong to?" You could hear an ant crawling across the floor. Daniel looked at Hal who was staring at Rick. The sergeant intercepted the look.

"Jordan, you know who this belongs to?"

Daniel swallowed. "No, sir."

"Alabama?"

"No, sir."

"Anyone?"

There was no response.

"I will give the owner one minute to step forward. If no one does, you will all serve detention." A wave of moans and groans followed.

Rick grinned, pleased no one had turned him in.

"Go back to G-6 and get your hiking gear on."

"YES, SIR."

Daniel and Hal joined the cadets as they marched back to the Guardian barracks, eyes cast down. *What a jerk,* Daniel thought, upset that Rick let them take his punishment. Nine hours of mountain climbing and desert trekking with no food and little water took its toll. When morning came, the tired marchers returned to shower for the day exhausted and angry. Ahead was a full day with no rest.

Daniel didn't complain. As he came out of the shower, Rick punched his shoulder. "Thanks, cowboy, I owe you one." It took everything Daniel had not to punch him in the face.

The sergeant tapped on the captain's door.

"Come in, Sergeant. What can I do for you?"

"A little mutiny in the Corps, sir."

"Let's hear it."

"The janitor found this communicator in his cleaning closet."

"Pretty serious offense."

"Yes, sir."

"What are you doing about it?"

The sergeant informed him of the overnight march. "Shall I put them on another night hike?"

"Would it produce the villain?"

"No, sir."

"Sergeant, I find this disturbing, but I like the Corps' loyalty. It achieves one of our goals for them, doesn't it?"

"Yes, sir, my thoughts exactly."

"Destroy the communicator. Do you know who it belongs to?"

"I've got a good idea, sir. It has New Jersey area codes in its directory."

"New Jersey? Keep your eyes on him then."

"Yes, sir."

"Dismissed."

Chapter Twenty-seven

December 31, 2022: Shotokan karate: The sensei entered the dojo. Immediately Cell 1 assumed the ready (yoi) stance: feet, shoulder-width apart; hands held waist high in fists.

"**Sensei,**" they yelled in unison.

"At ease, cadets." The sensei cleared his throat and held up his hand. "Last night, one of your own attacked the sergeant in hand-to-hand-combat." The room was still. "The young soldier from Tennessee is paralyzed. The sergeant is a master of Shotokan. He responded in self defense.

Daniel and Hal exchanged glances. Brad, the cadet from Tennessee, must have snapped. Cell 3 had just been on one of the sleepless overnight hikes supposed to make them tough. Instead, Daniel guessed, it had broken the young soldier.

The sensei continued. "Enough. Let's begin." The cadets moved through the four basic stances like robots, continuing to go through the punches, blocks and kicks as the sensei weaved in and out correcting each movement. To an outsider, the routine appeared synchronized. This was no dance though, but intended to teach them how to restrain attackers, neutralize the opponent's power and properly and safely use hand-to-hand weapons. Orange and yellow belts earned, in five months they would have their green and brown belts.

Despite Tennessee's accident, Daniel still loved the discipline, a required part of their Small Unit Tactics class. At the end of a class he felt strong and in control. The exercise released pent-up energy. The depth of concentration he'd developed through the martial art surprised him. After class, he returned to his locker changing from the oriental clothing into his regular Guardian issue.

"Daniel-san"

Daniel turned. "Hey, Hal, sad news, huh?"

"Yeah. He was all right, ya know?"

"I know... ready for yoga mumbo jumbo?"

"Better not say that too loud."

"Sorry, it's the mantra thing."

A voice interrupted, "Arizona, are you complaining?"

"No, sir...I mean yes, sir?"

"Which is it, soldier?"

"Sorry, sir. No, I'm not complaining."

"Criticizing?"

"No, sir. Better minds than mine have planned our training."

"Remember that, soldier."

"Yes, sir."

Daniel looked at Hal. Close call. He got off lucky. How did the sarge always manage to turn up at the most inopportune times?

Hal laughed. "Gotcha. Let's go relieve our stress."

The boys headed for yoga. They arrived at the meditation room and took their position on the floor. The repetitive Guardian mantras filled the air as each recruit added his voice to the murmur. *We are Guardians...we are strong... we are invincible...we are chosen...* over and over. The instructor entered the room. "Let's begin." The yoga master played music in the background, music without words and little melody—almost a hum. The monotonous music got on Daniel's nerves. What was the purpose?

After class, the boys walked back to the barracks. Today was their last day of basic training and tonight a special banquet in full dress uniform ended their first twelve weeks. Daniel showered, laying out his dress uniform on his rack. So far, all cadets survived except Tennessee. He spit-polished his shoes and yelled at Hal.

"Walk over to the mess?"

The boys, joined by three or four other cadets from their unit, headed for the mess hall. The group sat down, surprised to find linen tablecloths and upperclassmen serving the meal. Caesar salads and hot rolls, followed by plates containing roast beef, broccoli, mashed potatoes and gravy, completed the feast.

"They're making Mom proud tonight," Daniel said as the captain signaled for quiet.

"Gentlemen, tonight marks the end of basic training. You've come a long way but you still have a long way to go. Some of your classes will continue. New classes will be added and you will have to use your free time to maintain target practice and conditioning. In five months you will graduate as the Guardian Class of 2023—a toast."

"Here! Here!"

"While the waiters serve your dessert, we have a special feature—the new Guardian uniform to be worn when on duty representing the country. It is a product of research begun in the early 2000s. A brochure describing the attributes of this mechanical wonder is on your table. Check into the health center this week and get measured."

"Now relax and enjoy a special new movie, 'The Last Day'." Tomorrow Officer Training begins. You've done well. Only one Guardian from your class failed to measure up. Keep up the good work."

Anxious to check out the new Guardian uniform, Daniel signed up for an afternoon appointment. The nurse greeted him showing him into a dressing room where she measured him and then instructed him to put on the suit. First, he slipped the undershirt—netted with sensors that monitored his heart rate, body temperature and respiration—over his head.

"Look over here, soldier, and you can see the readings."

Daniel read temperature 97.9, respirations 18, heart rate 80.

"Whenever you put the uniform on, sensors telegraph your vital signs directly to the Guardian Control Center. The technician on duty will know if you are in a stressful situation and notify your commanding officer."

Daniel put on the silver jumpsuit, noting he could barely feel the lightweight material. A blue and red presidential seal appeared on his left chest. "Ma'am, what kind of material is this?"

The nurse raised her eyebrows. "Nothing you've ever seen before, soldier. The macromolecular fiber can close its pores between fibers to block out chemical weapons or bullets. You can program the fabric to mirror the surroundings and make yourself nearly invisible...but the best part for you is that the surface of the cloth detects the atmosphere above the surface adjusting the temperature inside the uniform to 80 degrees Fahrenheit."

"You mean when it's 120 degrees, I'll be cool."

"That you will."

"Wow!"

"A big $100,000 wow! The president spared no expense. And you haven't seen the best part yet."

Daniel watched the nurse reach for the silver helmet.

"Hidden in the wings are two small video cameras, along with a GPS system in the visor. It's two-way. The GPS informs you of your immediate position showing you a map with your location. By speaking into the voice sensor in the visor, you can ask or relate any information needed."

The uniform was amazing but the thought occurred to Daniel that with it on, every action he took would be monitored. He would be plugged into a living computer.

Chapter Twenty-eight

Not wanting to be late for his first Public Policy class, Daniel picked up his pace. Hal was waiting at the door. "You're late."

"Sorry, getting fitted for the new uniform. Have you seen it yet?"

"No, didn't have time to work it in yet. Cool?"

"Very."

The boys slipped into the third row as the instructor passed out the lesson for the day.

"You have in your hands the present structure of the United States Government. I'd like to give you a little history. In the 2000 presidential election both the democratic and republican candidate tied in votes. The Supreme Court decided the presidency. For many years the elected party tried to pass important legislation through the House and Senate. The opposing party blocked legislation causing the Congress to be constipated."

This statement brought laughter. The instructor continued, "Hard on the country."

"In 2020, President Blackstone appointed the Council of Twelve and each state governor to a Board of Governors to conduct business for the country eliminating the need for millions of dollars normally wasted on congressional campaigns. The Supreme Court has not interfered.

"The Guardians are the new edition to the government food chain. Each state will have its own Guardians. After an internship in Phoenix, most of you will return to your home states to help set up the Guardian units there. Now, let's see what one of the government initiatives looks like."

The instructor passed out another set of papers. Daniel looked at the handout realizing that he was looking at the Ascension Initiative. His heart began to pound and sweat broke out on his forehead.

"You all right, DJ?" Hal whispered.

He could hardly breathe. "Yeah, I guess... memories."

"You were there? At the first one?"

Daniel nodded, trying to tune Hal out so he could hear the instructor.

"The Social Security and national health care system were in danger of collapsing when the Council of Twelve and President Blackstone designed an initiative to allow people with terminal conditions or those over eighty to offer their lives for their country just as young combat soldiers do."

It wasn't volunteer, Daniel thought, as he recalled the legal summons his grandparents received to report to the Center for New Age Medicine.

"The Ascension's purpose is to equalize the numbers of old and young, to take the financial burden off the government and to provide older citizens an opportunity to serve their country. Millions of dollars will be saved without costly end-of-life surgeries and transplants."

A knot began to form in Daniel's stomach. *So his grandparents gave up their lives—to balance the budget?*

The instructor continued, "Our job is to assist with the president's initiatives. The Council and the president design the initiatives for the good of society—for the good of the many instead of the individual—a long overdue policy."

Daniel shuddered, thinking that the good of society might depend on how old you were — good for the people who were thirty but not so good if you were an eighty-year-old.

When they got out of range of the class, Hal asked him more about the Ascension.

"I'll tell you more about it someday, Hal. I just can't today."

"But DJ, I watched it on TV and it looked amazing."

"Not so amazing for my grandparents."

"They were in the 1st Ascension?"

"My grandmother needed major heart surgery. The hospital and the doctors refused because of instructions from the Council and assigned her to the Ascension. My grandfather, who was eighty, volunteered so he could be with her."

"And you saw them...."

"I saw them ...give their lives for their country."

"Wow."

Unnoticed by Daniel and Hal, Rick Hathaway followed a few feet behind. Rick took out a pocket notebook and wrote...Daniel Jordan's grandparents were in the 1st Ascension. He is negative about the Ascension. An anonymous note to the instructor would find its way into Daniel's file. After all, the administration instructed them to report any cadet who criticized the program.

Chapter Twenty-nine

As the weeks went by, Daniel heard the Guardian slogans repeated. The sergeant summed it up: "**If it's worth saying, it's worth saying again.**" However, the slogans seemed more like brainwashing and went against everything he'd experienced in athletics where he'd been encouraged to think for himself and to anticipate.

Then one night about 0130 Alaska woke Daniel chanting. Daniel tried to shake him awake. The young soldier was in for big trouble if Daniel couldn't get him to stop chanting. Although Alaska was in a deep sleep, he pushed Daniel away, swayed, then got to his feet and began marching. His mumbling grew louder like thunder roaring.

"Are you thinking, soldier? No thinking."

"Thinking paralyzes."

"Obedience gets results."

Alaska marched up and down shouting loudly, "We are Guardians...we are invincible...we are chosen..."

The lights flashed on. The sergeant bellowed. "Alaska, is that you?"

Alaska snapped to attention appearing confused. "Yes, sir... no, sir..."

"He's asleep, Sarge."

"Did I address you, Arizona?"

"No, sir. But he doesn't know what he's saying. He's asleep."

"That's all, Arizona." And with that the sergeant took Alaska's arm and marched him out of the barracks.

"What do you think they'll do with him, Daniel?" Hal whispered.

"Nothing good," said Daniel.

Cell Biology fascinated Daniel because he liked anything scientific. The instructor presented each cadet with a packet of slides. Daniel studied the DNA of cancer cells, multiple sclerosis, diabetes, Down's syndrome, and AIDS, learning the difference in the cell makeup.

The instructor told them that the elimination of disabilities and genetic errors was a responsibility of the state. Now he understood why the young woman and the Down's syndrome kids were in the Ascension. Controlling genetics made sense to Daniel in a perfect world, but this wasn't a perfect world. *Many people inherited bad genes and you couldn't eradicate all of them.* He would keep that thought to himself.

Social Psychology was not one of Daniel's favorite classes, at least not the way it was presented. *They should have titled it 101 Ways to Manipulate and Control People,* he thought.

The instructor spent a long time on personality types: Sanguine, Choleric, Melancholy and Phlegmatic. Daniel remembered the personality test he'd taken at the Center for New Age Medicine. The instructor spelled out the fact that all Guardians were powerful Cholerics with some Sanguine. *So that's why Joey was eliminated.* Joey was a Phlegmatic, gentle with animals, easy to get along with, a little indecisive.

"Are you with me, Arizona?" the teacher added.

"Sorry, sir, just digesting the material."

The instructor went on. "Knowing these personality types and how they think and react will help you manage people. You control people with surprise and authority."

Daniel thought about the Guardians at the Ascension, how they handled the crying children, struggling people and the picketers.

"When on assignment, you have the government's authority. How many of you watch the news?" No response. He shook his head. "Your assignment for the duration of this course is to head for the auditorium immediately after evening mess. We will use the news to develop Guardian situations. Dismissed."

After mess, the Guardians headed for the auditorium. Finding a seat, Daniel strained to focus on the news. Terrorists in Japan blew up the Nikkei Stock Exchange. A giant computer in Sweden registered participants of the World Financial Organization. (Daniel wondered if his dad had taken the number.) China announced nuclear missiles aimed at all bordering neighbors. Despite protests from the Arab countries, more Jews flooded into overcrowded Israel, and the first limestone block was laid for Israel's new temple as part of the seven-year peace treaty signed with the new global government.

A meteorologist followed the day's news with the latest weather disturbances. Daniel had never seen so much weird weather, hurricanes, volcanoes erupting in the oceans, temperatures out of control.

"And in Phoenix, an eight point earthquake cracked Bartlett Dam today sending raging waters into the Verde River, flooding northeast Scottsdale, the Verdes and the citrus and pecan groves run by the Yavapai nation."

Daniel bolted from his seat. His parent's ranch was in the path of the waters!

Chapter Thirty

Daniel ripped off his Guardian uniform, pulled on his jeans, and tennis shoes and raced out of the barracks unseen. Jogging out to the 331 bypass he did something he'd never done before. He walked into a convenience store, stopped a trucker and asked for a ride to Scottsdale, explaining his dilemma.

"I can only get you so close, boy. I'm not taking this truck into a #*#*! flood."

"It's okay. Just take me as far as you can."

Daniel climbed out of the truck, his heart beating as he saw the police blockades. He ran until the waters were so deep he could only continue by walking slowly and pulling the water with his hands. The churning water carried hay, horse manure and debris.

When he neared the ranch, he saw the waters had flooded his home. The cabins along the river, now swept away by the powerful current, made walking dangerous. Had his family escaped? He scanned the hills where the stables were, noting that although the water was waist deep, the stables were still there. He could hear the high whinnying of the terrified horses. Was his dad up there? Slipping on the mud as it broke loose under his shoes, Daniel climbed the hillside, giving no thought to his safety.

"Dad, Dad, can you hear me?"

The flood water had pushed the stable doors open but in the dark Daniel heard only the frantic horses. "Dad, are you in here?"

"We're here, Daniel."

Pinned to the back of the stable, his dad and one of the ranch hands stood shoulder deep, trying to force open one of the horse stall gates, the swirling water threatening to drag them under. Mud and debris caked their clothing. His eyes met his dad's.

"Dad, are you all right?"

"Help us move the horses, Daniel. Try to lead Sandy and Lad out. I think the other horses will follow, if we can just get them started. Lester and I will work this end and try to push the horses out of the stalls. Head west up through the hills. Put the horses in the northwest pasture if it's dry. Just move them to dry land, son. That's all we can do."

"Mom and Penny?"

"They're safe. We heard the roar and I told them to take the Land Rover and get out. Thought it was a flash flood."

"What about the cattle?"

"Gone...drowned. We'll deal with the ranch later. Let's just try to save the horses."

Harry and Lester opened the gates of the stalls while Daniel coaxed Lad and Sandy to follow him out of the stable. It was slow moving. He held tightly to their leads pulling them against the swirling current.

"Don't look back, son. The horses will follow," Harry instructed, wondering what price Daniel would pay for going AWOL? Prison?

Buffy, Penny's small blonde stallion, resisted Harry's tug. "C'mon now, Buffy. Don't be afraid. Penny needs you. C'mon girl, follow Daniel." Buffy broke loose swimming toward Lad and Sandy. "Good girl." Harry moved on. Thunder the big black reared up on two legs pounding the walls of the stall with his front hooves. "Thunder, down boy;

take it easy. You'll be all right." Harry couldn't get near the frightened horse. He and Lester moved on, speaking softly to each horse, coaxing them out of the stall. When he reached the brown and white pinto and her colt, Harry saw the little mare trying to lift her colt who'd apparently drowned in the waist deep water. "C'mon, Cinnamon. Let me help you. Lester take her reins, I'll get between her and the colt."

Daniel climbed slowly up the hill to the pasture land, leading Lad and Sandy, his dad and Lester following behind. Daniel knew flash floods carried cars, drowning people, trees and rocks but he'd never experienced anything like this. He felt sorry for his parents, twenty years of hard work buried under the floods. But at least they were safe. When the waters receded, his folks would work hard to put the ranch together again. Daniel wished he could stay and help his dad. What would the captain do with him?

"I called Mom, and she's going to meet us with the Land Rover. We'll take you back to camp. Thank you, son. I'm at a loss for words. Thanks to you, we saved the horses which will give us a new start. The insurance will cover ranch damage and, if it doesn't, we'll sell the Michigan cottage. Everything will work out. Now, let's make sure the horses can't get out. Lester and I will find some hay and water for them later."

Judith and Penny drove as close as they could without getting in the turbulent water. Harry's call said they were all right and to pick them up. She couldn't believe her eyes when she saw Harry covered with mud and debris. The dye from his old Stetson ran down his face, and he reeked with a disgusting stench. Lester dittoed everything she saw with Harry. But they'd saved the horses.

"Mom, isn't that Danny with them?" Penny said.

Judith eyes clouded. *What was Daniel doing here? Had he gone AWOL to help his dad with the flood?* She couldn't believe his foolishness. She had a sickening feeling that Danny had ended his career with the Guardians.

"Daniel? You've gone AWOL?"

"Leave him alone, Judith. If it weren't for Daniel we'd have no horses."

Judith bit her lip. She wanted to cry. All her sacrifices to get this boy into the president's elite Guardians thrown away in one night.

"Mom… Pen…you're all right?"

"I'll drop you off, Judith; then I'll take Daniel to Luke. Perhaps, if I explain..."

"Explain what, Harry? That Daniel's primary loyalty is to his family, not to the Guardians. That will go over big, I'm sure."

"Thanks, Dad. I did what I had to do. I'll take whatever they give me."

Daniel's sergeant checked the empty rack that should have held the Arizona Guardian. "All right. attention." The cadets staggered to their feet. "Can any of you tell me why this bed is empty?"

Silence.

"I'll ask my question once more. Can anyone tell me where Daniel Jordan is?"

Still silence.

"Alabama?"

Hal trembled. "Sir, the last I saw Daniel was in the auditorium watching the evening news as ordered, sir."

The sergeant tapped his walking stick. "Is that so…and what news caused him to leave, soldier."

Hal's face reddened. "I don't know sir…maybe the news about the dam breaking. That's when he left."

The sergeant squinted. "We'll handle this in the morning. Dismissed."

The sergeant left and the cadets climbed back in their racks. It was clear and certain—Daniel Jordan was in for it.

Chapter Thirty-one

"The military isn't very forgiving, Daniel. You violated their rules."

"What do you think they'll do, Dad?"

Harry thought a minute, "Son, you showed more loyalty to your family than to the Corps."

"I know."

"It may be a deadly mistake."

The gates of the Guardian School loomed before them in the early morning haze. Two Guardian MPs opened the truck door and pulled Daniel out, putting him in handcuffs.

"Go for a family visit, Arizona? We'll take him from here, sir."

Daniel remained quiet. He turned to his father. "Go home, Dad. Go home."

"The captain is waiting for you, kid."

His dad was right. He'd committed a crime in the eyes of the military, deserving punishment. Daniel was in for trouble.

Captain Stern paced his quarters, stopping to glance at the young cadet's file. One of the good ones. *Why, Daniel, why did you do it?* How should the captain handle the AWOL cadet? Should he transfer Daniel to a regular military prison to finish his five years, sending a warning to the other cadets? *What a waste.* The captain buzzed in the MPs.

"Bring him in." The captain ordered. "Take the handcuffs off. You're dismissed." The captain sized up the young cadet before him.

"Daniel Jordan."

"Yes, sir."

The mud-caked clothes showed Daniel's struggle with the churning waters that the captain had watched play over and over on the news.

"Your family's ranch was in the path of the flooding waters?"

"Yes, sir."

"Sit down, Daniel. Have you thought about your future?"

"I'm not sure I have any, sir."

"A wise answer, Daniel. Of course, you realize that I cannot condone cadets running off to save their family's ranches from disaster."

"I understand that, sir. I'm sorry."

"Are you really, Mr. Jordan?"

"Yes, sir, I know I've put you in a difficult position."

The captain rang for the MPs. "Put Daniel in solitary."

After they left, the captain scratched his head. He had to set a precedent so the cadets understood the serious consequences of leaving the base. In the regular military going AWOL merited a court-martial. But the Guardians weren't regular military, perhaps a court-martial with his peers as the judges. The captain made his decision. Daniel Jordan would be judged by his peers.

Rick, the New Jersey Guardian, slapped Alabama on the back holding up the summons. "Looks like your pal is in big trouble. You serving on the court-martial?"

Alabama winced, disliking the pleasure he heard in Rick's voice. "No, I'm testifying."

"Heard they put him in isolation."

Hal heard the rumor that Daniel was in isolation while plans for his court-martial went forward. "He saved your skin, Rick. Back off."

No shower, still wearing jeans caked with mud and manure, Daniel was his own worst enemy. The stench of the manure sickened him. His head ached and his stomach felt like someone had tied knots in it. What would the captain do with him? Did he have any future? Daniel sat on his bunk, holding his head thinking about the flood. Was it worth it, helping his family? Yeah, at least they had the horses to start over.

Several days passed and Daniel ate little, growing more nervous with each day. His Guardian instructor, the only visitor, said a court-martial was planned for the end of the week. Did a court-martial mean the end of his Guardian career?

Chapter Thirty-two

A t last, escorted by a Guardian MP, Daniel was taken to the showers and given a clean uniform. Not knowing what to expect, he entered the library set up as a courtroom. Six cadets sat at a long table and Captain Stern served as judge. The room overflowed with cadets. Everyone in his class attended. He recognized two of the six jurors—the Illinois Guardian and Rick. The other four must be from Cell 2 and 3.

The captain's voice rang out, "The court will come to order on the case of Daniel Jordan. Call your first witness."

"Hal Winslow, take the stand. Do you swear to tell the truth…"

"Yes, sir. I do."

"Mr. Winslow, when was the last time you saw Daniel Jordan?"

"The night of the earthquake at Bartlett Dam. We watched the disaster on the news together."

"And what was Daniel's reaction."

"He got up and ran out of the room. I didn't see him after that."

"Did he return to his rack that night?"

"No sir, he didn't."

"Thank you, that's all."

Hal turned to the court. "His parents' ranch was in the way of the floods."

"That's all, Mr. Winslow."

"I call Daniel Jordan to the stand."

Daniel steeled himself for the worst.

"Mr. Jordan, you left the Guardian School without permission. Is that correct?"

Daniel stared at his shoes. "Yes, sir, I did."

"To assist your family in the floods."

"Yes, sir."

"And how did you get to the ranch?"

"I hitchhiked with a trucker."

"Did you know you risked expulsion from the Guardian Corps?"

"To be honest, sir, all I could think of was my family's ranch in so much danger."

"You didn't think about the cost?"

"No, sir, I just knew I had to help save the horses."

"Your family runs a famous dude ranch?"

"They do; they did, sir."

"They lost everything but the horses?"

"Yes sir."

"Did you intend to return to the Guardian School?"

"Yes sir, I'm a Guardian."

"Do you understand we expect loyalty to the Guardians above any other loyalty?"

"I understand your expectation."

"Would you go AWOL again?"

Daniel wrestled with the question. He knew what they wanted him to say but in truth he'd do it again. "I respect the rules, sir. I'd hope not to have to make such a decision again."

"You are dismissed."

The six jurors were remanded to weigh the evidence and come up with a verdict.

Daniel waited, unsure what his fellow cadets would decide but afraid his career as a Guardian was over. The judge dismissed the assembly and set a time for decision. The longer they debated, the more doubts about his future Daniel had. Finally, he was called back into the temporary courtroom.

"Jurors, have you reached a verdict?"

"No sir, we have three votes for dismissal and three for a second chance."

Captain Stern studied Daniel's reaction, noting the intense strain on his face. "Do you think more time will help you make a decision?"

The jurors shook their heads. "No sir, we are split."

The captain sighed. The decision was his. "We'll recess till 0900 tomorrow. At that time I will state my decision."

The MPs shackled Daniel and pushed him from the room returning him to isolation.

If they gave him a second chance, Daniel walked a tightwire—one step and…

He lay down on the cot in the isolation unit and closed his eyes. He'd made a mess of it. None of the cadets would trust him, even if they did grant another chance. How did he go from honored scholar athlete to an AWOL criminal? The food delivered remained untouched, Daniel's appetite gone.

Tomorrow he'd learn his future but, either way, Daniel feared he'd entered the land of no sunrise or sunset—only perpetual gloom.

"Daniel Jordan, according to court-martial rules, it should be my duty to transfer you to a military prison for the duration of your five-year term in the Guardians. I pride myself in evaluating my cadets. In reviewing your foolish but brave effort to save your family's ranch, I instruct you to resume your Guardian duties and studies.

"You will have no privileges. You will continue your studies under severe scrutiny. Every move you make will be suspect. Every word you speak will be monitored. You will run four miles every morning alone and every night after the cadets are finished with their day. You will not complain. You will spend the next four weekends cleaning the latrines. You will, however, continue to be a Guardian. Dismissed. Take him to his unit."

Daniel saluted and left the courtroom. The cadets would treat him like a leper, afraid of associating with him in any way. Unlike high school where Daniel had many close friends, friends he could depend on and trust, he had made only one close friend here—Hal. He hoped Hal wouldn't give up on him, too.

Chapter Thirty-three

Weekends when he scrubbed the latrines, Daniel was ignored and shunned by the cadets like a disease they didn't want to catch. Hal still talked to him at night across the racks or in a class, but no one risked sitting with Daniel for chow. He was an island in the middle of a military encampment.

For the first time in his life, Daniel hated to get up in the morning and felt a victory just to get through a day, collapsing on his cot where thoughts about the life and friendships he could be having at the San Diego College overwhelmed him. Questions dogged his mind constantly: Who were the Guardians? What was their real purpose? Had Daniel been deceived in thinking he would be doing something good for his country? Would all the initiatives be like the Ascension?

But…it could be worse. He could have spent the next four years in a military prison, so he was thankful for another chance. Surely, time would help the guys treat him normally again. Until then he was a loner in a different kind of solitary confinement.

One evening Daniel headed for the news in the auditorium, taking a seat in the back of the room. News Around the World was followed by a meteorologist reporting the weather. It had been 140 days since Phoenix experienced rain. The land was scorched and forest fires ravaged the Prescott forest and Pinetop—a hundred thousand acres burned.

A news flash interrupted the program: "We go now to Rome where the pope is meeting with other world religious leaders." Daniel paid close attention as each world religious leader burned his sacred writings in the papal fireplace. The pope himself placed the Bible into the fire.

The announcer stated, "The new One World Religion will create an equality among peoples, replacing the basic hatred of Jew and Muslim, Catholic and Protestant, atheist and Christian ushering a new era of peace."

The network cut to a reporter in Chicago interviewing a man on the street. "Sir, what do you think of this new One World Religion?"

"It's about time. Most of the wars have been caused by religious fanatics."

"And you, Miss, how do you feel about the new religion?"

"Finally, we'll have something in common with all people. Love and equality. What's wrong with that?"

The reporter turned back to the camera, "You've seen it first here on World News Network bringing you the latest in world news."

Daniel got up to leave. He wondered what spin the Social Psychology teacher would put on this and what role if any, the Guardians would play with this new edict. Daniel sighed… Grandpa was right. It was going to be a very different world.

Chapter Thirty-four

Neal Matthews, pastor of the Church of the Good Shepherd, slid into the first row of pews, his attention caught by the light streaming in the stained glass windows creating an aura around the simple wooden cross. *"Oh Lord, give me courage to walk in truth and love. Help me not to deny You no matter what the cost for I do love this church and cherish the honor of its members."*

He returned to the rectory awaiting the ten a.m. service. As the time approached the pastor again prayed, *"Help me, Lord"* and entered the pulpit. His eyes scanned the parishioners as they drifted in taking their usual seats. (God help any newcomer who presumed to sit in one of the elder's rows.)

He stood and addressed his flock. "Welcome to the Church of the Good Shepherd. Please turn and greet someone and offer them the peace of Christ." He listened as a murmur arose like the tide swelling and breaking on the shore. Turning he offered the peace of Christ to his lay reader and to the choir director.

The church grew quiet as the choir sang one of Neal's favorite old hymns, "A Mighty Fortress Is Our God." A tingling sensation followed the nerve pathway from his head to his feet and Neal took it as a sign that God was with him. The last notes faded and an awesome quiet filled the church. All eyes focused on him. He allowed the people to feel the quiet, meanwhile searching for his faithful nucleus of believers. His eyes acknowledged each believer, sending a message to surround him with prayer, then he opened his sermon, not sure what words the Spirit would bring to his mind.

"We have entered a new age. We no longer have a Congress or active Supreme Court. We have a charismatic president, a vice president, Council of Twelve and Board of Governors. It is a new era but one prophesied thousands of years ago. Recently, our nation joined a World Federation that adopted a one-world financial policy. Each of you was instructed to get a mark on your hand that will be used to buy and sell. If you don't have this mark, you cannot purchase food, clothing or pay your bills. The Bible predicted this time and God's people are instructed not to take this number, as I've told you before.

"Please turn in your Bibles to Revelation 14:9 and read silently." He waited while the people found the passage and read to themselves. "This is God's word on the subject. If we follow Christ, we cannot take this buying and selling number.

"This week the religious heads of the world gathered in Rome to discuss peace. Terror has reigned since the September 11, 2001, attack on our twin towers in New York City. The Dalai Lama believes that separate religions are responsible for this terror. He presented the case for a new religion based on love and tolerance, asking leaders to give up their outdated, ancient beliefs and join together in unity and peace. To pledge their sincerity, these religious leaders burned their Bibles, Quran and mystical writings.

The "Bible, we are told, is no longer to be used as it causes division and intolerance by speaking of one way to God. The new religion states God loves all people equally."

Pastor Neal held up his Bible. "This Bible contains the Word of God handed down to many men through the inspiration of the Holy Spirit. It is a foundation for our faith, giving us truth and guidelines for living. It teaches us about Jesus who said, 'I am the way, the truth and the life. No one comes to the Father except through me.' It is a narrow way. A way that cost the God of this universe His only Son who died a hideous death stretched out on a wooden cross so that you and I might have a way into eternal life where before there was none.

"As long as I am the pastor here, I will continue to teach and preach from the Word of God. And I will follow the warning in this holy book not to take the mark to buy and sell. May the Lord of life give us mercy and wisdom in this new age."

Stunned, people made their way out of the church, each turning and asking, "How then can we live?"

Neal turned to look once more on the cross. "*I have delivered Your word, Lord. Whatever happens is in Your hands.*"

The church trustees received phone calls for an immediate session at five p.m. As head of hospitality, Nan Coleman, Dr. Hart's nurse and a member of Good Shepherd, was summoned to the meeting, realizing only after her arrival that the pastor wasn't present.

"Where's Pastor Neal?" she asked Gloria, head of the children's Sunday school.

"I don't think he was invited. The elders wanted an opportunity for free discussion and we already know how he feels."

Nan bit her tongue, promising herself to listen and report back to the pastor. Removing a small grocery pad from her purse, she decided to take notes. The meeting was called to order by one of the elders, Lowell Atkins, a person she could never remember seeing in any Bible study. He cleared his throat. "We're here to decide what direction we want our church to go. Let's hear from you."

"If we continue to use the Bible, won't we be going against our president?" a voice yelled.

Questions and comments bombarded the leader.

"One at a time," declared the chairman.

"I think our pastor is a good man but he doesn't seem in tune with the times," said Alice. "I've heard that if we don't adopt the new way, our church will be closed."

Voices sprang up all over the meeting room.

"Didn't Jesus say the world would know us by our love? It seems the new religion is being formed on Jesus' teaching to love your neighbor as yourself."

"I read somewhere that Peter said it was our duty to obey our government and God would take care of us."

"If you stop and think about it, saying we have the only way to God through Jesus is very narrow and leaves out a lot of people who think their way is just as good."

"Talk about the number," someone interrupted.

"Aren't we taught to be good citizens and obey our laws?"

"How will we pay our taxes or keep our homes, much less buy food."

Pastor says the Bible contains God's words but these are not his words for today. They are his words for the people who lived 2,000 to 4,000 years ago."

"I say we keep our church, get rid of our pew Bibles and ask the World Council of Churches to send us a new minister."

"God wouldn't want us to starve our children. He was the one who fed the five thousand."

The chairman pounded his gavel. "If everyone will be quiet, please, do I hear a motion?"

"I move that we ask our pastor to resign, contact the WCC for a new minister, remove all the Bibles..."Mr. Cavanaugh paused, then added, "...and perhaps we'd better remove the cross."

"Here, here."

"Do I have a second?"

Janice Rose stood to her feet, "I second the motion."

"Well maybe now we'll hear more about love and kindness. We can become a church of joy," Gloria added.

"That's a wonderful thought. Could we change our name from the Church of the Good Shepherd to the Church of Joy?" asked Mary.

The suggestion was met with almost unanimous approval. Chairman Atkins finished by saying, "I'll notify the pastor."

Nan could hardly believe her ears. She had waited for God to move her to speak but felt only a quiet peace. She rushed to her car, hoping to get to the pastor's home before Mr. Atkins' call. She spun around the corner, jumped out of her car and knocked loudly on the door.

Pastor Neal lived with his sister Nellie who opened the door.

"Is he here, Nellie? I need to speak to him."

"Mercy, Nan, you're awfully upset."

"Wait till you hear. Pastor!"

"I know, Nan, the Lord impresses my heart that my time here at Good Shepherd is drawing to a close."

Nan gasped, "Your time at the Church of Joy."

"He has new work for me, Nan. Never fear."

"But, Pastor, they're going to remove all the Bibles and the cross."

"I expect they'll have to. The Bible will have no importance in the new church of love."

"Love without Jesus."

"Yes, isn't it sad." And with that the pastor took her hands in his and led her to the door. "Now we will truly become an underground church. The elders have made it simple for us to know who to involve. Those who don't stay with the church will come to us."

Nan nodded. "What must the Lord think?" she said softly.

"Remember, He knows men's hearts better than anyone. It was the religious leaders who killed Him."

Judith turned on the T.V. "Harry, come here, the president is saying something important."

Harry took out a doughnut and walked mechanically into the great room. "You know..."

"This is important, Harry, listen."

The president sat in the oval office. "Today is an historic day. It marks the beginning of a unified world, peaceful and without terror. As you saw on satellite, this week in Rome all religious leaders joined to form a new religion." The president turned, "Run the news from earlier in the week." As they watched, Judith and Harry saw the pope and religious leaders from all nations separate themselves from their holy writings, throwing their scriptures into the fire as a symbol of newfound unity. "These world leaders have taken an oath to participate in a new religion of love and tolerance. I want America to take the lead in this movement."

Judith looked at Harry, not knowing what to expect.

"Does this please you, Judith?"

Caught off guard, Judith swallowed, "I think it's wonderful that all these leaders want to have peace. To think that wars will cease. It's an unbelievable effort they are making and, yes, I guess I do think this is rather wonderful, don't you?"

Harry sighed. He thought of what his father and mother would have said and was so glad they weren't here to see this latest development. "No, I think it is the saddest thing I've witnessed so far in this presidency. I can't even imagine what people like my parents will do now. If they try to follow their beliefs, they will be ostracized. And more than that, they may be persecuted and treated as dissidents."

The following days, the newscasts showed churches being closed down and Bibles being burned in a great show of unity for the president's speech. Harry had become a prophet.

Chapter Thirty-five

May 2023

Daniel walked quickly to the seats assigned Cell 1, choosing a seat to the back and rear of his group. The members of his cell continued to avoid him. Even Hal limited contact to a few words in the shower. Daniel longed for things to get back to normal. Tomorrow the War Games began.

The sergeant's whistle called them to attention. "The War Games are a final test of leadership and teamwork. Each cell will try to bring home the coveted trophy. Tonight you will elect your team captain and plan your strategy. As you can see, Cell 1 is the Red team, Cell 2—the Blue team, Cell 3—the Gold team. You will have five hours to accomplish the objective: discover the goal, plant your flag and return to Command Center.

"If you encounter the other teams, seize their flags and eliminate their soldiers. Each soldier will be issued light lasers. If you are shot, you will turn fluorescent green and will return to Command Center. At 0700 each cell will be given a map. All maps start at a different location but are equidistant from the goal.

"Cell 1 you will take these red armbands and go to the library; Cell 2 you are the Blue team, go to the gym; Cell 3, the Gold team—the barracks. Are we clear?"

"YES, SIR."

Cell 1 sat down at the library tables—seventeen cadets. No one spoke. Finally, Daniel broke the ice. "I think we've got to be a team and look out for one another."

"You want to be our leader, Arizona?" asked Craig from Louisiana.

Daniel realized his team would be reluctant to follow anything he suggested. "No, but I have an idea. What if all of you put your ID badges in a hat and let the librarian draw one out? You've all had the same training. Any one of you can be the leader."

"Good idea, Daniel."

Everyone agreed and they asked the librarian to do the honors. Hal's name was drawn.

"All right… Hal."

Several voices yelled, "Got any ideas?"

Hal scratched his head. "We're fast and we've got the best sharpshooter in all the cells — 'Family Man.' He pointed to Daniel and everyone laughed. "Louis, you carry the flag. You other guys move out and protect Louis. Remember the other teams will try to steal our flag. Daniel and I will bring up the rear. Doug, you and Hank take the map and be our scouts. Everyone stay alert; watch each other's backs."

Cell 2 reconnoitered in the gym. Rick Hathaway took control of the meeting. "This isn't about being a good guy. We need to achieve our goal any way we can. This is war but we have a secret weapon."

The Cell 2 cadets grumbled under their breath. "Is that our map?"

"Could be...and what if I told you I figured out where the goal is?" Rick laid the map in front of them, pointing to an area in the mountains behind the target range. "I say we go directly to the goal, forget the map, plant our flag and set ourselves up to ambush."

"Good plan, Rick."

He continued, "Then we wait for Red and Gold, pick them off and steal their flags."

The group had a plan; Rick was the leader. They all agreed that winning was the goal—any means as long as they achieved their objective.

Cell 3 made its way to the barracks. When they arrived, the small group gathered around their bunks. "Any ideas?" a voice called.

Toby Allen, the cadet from Virginia, spoke up, "We all know Daniel Jordan is the best sharpshooter. Rick Hathaway is a master planner. I say we figure out who the leaders are and try to nail them. That will paralyze their cell. Then we move in, plant our flag and we're home free."

Toby's idea caught on. The cell selected him as captain of the Gold cell, and then they made a list of whom to target. By the time the Blue and Red team returned to the barracks, the members of the Gold team had their plan and were in the showers.

Next morning all three cells dressed for a hike, ate breakfast and reported to the target range. The sergeant was waiting for them. "Team captains, report here please."

Hal, Rick and Toby went forward.

"You understand the mission?"

"Yes, sir."

"You all understand if you're hit, you return here to the Command Center?"

All heads nodded in agreement.

"All right, leaders here are your maps. When you hear this blank fired, you will begin." The sergeant allowed the cells five minutes to study the map, then fired his gun.

The Red team took off, keeping their flag bearer in the center protected by cadets from all sides. They didn't concern themselves with where the Blue and Gold teams were, but moved as one man according to the map.

The Gold captain huddled his men. "I'm sure our paths will intersect Red and Blue. Move quickly until that time, then look for and isolate our enemy targets."

Blue team studied the map, seeing that it was the same map Rick had shown them. (No one wanted to know how he got the map.) They took the shortcut Rick suggested, buying his philosophy that "All was fair in war." Within an hour, they planted their flag and positioned themselves for an ambush.

Daniel thought Hal was a good leader. The two of them moved behind the unit guarding the flag bearer and keeping watch in all directions. After a half-hour following the map they heard movement and saw gold armbands.

"Be ready, Daniel."

Daniel took aim hitting two Gold cadets. The Gold team bombarded them with the light lasers, eliminating half the Red team. "Daniel," yelled Hal, "move up. They're targeting you. We need you to stay alive."

Daniel moved up closer to the flagman. They'd lost eight Red cadets to the Gold, but hadn't seen any of the Blue team.

Rick's men waited. The terrain provided minimal camouflage but there was some scrub brush, and a cave. He signaled a couple of guys to climb up into the paloverde trees.

The men were in place; now they would wait. It was a good time to be patient.

Gold's map intersected Red's for awhile. The Red team had taken a lot of casualties. Of the seventeen, Daniel, Hal, the flag bearer and five others were all that remained. Daniel was glad the map separated the two teams for a while. Maybe their smaller unit could make better progress.

Toby, the Gold captain, was satisfied that they'd wiped out nine Reds. "Good work, team. Let's get to that goal. Heads up."

Sitting in the arm of a paloverde tree, Rick heard the sound of troops moving. He waved at the soldier behind a nearby boulder who passed the signal.

The Gold scout rushed back, "Blue's flag is planted, Toby," he reported.

"Did you see any Blue soldiers?"

"No, no soldiers."

"Maybe they've started back. Let's steal their flag and plant ours. Send in a contingent. We'll cover them."

Rick waited until Gold approached the goal, then he whistled and lasers pelted the six-man Gold contingent. One of the lasers hit the flag bearer who dropped the Gold flag.

"We've got to get our flag," the Gold captain yelled.

"We can't, Toby. They'll pick us off, too. We better retreat and make a new plan. Leave a couple of guys to shoot anyone who goes for our flag (the Gold flag lay about ten yards from the goal). The remaining four Gold cadets retreated.

Toby didn't see the Red team or flag. Taking off his shoe, he removed a white sock and tied it to a mesquite branch which he handed to his scout. "Go for it, Mike," he said. "If you can get the Red team to join us, we might have a chance. The way I figure it, Red is down to about seven men. Rick's team outnumbers us two to one."

Daniel and Hal moved slowly, sure they would meet Blue or Gold any minute. Then Daniel saw a white flag. "Hal, you see what I see?"

"Yeah, what do you think?"

"It could be a trick, but that should mean they want to talk."

"Shall we risk one guy?"

"What have we got to lose. Send Nate. Okay, Nate?"

Nate agreed and took off one of his shoes tying his white sock to a branch. Ready, he made his way toward the Gold peace envoy.

"It's risky," Hal said.

"I know," Daniel answered.

No one shot Nate. When the two cadets met, the Gold team member told him about Blue's ambush. "I don't know how they got there so fast, but their flag was planted and they were in trees, behind rocks and shooting from the caves. We don't have enough men to take them on, but if we team up..."

Nate returned to his group and reported his findings and the startling information about the Blue ambush. Daniel listened as a plan formed in his mind. "Hal, I think if the Red team circles around behind them and the Gold team causes a diversion to draw them out, we might stand a chance. We've got two hours left and it'll take one to get back; the Blue team will have to move out."

The Gold team agreed to be the decoys and the plan went into action. Daniel and Hal and their small cohort hiked behind Blue until they were in position. At a prearranged time, Gold created a diversion to draw the Blue team out. As

Blue moved out of their hiding places, Hal and the Red team took aim and finished off the Blue team. Defeated, the Blue team made its way back to the Control Center.

Hal and Toby placed their flags side by side on the goal. Only two Red and two Gold survived.

The sergeant looked at his watch and counted the cadets before him: 16 Blue, 14 Red, 14 Gold, four cadets missing—two Red and two Gold.

Daniel and Hal, Toby and Mike emerged walking together, white flags waving. "What's going on?" the sergeant yelled.

"Teamwork, Sergeant, isn't that what this is all about?" said Toby.

The sergeant grinned. "You satisfied to share the glory with each other?"

"Yes, sir."

"All right, I declare a tie. The War Games are over. Report to the mess."

Laughing and patting each other on the back, the Red and Gold teams headed for the mess hall. Sullen, Rick, followed by the Blue team, joined them.

"It was a good plan, Rick, they just pulled one out of the hat."

Rick shrugged. *What had happened? It had been an unstoppable plan.*

After evening mess, the cadets returned to the assembly hall. Tension electrified the air. Tonight they would learn who their partner was. Daniel hoped he got someone like Hal. His partner would be with him day and night and they would be judged as a team.

The captain waited for the room to quiet. "I know this has been an exciting day and now an exciting night. Your officers chose your partner with care. Each of you will receive a card with a number. Your partner will receive the same number. Your job is to find the person who matches your number. Good luck."

Daniel held No. 8. Who was an 8? He watched a few of the guys discover each other. He saw a few, like himself, waiting to be approached. He didn't have to wait long.

"Well, cowboy, did I get so unlucky as to draw you?" Rick Hathaway held out his hand. In his palm rested the No. 8. Daniel felt like someone kicked him in the gut. He was disappointed. Grossly disappointed. How would he ever work with someone he didn't trust, much less respect. Rick was the one Guardian he'd never have picked for a partner. It must be some terrible mistake. Why would they pair him with Rick? Was it the AWOL thing? The fates had dealt him a low blow.

The captain's words rose above the clamor, "The next two weeks you and your partner will become a unit—one mind, one heart and one purpose. A real team."

A real team, Daniel thought. Daniel assessed Rick as a man who didn't play by the rules and who'd promote himself at anyone's expense. Perhaps, they hoped Rick's blatant unquestioning attitude would rub off on Daniel. *Over my dead body*, he thought. But to Rick he said, "Let's make it work."

The new partnership challenged Daniel. Rick was cold-hearted, efficient and obsessed with getting the job done. Perhaps that was good. Daniel held his own in the relationship for two important reasons: Rick respected his ability as a sharpshooter, and athletically, he surpassed Rick.

Daniel could be tough if he needed to be. But then that's exactly what the Guardian officers were trying to accomplish—a performance team, functional and balanced. Daniel had no illusions about Rick. If he showed any weakness,

Rick would take advantage of him. Daniel hoped they would not be put in circumstances where this would happen.

Although the last two weeks of training went better than Daniel expected, he struggled to prevent Rick from taking charge of their partnership—a subtle tug-of-war. Daniel hid behind a tough exterior. The real challenge was keeping Rick out of his head. Daniel didn't want to be a steppingstone to Rick's rise in the Guardians. Daniel had two strikes against him, a third would end his career in the Guardians. Rick might be his partner but he definitely was also his enemy.

Chapter Thirty-six

May 31, 2023

Disappointed, disillusioned and dejected, his future looking dismal with Rick as a partner, Daniel wondered what else could go wrong

"DJ, seen your assignment yet?"

Daniel looked up, "Not yet, Hal…afraid to look. All I need is for them to make us MPs."

Hal lowered his voice. "Hey, man, I'm sorry you got Rick…dumb luck."

"Dumb luck, all right. I just hope we can work together. Why do you think they did it?"

"Maybe they were hoping you'd rub off on him."

"Or the other way around."

"No, DJ, they're smart. They probably figured you'd be a good balance for him, keep him in line."

Daniel rolled his eyes. "You wanna be a trainer, right?"

"I'm hoping."

"You'd be good, Hal. That's where I'd like to serve. Gonna be okay with Craig?"

"I think so. He's pretty low-keyed, not an agitator like Rick."

"Picked up your uniform?"

"After I get my assignment. Want to walk over and get the news?"

As the two boys entered the building, they saw the electronic billboard surrounded by cadets searching the lists. Hal found his name on the Guardian trainers and a big smile broke out on his face. Daniel kept looking, finally discovering his name on the list of regular Guardian corps assigned to the Center for New Age Medicine. He was disappointed.

"A bummer, isn't it," said Rick behind him. "Now we get to be an escort service for all the losers."

Daniel ignored his comment, not wanting to start an adversary relationship. "Wanted MP duty, right?"

"Right. Somebody made a mistake."

Daniel and Hal headed to the health center, picked up their uniforms and made their way back to the barracks.

"See what you mean about Rick," said Hal.

"At least they have us scheduled to live in the Guardian dorm in Phoenix and I can go home on my time off. Glad you got the school, Hal. Remember how green we were?"

"YES, SIR!"

The shrill blast of the emergency siren screeched wave after wave of ear-splitting sound. The two dropped their uniforms on their racks and dashed to the auditorium.

"Wonder what's up?" asked Hal.

"Must be something important; they've never sounded it before."

The signal caught cadets in every location and state of dress. Everyone waited to hear the captain's news.

"Guardians, there's been a change in plans. You were scheduled to graduate this weekend and go home on a two-week leave but the vice president asks that you assist with a national emergency. This will be your first test as a Guardian." He signaled and a video appeared of six Guardians entering a church where they removed crosses and Bibles, depositing them on a huge bonfire in front of the church. Next, they boarded up the doors and windows of the church. The film clip stopped.

"You and your partner will be assigned to a six-man unit. You are now on duty for the president's newest initiative—Operation Clean Sweep. Each unit will be given a list of dissident churches. Your mission is threefold: remove all Bibles and crosses from each church, take down all church signs and board up all doorways and windows of the dissident churches.

"This new initiative is designed to support the recent creation of the One World Religion. Churches not cooperating with the government have been designated 'dissident churches' and you will aid in their closure. Is that understood?"

"Yes, Captain."

"Report here at 0700. Each six-man unit will be assigned a Guardian leader and a Hummer craft. This mission will continue until Phoenix is a model for the One World Religion. America will set the pace for the rest of the world. Do not let the media interview you. Resist confrontation with civilians. Complete your assignments.

"Unfortunately, graduation will be postponed until this operation is complete. Your families will be notified. Dismissed."

Daniel and Hal walked slowly to the barracks. Rick pushed past them. "Some real action for a change," he yelled. "Meet you at 0700."

The next day Daniel unpacked his uniform, putting on the net undershirt which connected him to the Guardian Command Center. He shot a look at Hal. Neither spoke.

Daniel finished dressing and as he put the silver helmet on, he immediately heard the voice from command center.

"Set your GPS by verbally stating your street location."

Daniel and Rick joined a four-man team and Hummer craft. The Guardian trainer studied the list of dissident churches, climbed into the Hummer craft, set the automatic pilot for the first address and motioned the team aboard.

Daniel wondered if any churches survived the list. Looking over the trainer's shoulder he noticed that a lot of the dissident churches had Baptist or Bible in their names. "Sir," he said to the trainer, "think the government will allow any churches to continue?"

"Sure, any that join the One World Religion."

"This is Channel 5 live in Scottsdale at the corner of Shea and Miller. We're at the site of the big Scottsdale Bible Church where silver-clad Guardians are closing down the church. In the center of the courtyard an enormous fire is burning." The camera moved in on Guardians taking down a big wooden cross, which they hefted onto the roaring fire. Other Guardians formed a line emptying a small on-campus bookstore. Last, the large "Scottsdale Bible Church" signs were thrust on the fire.

The reporter continued, "Looks like any church with Bible or a reference to Jesus Christ in its name will be closed." The reporter moved to an old man who watched quietly. "Sir, are you a member of this church?"

Startled the man stuttered, "Yes, over thirty-five years."

"And what are your thoughts today?"

"It's a very sad day for me and I think for America."

Noticing few Bibles on the bonfire, the young reporter turned again to the old man, "If this is a Bible church, why don't we see more Bibles?"

The old man smiled, "Each person brings his own. They won't find many here." Not waiting for any more questions, the old man walked away.

Daniel and Rick unloaded lumber and carried boards to the open doors. They blocked all entry and exits to the series of church buildings. Their team leader provided them with electronic hammers. He cautioned them, "Wait till the Bibles and crosses have been removed, then go door by door and seal the church up."

"Yes, sir."

Daniel's head was spinning. Relieved that the main church building was empty, he turned his head to see a small group of people standing in front of a building labeled Chapel. The people carried signs which read, "God is watching!" "Freedom to worship!" "One Way —Jesus Christ." He watched as the Guardian MPs took the signs and threw them on the burning pile, meanwhile shoving the protestors into a military police vehicle. *Nothing good will come of that,* Daniel thought.

Penny flipped on the T.V. Dad had told her to watch the weather at five p.m. and let him know what the weekly forecast was. She hesitated when she hit Channel 5. *Were those Guardians?* "Mom, Mom, come quick, I think Daniel's on TV."

Judith rushed out of her office.

"Look, Mom, the silver suits...it's the Guardians...do you see Danny?"

"No, honey, the camera moves around too fast but you're right, it is the Guardians."

"Well, folks, a lot of people will have no church to attend. The Scottsdale Bible Church had seventy-five hundred members. Let's go to Fountain Hills and our reporter there. Sue, what's happening in Fountain Hills?"

"Well, Andrew, we're at Christ's Church on East Bainbridge Street. There are three buildings here being boarded up. The Guardians have taken down the signs saying Christ's Church."

"Think any of the churches will reopen?"

"I'm told they can only reopen with an approved minister by the World Council of Churches and a change of name. This church will never be Christ's Church. Some of the neighborhood kids have decided to make a wiener roast out of the Bible bonfire. Guess the activity of this church will be limited to the skateboard park they built for kids. Back to you."

"All across Phoenix, it's the same story. Only churches willing to practice the new religion of love and peace will be allowed to meet. This is Andrew Hale signing off for Channel 5."

Penny looked at her mother. "Those books they were burning...were they like Grandpa's?"

Her mother nodded. "Yes, I think the World Council of Churches finally realized the secret to peace is in mutual respect and equality. The new religion makes everyone equal whether they are in Africa, India, Iraq or here in the U.S."

"Would Grandpa be happy?" asked Penny.

"No, your grandparents were too old to change. They'd have been unhappy. We'll have to watch again at ten p.m. and see if we can see Daniel. Aren't you proud of him, Pen?"

Penny nodded.

Bone tired, Daniel hit the showers as soon as they returned. His muscles ached from nine hours of lifting boards and sealing up doorways. Still, he was glad he wasn't assigned to collect and burn the crosses and Bibles, something that would have hurt Grandpa if he were still alive.

He lay on his rack thinking about his grandparents. He remembered Grandpa's words, "There will be very difficult times coming." On the campout, Daniel had read only a little of the old Bible but enough to make him wonder why a holy man who did only good things healing the sick, the deaf and the blind, and dying two thousand years ago could cause so much furor that the president would actually try to erase Him and His influence.

Daniel thought about the lawless man who the Bible said would change times and laws. The United States—and yes, the world—had undergone a lot of changes in the past year or two. Were the changes good or bad? Daniel hadn't decided. While the new religion sounded good, he felt bad boarding up the churches—like he was taking away a lot of people's rights.

Perhaps the Guardian theology was right, thinking was deadly. Thinking confused and upset him. As a Guardian, Daniel worked for the president. His job was to carry out the initiatives, not question the president or his council. Daniel blocked his questions, rolled over and tried to go to sleep. Tomorrow would be more of the same.

Dr. Hart's nurse took advantage of a lull in the appointment schedule to check the news. She watched the military surround the church on Shea and tear down the cross atop its roof. "Doc, got a minute?"

Dr. Hart left the surgical area and stood watching the screen. "Taking apart a church, are they?"

"Looks like it."

"What will happen to your church, Nan?"

Nan hesitated. Should she be open with the doctor? She'd known him for a lot of years. "Nothing, Doc. Our board fired our minister and applied for an approved one. They changed our name from the Church of the Good Shepherd to the Church of Joy."

The doctor frowned. "I guess they were smart."

"Yeah, I guess...but...I won't be going anymore."

"No?"

"No, promise you'll keep this to yourself, Doc, but we're going to start meeting in homes, those of us who don't want to be part of the One World Church."

Dr. Hart knew Nan was a devout Christian. He honored that. "I'll keep your secret, Nan. Going underground, are they?"

"Well, if not underground, other ground." She paused. "Doc, there's something I've been wanting to tell you."

"Go ahead."

"I think you are at risk helping the old people. Don't you think the other doctors in the Center will get suspicious when they see you doing so much surgery?"

"It's a risk." Dr. Hart sat down. "Is it that obvious?"

"I'm afraid so. You need a safer place to work if you're going to try to help these young girls and old people."

"I know. I bought a ranch a few hours from Phoenix before the number thing came up."

"That's what our underground church is finding out about...safe ranches where people who can't live with the system can go...where is this ranch?"

"It's about three hours south of Phoenix near the New Mexico border. It's run now by a Mexican family. They call it Rancho Christo."

"Doc, have you taken the number?"

"No, something inside me just won't let me. Thank goodness I don't have to use a number to order provisions. I've been shifting some supplies to Rancho Christo. I may want to use it to send some people. It would be dangerous but..."

"... You just can't go along with these initiatives."

A tired smile crossed the doctor's face. "I'm a doctor, Nan. My oath is to do no harm. If I help them, will you still be my nurse?"

Nan put her arm around the doctor's shoulders. "I'm with you, Doc, for better or for worse."

"Hey, that wasn't a marriage proposal."

The two laughed. It felt good.

Chapter Thirty-seven

Graduation...the Big Day! The barracks echoed with excitement and good-natured joking.

"Hey, Arizona, you got vacation plans?"

Daniel turned toward the voice. "Going home...gotta help my dad."

Hal fastened the silver suit. "My dad and I are gonna do a little fly fishing in the Gallatin River up by Bozeman, Montana, and Big Sky...a little white water rafting... some fine hiking. Wish you could go along."

"Thanks, Hal, but Dad needs my help—the flood. So much damage. They barely had a season. I don't know what Dad's working on but I know he needs me. It sounds great though, thanks for asking."

Daniel added the silver helmet and spoke to the Control Center. "Set it at 80 degrees." He looked at Hal. "Well at least when my little sister tells me how cool I look, I'll actually be cool."

All networks were televising the Guardian graduation. Vice President Prophet had flown in to present the cadets for commissioning. Calm, Daniel lined up alphabetically by states meanwhile searching the audience for his family. *It would be good to be home for a couple of weeks*, he thought.

"There's Daniel," Penny yelled. "He looks so handsome, doesn't he, Mom?"

Judith beamed as she watched her tall blond son in the silver uniform await his commission. She had pushed Daniel in his decision to leave a sport's career behind but it was worth it. Now he might really be able to do something important…something for the president and the country. She was very proud of Daniel.

Harry was proud, too, only worried. What effect did the court-martial and boarding up the churches have on his son? Although Judith was impressed with the Guardian's assignment to close down the churches, Harry knew this would not have been easy for Daniel, having spent so much time with Grandpa before the Ascension. And what in the world would Daniel do if they assigned him to the next Ascension?

Harry was tired. Putting the ranch back together after the dam broke left him exhausted. He'd pushed himself and the hands to the breaking point. Judith sold the Michigan cottage when the insurance informed them they had no flood coverage which made him feel like he'd failed his parents and lost his youth. He needed a rest. Maybe he'd take some time while Daniel was home, go fishing, just the two of them. He envied his dad and Daniel's camping trips. His thoughts were interrupted by the vice president.

"Good evening America, Guardians, families and friends. Tonight a fine class of Guardians graduates and will be commissioned." He turned to address the Guardians. "Today, you earn the title of Guardian. You are trained for national emergencies, terrorist attacks and natural disasters. Each of you has received your duty assignment. The nation is proud of you.

"When I call your name, you will come forward and receive the Guardian Command watch. Your name has been engraved on it and it bears the seal of the president. I extend congratulations from President Blackstone, the Council and the Board of Governors.

"Alabama...Alaska... Arizona..."

After the commissioning service, Daniel joined his family who would never know what he'd been through to get this far.

"Oh, Danny, you are the coolest of the cool, isn't he?" Penny grabbed him. "I wish my friends could see you in uniform."

Daniel hugged her then saluted his mother and father. His dad shook his hands and patted him on the back, his love and pride visible, his mom shooting a video with her smartphone.

"For posterity, Daniel," she said.

"We should do something special to celebrate," added Penny.

"It's special just going home, Pen. You guys walk around, I'll change into some shorts and join you in a minute. Have a great vacation, Hal," Daniel yelled. "See you some weekend."

Chapter Thirty-eight

The dam breaking wiped out the 2023 tourist season at the ranch. Daniel's mother was already starting on next year's agenda. The ranch furniture had been replaced with new leather furniture but, except for a dank odor that lingered in every room, the ranch itself had been salvaged. How did they get it back to normal so fast? Filled with questions, Daniel strolled out to the work shop in search of Dad. "Dad, you in there?"

"Come in, Danny."

"What are you up to?"

Harry looked up. "Would you like to go up to the caves… just you and me?" Harry waited for his reply. "Just a few days, I know you want to spend time with your mom and Penny."

Daniel couldn't remember the last time he and Dad had gone fishing. "You mean where Grandpa and I camped?"

"Yes, I think your grandfather rode up there the morning …the morning of the Ascension."

"He did, Dad, he left me something."

"His Bible?"

"Yeah, his Bible. But he had it marked with strips of paper with numbers. I haven't had time to read all of them."

"Do you think he was trying to tell you something?"

"I'm sure of it, but I haven't figured it out yet. I didn't have time to go through all the slips. I'd love to go fishing. It's been a hard year; it would be good to unwind. What about Mom?"

"She'll be okay. She knows I need a break. She hates camping—sleeping in bedrolls has no appeal."

"And Pen?"

"Pen can't go; she's playing spring soccer. Tomorrow evening? That'll give us time to pack up. We'll ask Mom to get us some supplies."

"Didn't you get the number yet, Dad?"

"I'm not getting the number, Daniel." Harry looked him in the eyes. "It's my way of honoring your grandpa. Mom's our shopper. She's part of the new regime."

"But Dad, won't you have to get it sometime or…" Daniel didn't say anymore. His dad could be stubborn, too, and he could tell by the look on his face this was a non-negotiable decision. Good for Dad. Daniel just hoped he wouldn't end up in trouble. What did the government plan to do with the people who refused the number? Daniel had one more year and he'd be forced to make the same decision. Saying "No" would bounce him right out of the Guardians and probably into one of the prisons for dissidents. He wasn't sure he had that much courage.

The weather was perfect for May—80s to low 100s. Bees buzzed the white flowers atop the saguaros. A few low clouds reflected the colors of the sunset. When they arrived, Daniel put their supplies in the cave while his dad built a fire for the cookout. He watched his dad place the kindling then lay old saguaro wood on top, finishing with some mesquite to give the steaks flavor. Dad was a simple, solid man—a person you could always count on.

Daniel didn't think Dad felt appreciated but as far as Daniel was concerned, he was the rock the family was built on. The pungent odor of the steaks reminded him how hungry he was. "Dad, where did you learn to cook like that?"

"I used to work at a camp, remember? That's actually where I met your mom."

"What was Mom's job?"

"She helped in the office, solved problems with the kids, handled the parents…that sort of thing."

The stars lit up the desert and for the first time since he left home, Daniel relaxed. He closed his eyes enjoying the gentle wind blowing across the camp and let the tension drain out of his body. "It was hard going back after the dam broke."

"I knew it would be. Want to talk about it?"

"Not really. Water over the dam." He grinned.

"Things got back to normal."

"No, not till after the War Games. I wasn't the guy to hang with if you get the picture."

So Daniel was ostracized.

"I was disappointed to end up with Rick Hathaway for a partner. He's the biggest jerk in the group. And I'd like to have been a Guardian trainer, but I got assigned to the doctor at the Center for New Age Medicine."

Harry looked thoughtful, "Does that mean you'll have to assist at the next Ascension?"

Daniel was quiet. "Yeah, that's what it means."

"How do you feel about that, son?"

"It makes me think about the Grands. It's like living it all over. Even closing down those churches reminded me of Grandpa."

"The Bibles are forbidden now, you know. But your grandparents lived their life according to it. Grandpa said the Bible contained 'words of life'."

"Have you read it, Dad?"

"No, I guess mostly I just remember stories from my Sunday school class. The New Testament describes the life of Jesus."

"I read a little about Him."

Harry thought back through the years. "I remember we used to celebrate His birth at Christmas."

"Winter break?"

"It wasn't Winter break then. It was Christmas. We always had a tree, lights, special food. My Sunday school teacher said Jesus was God's only Son. He was born to a poor carpenter's family. His mother was only fourteen or fifteen years old. Pretty young to have a baby, but those were ancient times, the girls married young and people didn't live as long."

"They killed Him."

"Yes, the Romans hung Him on a cross but that was God's plan to save mankind—Jesus paid the price for sin. It's complicated." Harry shook out his bedroll. "Time for a little shut-eye."

Daniel was too keyed up to sleep. He dug up the wooden box and took out the Bible opening it to the next marker and, amazingly, it was the story of the birth of Jesus. What stood out to his mind was that the mother of Jesus was only fifteen and that somehow the girl became pregnant before she was married. He put the book away and dozed off listening to an owl hooting softly. He awoke to the scent of coffee and bacon.

"Dad, you're killing me!"

Harry smiled. "Are you up for fishing or would you rather take a ride?"

"Let's ride." They put out their campfire and rolled up their bedrolls. "I'd like to see those petroglyphs again.".

"The Indian ruins? Good idea. I'll throw some tins in my saddlebags. We'll have lunch up there."

Riding through the familiar high desert with its cholla, saguaros and ocotillo cactus, Daniel knew he was truly home. As he rode, the loneliness he'd experienced the last few months melted away.

The next morning he reburied the old Bible under the tree in its box. Only Dad would know it was there. He and Dad caught catfish, took some hikes and rode the horses. Finally, they headed back to the ranch.

Daniel spent the rest of his time attending Penny's games and enjoying his family. On his last morning, he dragged himself out of bed, amazed that everyone was up for his last breakfast.

"We have a surprise for you, Daniel. Come outside," said his mother.

Daniel walked outside not knowing what to expect. He couldn't believe his eyes. Parked in the road was the hottest black Honda motorcycle—a real dream machine. A matching helmet hung from the handlebars. Daniel's eyes smarted. "How did you know...it's perfect...just what I need...now I can come home on weekends."

"You deserve it, son. Maybe you'll find it useful."

Daniel thought that must be the understatement of the decade. The motorcycle would give him a break from Rick.

Dr. Hart looked at his appointment book for the following weeks. "Nan, schedule some time to orient the new Guardians next week."

"It looks like we were assigned about one-third of the cadets this year."

"Yes, we were. Actually, I asked for our Arizona cadet to be assigned here."

Nan was surprised. "You mean the young man whose grandparents were in the first Ascension?"

"Yes, Daniel Jordan...something different about him. I'm hoping he'll be more considerate with the Ascension candidates, having experienced his grandparents in the Ascension."

"Might be a little hard on him, Doc."

Dr. Hart pretended not to hear the last remark. It would probably be very hard for Daniel but it was part of the doctor's plan to run a center that cared about people, even if it was only able to handle them more gently.

Chapter Thirty-nine

"**D**ad, can you help me move my stuff to the Guardian quarters?"

"Your motorcycle won't hold that much?" his dad joked. "When do you want to move in?"

"I think, Sunday night...and Dad...just *you* this time, okay?" Daniel didn't want Penny and his mother running around taking videos and saying how "cool" everything was. He was, after all, in the military.

"Do all the Guardians live downtown?" Harry asked.

"No, just the ones assigned to the Center for New Age Medicine. The trainers live at the school and the MPs have their own housing at Luke."

Daniel and Harry searched for the address, 109 W. Courtland Street.

"These one-way streets are a maze," said Harry as they back-tracked the Roosevelt area.

"The GPS shows a sharp turn and then Courtland. Yes, here we are."

A series of three-story buildings surrounding a grassy court fit the address. Each building had its own underground parking. Daniel and Harry parked in the lot for Building 3, unloading Daniel's personal luggage and rolling the motorcycle down a ramp off the truck.

"Well, you're right downtown in the new reclaimed district."

"Yeah, let's explore, Dad, but first let's find Suite 219A." They rode the elevator with Daniel's luggage to the second floor where they discovered his two-bedroom apartment equipped with a kitchen butler and media center. The great room looked east over the city. Tall palm trees surrounded the wall-to-floor windows walking out to a covered balcony.

"Very cool," Daniel said.

"They take care of you, don't they?"

"All the good stuff is on the third floor level."

"All the good stuff?"

"You'll see, Dad. C'mon. I'll show you."

They climbed the stairs to the third floor. Palm plants and tropical flowers formed an indoor atrium with a rock water-fall. Behind the atrium, cadets and their families sipped cool drinks under a vine-covered deck surrounding an Olympic-sized pool. "Let me treat you, Dad." The two sat down at a table. The city stretched out before them. They were comfortable with the silence.

"Will you be coming home on weekends?"

Daniel grinned. "The Black Mustang and I will definitely be coming home. You just don't know the freedom that motorcycle gives me. Thanks, Dad."

Harry surmised as much and had no trouble getting Judith on board for the gift. She wanted Daniel to come home as often as he could.

They finished their drinks and continued their tour. To the west of the swimming pool they could see a gym equipped with a massage and stress center; to the east of the pool—a private restaurant available for Guardian meals.

Daniel worked off stress swimming laps but having a masseuse was over the top. Things weren't all bad.

After his dad left, Daniel unpacked his gear and plugged in his communicator. The Command posted assignments on the Guardian channel. Daniel entered his password and found instructions for the next day.

0815—Meeting with Dr. Hart @ the Center for New Age Medicine.

Rick barged into the apartment. "Checking your assignment? My appointment is 0800."

That was odd, Daniel thought, *why weren't they being interviewed together if they were a team?*

"When's yours?"

"0815...fifteen minutes after yours."

"Wonder what Dr. Quackeroo has for us to do?" Rick quipped.

"We'll know tomorrow, I guess." Daniel said. He wished Rick wouldn't make those kind of statements. Daniel had a feeling these rooms might be bugged or at least connected to the all-seeing Command Center. He reminded himself to say something to Rick when they were alone. He watched Rick unpack a cooler of beers.

"You got a false ID, Rick?"

"Yeah, friend from New Jersey makes them. Comes in handy. Want one?"

Daniel shook his head "no" but accepted the beer not wanting to alienate Rick. After about three beers, Rick picked up the keys to the Jeep they'd been assigned. "Want to come along?"

"Not tonight, gonna go up and work out, hit the rack early." Daniel hoped Rick didn't have a drinking problem. With his tongue and attitude he could get in a whole lot of trouble. "You good to drive?"

Rick shrugged his shoulders. "You're my partner not my keeper."

Daniel knew he was right. He wasn't Rick's keeper or his conscience but if he got in trouble, it might pull Daniel in whether he wanted it or not.

Daniel and Rick showered, put on their utilities, jumped in the Jeep and headed for the Center for New Age Medicine, a few blocks away. Daniel would be careful in his interview. He knew what the doctor wanted to hear—what they all wanted to hear—no questions, quick response to carry out orders, loyalty to the government.

Rick had his interview and came out loaded with paperwork. He signaled Daniel to go in.

Dr. Hart greeted him but appeared on edge. Daniel guessed Rick had that effect on a lot of people.

"Daniel?"

"Doctor."

"Sit down and let's talk about your work. I have a few questions for you. I may have some assignments for you that I won't need Rick for. Will that be all right with you?"

Daniel assured the doctor it would.

"These assignments could be at night, after hours or on the weekend. Would that be a problem?"

"No, sir. I'm at your disposal. I do go home on weekends so I'd have to know ahead of time."

"I'm sure that could be arranged."

"I don't know how Rick will feel about this."

"I'll take care of Rick, Daniel. I have some special assignments for him, too. I want to see how you work together and apart so I can utilize you for the greatest benefit. Your first assignment will be together. We're getting ready for the next Ascension and you'll be bringing in some of the candidates. Not all of them will be chosen." The doctor watched Daniel's face. He saw his hands tremble. He was counting on Daniel to be that special person he needed. Was he wrong? And then he realized it was the handshake at the end of his

Guardian interview that made him think Daniel was special. A handshake.

The next day when the fifteen cadets reported to the Center, Dr. Hart handed them an address. "I've assigned each team to a candidate for the Ascension," he explained. "You will drive to their home, and courteously escort them back here to the Center. Is that understood?"

Familiar words those last. "Yes, sir," the cadets replied.

The doctor handed each team keys to a van located in the underground parking garage. For each trip they were to record the time of departure, the time of return and the mileage. Rick reached for the keys. "I'll drive, okay with you, Daniel? You navigate since you're the one who knows Phoenix."

Daniel nodded, aware that Rick was again trying to take control of their partnership but feeling he could do a better job navigating the city. "Our first pick up is in Sun City on the west side of Phoenix," Daniel instructed. "We'll take Grand Avenue." Daniel switched on the GPS which showed them where they were and how to get to Grand Avenue."

Rick started the motor. "Roger that."

Daniel dreaded confronting the old people. He knew from his grandparents that they must have a health problem or be over eighty. Rick rang the bell.

Sadie and John sat staring at one another. "I'll go," said Sadie, hesitantly.

"No, Sadie, let me get it," returned John. He crossed the tile foyer and looked straight into the Guardians' eyes. "What do you want?"

"We're here to escort you to the health center," replied Rick.

"We've decided not to go," shot back John.

"Sir, you have no choice. Now get your things together."

John walked back into the cozy kitchen where Sadie sat warming her hands on a cup of tea. "I told them we aren't leaving," said John.

"Now, John, we've been through this before. We've been told to see Dr. Hart today at two p.m."

John stared straight ahead.

Daniel watched while Rick moved through the open door. His face was grim. Rick didn't like resistance. The old couple had lit his short wick—he was ready to explode. He wouldn't let two old people keep him from accomplishing his first assignment. Daniel sensed the problem. Something was wrong with one of the two. They were afraid and becoming stubborn. If they didn't leave their safe little bungalow, nothing bad would happen. If they did, life as they knew and loved it would be over.

Daniel thought of his own grandparents, he noticed Rick reaching for the handcuffs which were hidden under his jacket. Daniel interceded before Rick could force them to comply. "Good afternoon, folks. My name is Daniel Jordan. My partner and I are here to escort you to your doctor's appointment. Don't want to be late. You'll like Dr. Hart. He's a real nice doctor. Here Sadie, take my arm."

Sadie smiled trustingly. She got up and took Daniel's arm. "Come along, John," Sadie called, "we'll be late."

John rose slowly when he saw Sadie take Daniel's arm. Hope drained from his face. The battle was over and he'd lost.

Rick's face was flushed. He would have handled these old people differently. Who did they think they were? Rick knew. They were old, unproductive people who had lived too long draining society. He had no use for them. He knew what lay ahead for them. *Good riddance*, he thought. He had to hand it to Daniel; he had manipulated the old people into doing exactly what the Guardians wanted. He stared at

Daniel's back. Was Daniel a genius or had Rick just witnessed Daniel's weakness? Did Daniel actually care about these people?

Daniel also knew what lay ahead for Sadie and John. From the looks of it, they had worked hard and retired in Sun City hoping to live out their years. Daniel winced. He'd betrayed them. He refocused his mind. Only the weak allowed such thoughts. He shouldn't get involved with the people assigned. His only job was to escort Sadie and John to the Center for New Age Medicine. What happened next wasn't in the parameter of his job. He was gentle and kind. He'd kept Rick from using force on the old couple.

Chapter Forty

The following week, the boys were assigned to bring in a fifteen-year-old girl for the Lamb's Project. When they arrived, Daniel was surprised to find the pickup was Katy Brown, the girl he'd rescued from the ski accident at Lake Pleasant. *She was scheduled for the Lamb's Project?*

"Hi, Danny, I heard you were a Guardian."

Daniel smiled. "Hi, Katy, this is my partner Rick Hathaway. Ready to go?"

"It's a thrill to be picked up by two handsome Guardians," she flirted.

Daniel watched Rick's eyes light up as he grabbed her arm and opened the door to the van. "You're our first pickup today. Guess we got lucky." Rick winked.

The waiting room at CNAM was filled with fifteen-year-old girls. Dr. Hart's nurse passed out a questionnaire. Then the room darkened and a video began to play. Similar to their training videos, it explained procreation, the wonder of perfect genetics and the news that if the girls were chosen they would become the mothers of a new generation of children. The announcer assured them to be chosen for the Lamb's Project was the greatest honor any young woman could receive.

A shiver ran down Daniel's spine. Were they saying that the president was making his sperm available to create children for the world? Daniel knew from studying World War II that Hitler tried to create a race of blond-haired, blue-eyed children. This president was going for genetic purity and he apparently was the control factor. *Unbelievable.*

Following the genetic explanation, a flashy promo showed young women at a special resort—Club Stork, a health resort converted for the government's private use: luxury suites, gourmet food, swimming pools, walking trails, libraries, table tennis, even computers. The voice on the video crooned, "It will be the best year of your life."

Right, thought Daniel, *all you have to do is get pregnant and have a child.*

When the girl and her parents signed the contract, they were promised a four-year scholarship to the Arizona university of their choice. Daniel was worried—Penny was thirteen.

"C'mon, Katy, let's get you home."

The boys loaded her into the van. "So what'd you think, Katy?" Rick asked.

"It looked like a Caribbean resort…so beautiful…and a four-year scholarship!"

Daniel swallowed his thoughts. *Why was it every assignment appalled him. What was the matter with him?* They pulled up at Katy's house and before Daniel could get out to open the door, Rick bounded from the driver's seat.

"Hey, sweetie, what are you doing this weekend?"

"Nothing, Rick, what did you have in mind?"

Daniel listened. He could see there was some magnetism between the two. He waited while Rick made a date to pick her up Saturday night. When Rick got back in the van, Daniel let him have it.

"Are you crazy? This girl may be selected to have a kid for the president. It's not worth it, Rick, she's only fifteen."

"Yeah, fifteen. Did you see those legs? She's gonna be dynamite. And I've always liked them young. That way, you can teach them what you want them to know."

"Knock it off. It's not worth risking your career."

Rick sobered up for a second but Daniel could see that he was pulling the same mentality he'd had in training—he wouldn't get caught and nothing bad would happen.

"Don't worry, I just wanna have a little fun with her."

"I thought you had a girl in New Jersey. Why don't you leave Katy alone."

"Wait… she knows you. You got some history with this chick?"

"You could say that but not what you think. She's just a nice kid. You need to leave her alone."

"Maybe she has a friend," Rick said. "You don't have to go home every weekend."

Daniel shook his head, "You just don't get it, do you, Rick? She's not worth the risk."

Rick was unconvinced. "She's cute; she's here."

"Where do you plan to take her?" Daniel asked.

"Mario's…a little dancing…a little wine…a little…"

Daniel gave up. He wasn't going to convince Rick, but he knew Rick was ambitious. He hoped that would be enough to deter him. His real worry was Rick's drinking. If that got out of control …

Saturday night Daniel watched Rick get ready for his date with Katy. They hadn't talked anymore about it. Rick left and Daniel struggled with himself. Should he intervene? Was this why they'd put Rick and Daniel together? How many beers had Rick drunk before he left?

Daniel revved his motor, put on his helmet and headed for Mario's. Rick was his partner. He parked the cycle and made his way into the dimly lit dance club. He didn't see

Katy, but finally located Rick playing cards at a table in the back. Rick looked annoyed when he saw Daniel.

"Where is she and how did you get her in here?"

"In the ladies' room. I knew you'd show up." He flashed an ID that showed Katy looking eighteen. "Want to sit in?"

"We'll see." Just then Katy came back. Her dark hair was piled on top of her head and she wore a strapless tube top with a sheer, long-sleeved blouse and a miniskirt. She didn't look fifteen.

"Hey, Daniel."

"Katy." Daniel watched as Rick left the poker table to dance with her. He pulled her close, running his hand across her miniskirt. When they returned, Rick ordered two more beers and offered to buy Daniel one. Rick was getting smashed.

Daniel decided on a course of action. He'd act interested in Katy and sucker Rick into a poker game.

"What shall we play for?" Rick challenged.

"Let's play for Katy."

That surprised Rick, but he couldn't back down. He didn't know what kind of poker player Daniel was, but Rick was good. He'd spent a lot of time in pool halls and bars in New Jersey. He smiled. "Fine, you don't mind us playing for your company, do you, Katy?"

Katy looked flattered. Two handsome Guardians fighting over her. She shook her head.

Rick dealt five card draw. "One hand, winner takes all. Cut for deal."

Daniel drew a 10—Rick a King.

Rick dealt the cards slowly, picked up his hand and grinned.

So he got a good hand. Daniel looked at his cards... Jack of clubs, Jack of diamonds, and two eights. "One card," Daniel said. Rick frowned. Daniel held the card while Rick took two cards. Daniel turned over, a third eight—a full house.

Rick played his cards—three Kings.

Daniel quietly laid down his full house—two Jacks, three eights.

Rick looked disappointed but saluted and left for the bar.

"C'mon, Katy, we're getting out of here." Daniel led the girl out of the bar and asked her if she minded riding on his motorcycle. He handed her his helmet hoping it would fit and they left Mario's. When they arrived at Katy's house, Daniel took her hand. "Don't go out with him anymore, Katy. He's trouble. And going out with you will get him in trouble, too. Do you understand?"

Katy shook her head. "Thanks, Daniel, I guess you're my guardian angel." She turned and walked into the house.

You don't know what a close call you had, Katy girl!

Chapter Forty-one

"She's screaming, Doctor. Out of control. I can't get the baby away from her. Can you fly down here right away?"

"Calm down, Rose. I want you to give her a sedative."

"I've tried that, Doctor. She bites me if I come near her. She's out of her mind. Please, hurry." And with that the connection broke—a young girl screaming in the background.

Dr. Hart put the communicator down checking the time—three a.m. It was dark, but if he hurried he could make the resort near Tucson before dawn. Maria Sanchez, the teen in question, had seemed gentle and reserved. What in the world caused her to lose control?

He threw on some shorts and a golf shirt, rubbed his overnight chin growth deciding not to shave, grabbed his medical bag and ran to the heliport on top his building. If he flew low enough, he wouldn't need a flight plan. Thrusting the key in the engine, he revved the motor. The wings unfolded from the sides of the car and began to rotate. As the aero-car lifted, Dr. Hart flew in the direction of the Tucson mountains.

The sun was pushing the purple night clouds away as he landed. He strode toward the birthing hospital. Rose, the nurse who'd called, intercepted him. "Doctor, I locked her in her room. She was so violent."

"No drugs?"

"No, sir. She says she'll only talk to you."

Dr. Hart unbolted the door, warning the nurse to stay back, and closing it behind him.

"Fine," Rose huffed. "She's all yours. Just get her out of here before she upsets the other girls."

"Maria, are you all right?" he asked softly.

"Yes, Doctor, but they tried to take my baby. They said he was below standard and they would dispose of him." Tears ran down her face. "He's a person, a real living person. They can't just treat him like he's garbage."

Dr. Hart stroked her hair, a plan forming in his mind. "He has Down syndrome. Down babies are automatically listed for the Ascension."

"But he's a baby, Doctor, just a sweet little baby." She held the baby tightly.

"Do you want to keep him and take care of him, Maria?" he asked.

Maria nodded, trying to stop the choking sobs that continued to spill out.

"What about your parents?"

"I don't know. They teach me all babies are a gift from God, even sick ones."

The nurse had vanished for report so Dr. Hart wasted no time. He gathered Maria and the baby helping them into his aero-car. "Wait here. I'll inform the nurse." He walked purposefully into the nurses' meeting. "I'll remove Maria from the resort. It's better that way. I don't want her hysteria infecting the other girls. Do we have any deliveries due today?"

"No, sir. And the other newborns are normal and being nursed by their mothers."

"Fine. Thank you for calling me."

Climbing into the plane, he smiled at Maria. "It's going to be okay, Maria. I'll take you to your parents' house and we'll make a plan. Have you named the baby yet?"

"His name is Carlos, after my daddy."

"Carlos, you're quite a little man."

Dr. Hart had a soft spot in his heart for Down children. They were usually loving and trainable. He had a full surgery schedule but perhaps he'd send Daniel Jordan to take Maria and the baby to Rancho Christo providing her parents were willing. Elena would be delighted.

The girl's genetics puzzled him. The tests showed no link to Down or she'd never been chosen...unless...the president.

After discussing the situation with Maria's parents, Dr. Hart arranged for her to move to his ranch in New Mexico where she could nurse the baby and help with his care. Later, she could see if she wanted to return to high school. He doubted the offer for free college was still valid.

Daniel showered, then turned on his laptop to read his assignment for the day. A note instructed him to report to Dr. Hart for a special assignment. He looked over at Rick who was pouring a cup of coffee.

"You on special assignment?" Rick asked.

"Yeah, I guess."

"Well, at least we're spared a day corralling old people."

Daniel ignored him, dressed quickly and headed for the Center. Nurse Nan looked up when he came in. "Feel like a drive, Daniel? We'd like you to pick up someone and take her to Rancho Christo."

"Thanks, Nan, I need a day off." Daniel took the card with the girl's address and went to the garage to sign out the van. He'd taken supplies to Rancho Christo a half-dozen times but never a person. Elena, the Mexican lady who ran it, spoiled him with her Mexican burritos and chicken enchiladas. He signed for the van, listed its mileage and told the GPS Maria's address—45 University, Chandler.

Maria's address was in an area of Phoenix where the Mexican population was predominant. He knocked on the door and a pretty dark-haired girl carrying a baby answered.

"Hi, I'm Daniel Jordan. I'm here to take you to Rancho Christo. Are you ready?"

"Uno momento, Daniel. Mama, Papa, the Guardian is here. I'm leaving now." She kissed them good-bye. Daniel reached over and picked up her duffel bag. He glanced at the baby tucked in her arms and he knew...a Down syndrome baby. He touched the menu selection and pushed "baby car seat." Immediately a baby seat unfolded from the floor. Maria placed the baby gently into the seat and climbed in next to him, clasping the baby's tiny hand in hers.

They drove awhile in silence, Daniel watching the girl in his rearview mirror. "Are you from the Lamb's Project?" he asked.

Immediately fear flashed in her eyes. "Si."

Daniel saw that he'd upset her. He touched the communication panel and soft rock filled the van. "Is this music all right?" he asked.

The girl looked up. "It's fine, senor. I think I'd just like to sleep. I was up all night."

That was fine with Daniel. He drove until they reached the ranch. Elena saw them coming and flew out of the house. "My children, come, come. Give the precious one to Elena. You look so tired and hungry. I have nice food for you— Daniel's favorite."

Daniel blushed but he and Maria followed Elena back to the house listening to her coo and sing to the baby. Daniel turned to Maria. "You don't have to be afraid, Maria. Elena will take good care of you. Let's see what she's cooked up for us."

After dinner, he said good-bye, filled his gas tank at Elena's pump and climbed into the van. If he drove eighty, he'd be back in Phoenix by midnight. Why had the doctor sent Maria to the ranch? Then Daniel remembered the Down children in the Ascension and suddenly he understood. They'd probably tried to take her baby and she was afraid something bad would happen to it. What was Rancho Christo?

Sleep eluded Daniel. Something was needling him like a burr caught in his sandal. Restless, he got up put on his swim trunks, grabbed a towel and headed for the pool. Maybe if he swam some laps this irritant would go away.

Daniel pounded the water...forty laps and still...then in an instant he knew. Fifteen. The girls were fifteen. Maria was fifteen. The Bible girl who gave birth to Jesus was fifteen. That was it, but...Daniel continued to swim...there was something more. He tried to remember. The girl in the Bible was unmarried, a virgin. Jesus' father was the Spirit of God. Was Daniel adding two and two and getting four? Was it possible this president who was having Bibles destroyed and churches shut down knew the Bible well? Was he mimicking the virgin birth with his Lamb's Project using fifteen-year-old virgins and playing God by fathering the babies?

Daniel swam faster, trying to outdistance his thoughts. Did the president think he could control both life and death? Dripping and exhausted, Daniel lifted himself out of the pool, panic pumping through his veins.

He wrapped his towel around him and dragged himself to bed. Tomorrow was Saturday. He'd drive home for the weekend, maybe talk to his dad, tell him his suspicions.

Chapter Forty-two

Daniel and his dad retreated into the den and closed the door. Harry sensed Daniel was upset and wanted to talk. "Something bothering you, son?"

"The Ascension's Sunday...I don't know if I can get through it."

Harry lit his pipe. He wasn't surprised that his son was having difficulty. Unlike Judith who thought the Ascension was a beautiful historic event, both he and Daniel had been traumatized by the death of Harry's parents.

"Go on."

"And Rick bothers me. He's a company man. He thinks everything the government comes up with is great. Drinks a lot...has a big mouth...he's trouble, Dad. He's always playing the game, putting both of us in danger and then retreating in the nick of time. I wish I'd gotten Hal for a partner, someone I could trust."

"They probably put Rick with you so you could keep an eye on him. Not to change the subject, Daniel, but how did you feel about boarding up the churches?"

"I kept thinking about Grandma and Grandpa. What would Gramps have said, especially when they burned the Bibles? I felt sad. At least we didn't hurt anyone."

"What are you working on now?"

"The Lamb's Project, the president's new initiative. Daniel explained the program, watching his dad's face as he digested this new initiative. Harry's usually kind face turned to granite as he tried to digest the news and Daniel saw deep anger flicker in his eyes.

"Why haven't we heard about this on the news? Who approved this project?"

"I don't know, Dad. They're treating it as a private contract between the girl, her parents and the administration. The girls seem to think it's a good deal. But...it just doesn't seem right. They're trying to do a genetic project that will create special kids—the President's Kids. But these kids will have no mothers or fathers just caretakers."

Harry was outraged. *Who did Omega I think he was? God?*

Daniel interrupted his thoughts. "Dad, if anything bad happens to me, you'll understand?"

Harry nodded. He understood more than Daniel guessed.

September 10, 2023. Daniel struggled to sleep ...two a.m., four a.m. When would the night be over? Near dawn he fell asleep only to be awakened by Rick's shower and loud singing. He dragged himself out of bed, programmed his breakfast from the kitchen butler and wandered out on the verandah. Rick joined him.

"Excited, Danny boy?"

"About as excited as going to a funeral."

"You got it...but what a classy production. You saw the last one?"

(Rick already knew this but baited Daniel to see what he would say.)

Daniel guarded his words. "My grandparents were in it. As my mother said, 'It was a historic event'."

"What's the Guardians' job?" Rick asked.

"Escort the participants and prevent trouble, I guess."

"Sounds simple."

"Simple, if it's not someone you care about."

Rick made a mental note to document that statement. Couldn't hurt. Daniel didn't seem to be in tune with Omega I's health initiative for eliminating the useless and deformed. After all, the old people had lived their useful lives. At this point they were only a drain on society.

They finished their breakfast, dressed in utilities and joined the Guardians waiting for the bus to Sedona. Today was setup. Tomorrow they'd drive participants to the event.

"Sedona as cool as it looked on satellite?" Rick asked.

"You got it...but..."

Rick raised his eyebrow. "Daniel, get over it, think of your grandparents as heroes."

Daniel withdrew. What was he thinking, telling Rick what he actually thought? Rick was the enemy. Heroes, that's what Mom had said. Think of them as heroes. *Heroes who didn't have a choice? Heroes because they were old and sick and no one cared? Heroes because some evil men decided to solve the country's financial problems with this "one should die for the many" program?*

No matter what spin Daniel put on the Ascension, there was nothing positive to him about helpless people herded against their will into a mass sacrifice. And the only thing that would make him feel better was to punch the lights out of anyone spinning the hero talk—especially Rick. No offense to his mother.

Upon arrival in Sedona, the sergeant led the Guardians to the stage and walked them through the ceremony. Finally, Daniel and Rick received their assignment to set up the chairs for the orchestra, and assist the special effects man whose job was to produce clouds surrounding the ascendant. They set up the atmospheric smoke machine, a compressor feeding vapor over dry ice.

Other cadets positioned the satellite for broadcasting, set up the sound system for the musicians, even placed trash containers at intervals. Kept busy, Daniel had no time to think—and Daniel knew thinking was not productive.

The cadets finished the setup and piled into the bus which took them to The Hideaway for spaghetti. The large-planked porch held tables with red and white checked tablecloths. Suspended over a canyon, the tables overlooked the top of ancient aspen trees. The sound of Oak Creek echoed below.

Everyone was in a festive mood, whistling at the waitresses and telling jokes but all Daniel could think about was tomorrow when hundreds of people would die in the second Ascension.

Chapter Forty-three

September 11, 2023–Ascension II.

The day of the Ascension, Daniel checked the pick-up schedule, relieved not to find Sadie's name on their list. He knew she'd been diagnosed with Alzheimer's. They had four clients to deliver to Sedona. This time, he signaled Rick that he would drive. Rick shrugged, deciding not to push Daniel's buttons although he thought Daniel was weak for letting his grandparents' Ascension get to him. Rick's grandparents died years ago. You were born…you died…what difference—natural with a lot of pain, or quick and easy like this.

The second Ascension followed the pattern of the first. The Native American flute player warmed up the crowd, followed by the Phoenix Symphony. The president in his somber navy suit and blue tie thanked the families for their sacrifice and the event began. Daniel stood in line until it was his turn to accompany a participant. He looked over to see who he matched up with. A lovely blonde woman about thirty sat in a wheelchair waiting her turn. She handed Daniel a card which said, "Paralyzed in auto accident—roll chair to center stage and leave."

Daniel wheeled the young woman to the center of the stage. Her eyes searched his face…dark, sad eyes…eyes he'd never forget. Then the girl and the chair fell into the vault and Daniel was nearly overcome by the sickening odor of lethal gas. He left the stage and ducked behind the backdrops, gagging, the realization finally getting through his soul that the victims were gassed and he was enabling their death. He was finished. No more...he couldn't do it.

"Something wrong, soldier?" a Guardian military policeman asked.

"No, no, I guess not." *Another lie.* Daniel joined the cordon of cadets making a human fence around the candidates. He wouldn't take another...he'd stay in the line.

The Ascension ended with the playing of the Star Spangled Banner. The sergeant led the boys behind the stage. "I'll explain this once. It's simple. The ascendant is given a heavy lethal dose of gas, falls into this crematorium and by morning ashes to ashes. Tomorrow, you will take an urn of ashes with the individual's name, date and inscription 'that one may die for the many' to the family with a video of their heroic sacrifice. Is that understood? Dismissed."

The van was quiet on the way back. "Drop me in the parking lot, Rick I've got something to do."

Rick nodded, stopping to let Daniel out. Daniel headed for the Black Mustang, grabbed his helmet, revved the motor and peeled out, dust and gravel ricocheting behind him. He headed up Highway 17 the wind biting his face, dirt stinging his cheeks. He pulled off at the Black Canyon exit and gassed up at the cafe. Calmer, he decided he couldn't go back to the Guardian apartment. He was sick of Rick. He was sick of the Guardians. He just wanted to be home.

Harry heard the door creak and knew it would be Daniel. He got up and slipped out of the bedroom, trying not to wake Judith.

"Daniel, is that you?"

"Yeah, it's me, Dad."

Harry didn't have to ask what the matter was. He knew. He'd watched Daniel take the young woman to the stage on TV. "You okay?"

"No, I'm not okay. I'm tired of hurting people...aiding a government that doesn't care about its people...I don't want to take ashes in an urn to remind the family they had a loved one killed."

Daniel put his head in his hands. "I don't know how to explain it. I stuff my true feelings until I'm ready to explode. I loved the Guardian training, Dad. But I don't like what we're asked to do. My head is full of questions and we're told not to question.

"I'm afraid to have a friend...afraid I might say something...and get reported. I don't believe in any of the initiatives we're asked to carry out. I'm doing things I never thought I'd be asked to do. It's turning me into a liar and pretender." Daniel stopped.

Harry and Daniel's voices woke Judith. Although she couldn't hear their conversation, she could tell by the tone of Daniel's voice that he was really upset. She turned on the security system and flipped through each room until she located them in the den. Then she listened.

"They gas them, Dad. They fall into a crematorium. They don't ascend; they descend. Ashes to ashes. And tomorrow our job is to take an American flag, a memorial urn with ashes, not even their own ashes, to the families and thank them personally."

Judith tiptoed to her office. The letter laid waiting. Tomorrow, she'd call.

Chapter Forty-four

J udith reread Captain Stern's letter. One paragraph caught her attention:

"If you notice a change in your son, discontent, anxiety over his duties, or unhappiness in his assignments, please call me on my personal line—602 478 0399. Your information will be handled by our professional staff."

The letter was old, but Judith took a chance that the number for Captain Stern was correct. He would know how to help Daniel. She picked up the phone and dialed the captain's private number. As a mother, she had to do something, Harry only listened. The phone rang five times before a man's voice answered.

"Captain Stern."

"Sir, my name is Judith Jordan. I'm the mother of Daniel Jordan, a new Guardian."

"Yes, I know Daniel. How can I help you, Mrs. Jordan?"

"I received a letter when Daniel graduated instructing me to report any problems."

The captain turned on a recorder. "Please continue, Mrs. Jordan."

"Well, Sir, Daniel comes home nearly every weekend. *She had to be careful how she worded this.* "He's always been enthusiastic about his Guardian training and assignments, but something's changed. I hear him talking with his father. I think it's the Ascension. Daniel was close to his grandparents and they were assigned to the first Ascension. Perhaps he isn't over losing them. I don't know. I just think there's a problem."

"Do you expect him this weekend?"

"Yes, I think so."

"We'll take care of him, Mrs. Jordan. You did the right thing to call."

Captain Stern typed Daniel's name into his office computer. The young cadet's training record appeared. The captain remembered the court-martial as he continued to look over Daniel's record. His sergeant commended him as a good team player and a sharpshooter. Captain Stern checked Daniel's high school academic record. Intelligent. *Maybe that was the problem, perhaps Daniel was a thinker.*

There were two code alerts. One was a note from his partner, Rick Hathaway. *"Daniel seems disturbed by the Ascension. I heard him say, 'The Ascension is fine unless someone you care about is involved.'"*

The other code alert was from the garage—Daniel was signing vans out after hours. The garage showed six trips, two a month, each putting four to five hundred miles on the van. *Where are you going Daniel?* What have you been up to?

Captain Stern picked up the two-way radio that connected him with the Guardian Military Police. "Pick up Daniel Jordan at 25821 Trails' End off Dynamite Saturday night. Take him to the Fort Thompson Retraining Center."

To follow up Captain Stern sent a fax to Fort Thompson: *"Sending Guardian Daniel Jordan for retraining. Expect him Saturday, late night. His file will explain. Keep in touch." Captain Stern.*

Eager to get home after a difficult week, Daniel mounted his motorcycle and left the Guardian condo. The twenty-four-hour leave kept him sane. His weekly talks with Dad helped him unload his worries and questions. And his mom always planned a favorite meal. He pulled into the driveway, climbed off the motorcycle and ran into the house.

Hi, Mom, I'm home."

Judith turned off her computer. "Ribs tonight, Danny."

"Mom, you're the greatest."

After dinner, Daniel and his dad sat down to a game of chess. Penny kissed them and left for a sleepover with her friends.

"Have fun, Pen. Watch out for those vampires!"

"Daniel!"

Daniel and Harry watched the ten o'clock news and then Daniel crashed. The Ascension had taken a lot out of him and he was bone tired. At midnight, he heard a screeching sound. *Was it a coyote?* No, someone was pounding on the front door.

"Open up."

Harry rolled out of bed. *Who could be at the door at this hour?* He grabbed his rifle. Midnight visitors might mean trouble. "Hold your horses, just a minute."

Two military police armed with stun guns stood in the doorway.

"What do you want?"

"We're here to pick up Daniel Jordan. Is he here?"

"Yes, but he's sleeping."

Harry pointed up the stairs. The MPs wasted no time. Jerking open the bedroom doors, they continued down the hall until they reached Daniel's room.

"Daniel Jordan?"

Daniel was wide awake now.

"We have orders to pick you up."

Daniel felt strong hands grab his shoulders on either side. The MPs lifted him to his feet. One handed Daniel his pants then shoved him out the door and down the stairs.

Judith flew out of her bedroom "What is it? What's going on?" Her heart beat faster as she saw the two MPs manhandling Daniel. "What do you want with Daniel?" she asked.

"Captain Stern's orders, Ma'am."

Pushed into the military Jeep, his head spinning, Daniel asked, "Where are you taking me?"

"Better if you don't ask too many questions, son. Our orders are to take you to Fort Thompson."

The retraining center...cold fear chilled Daniel. Who had reported him? He'd been so careful to keep his questions to himself, always giving the politically correct answer. The only place he'd spoken from his heart was...at home. His dad was the only one who knew his concerns.

Harry stood frozen. "Why are they taking Daniel?"

Judith bit back tears. "It'll be all right. Captain Stern said they would help Daniel."

"Judith, my God, what have you done?"

Chapter Forty-five

Fort Thompson rose out of the desert like a concrete cloverleaf. The moonlight lit up three round buildings connected by a circular desert garden. Daniel had heard tales of reprogramming as a cadet and it was the last place he'd ever hoped to see.

The MPs shoved Daniel out of the car. He stumbled in his effort to follow them. They unlocked a steel door with a touchpad depositing him in a small windowless room. A thousand questions flooded his mind. Why was he here? What would the retraining be like? How long would he be a prisoner? What would happen to him after he was finished? Would he still be a Guardian? Exhausted, he fell asleep on the single bed.

The aroma of bacon awoke Daniel. A large breakfast waited on a small table in the room. Further inspection found a leather chair, desk with a communication center, and a shower.

A soft sensual voice droned constantly through a piped-in sound system. He listened. "You are a Guardian…a soldier of the president's elite corps…you are to obey your commanders…loyalty will be rewarded…do not question… only accept the wisdom of minds seeking the good of the many"…and on and on. *Well, that robotic chatter would drive him crazy if he wasn't already,* Daniel thought.

He tackled the breakfast trying to make the best of the situation. A note on his tray instructed him to shower, put on the clean Guardian uniform that lay on a chair and be ready for an interview with Captain Taylor at ten o'clock.

At ten o'clock sharp, the metal door to his room slid open. A different MP led him to the private office of Captain Taylor. When he entered, Daniel faced a glass wall that looked out on the circular cactus garden he'd seen last night. The sounds of a small rock waterfall caught his attention. Captain Taylor sat at a desk directly in front of the garden studying a file.

"Daniel, take a seat." Daniel could feel the captain's eyes looking him over. The silence was heavy as he waited for the captain to continue. *Be careful, Daniel.* Ever since he'd been picked up by the Guardian MPs he'd asked himself, *Why? Who had betrayed him? What was he supposed to have done?*

"As I told your mother on the phone, we are here to help you. She said you were having some problems?"

Daniel closed his eyes. *Mother.* She must have overheard him talking to Dad. But how could she think reporting him to Captain Taylor would help? Daniel said nothing and the captain continued,

"I have two areas of questioning for you, Daniel. First, tell me about the Ascension of your grandfather and grandmother."

Daniel winced. The captain had taken aim and hit the bull's-eye. "Sir, as my mother would put it, it was carefully and beautifully executed."

"I want to hear your view, Daniel."

Daniel decided to be honest with the captain.. "It was painful, sir."

"In what way?"

"Sir, I loved my grandparents, I miss them very much."

The captain relaxed, relieved that Daniel said nothing political—nothing against Omega I's policy of euthanasia. He made a note to test Daniel with the thought analyzer to determine the depth of his emotional trauma. The test would give the captain a basis to plan treatment.

The captain had addressed two notes in Daniel's file. Now the third, "Tell me, where do you go when you sign out a van on the weekend?"

Caught off guard, Daniel hesitated. *What could he say?* "I don't understand, sir."

"You are signing a van out putting five hundred miles on it at least once a month, Daniel. Surely, you are going someplace."

Puzzled, Daniel tried to think. *Was Dr. Hart doing something on his own? If he explained, would he endanger the doctor and the people at Rancho Christo who had become his friends?*

"I'm waiting for your answer."

"Sorry, sir. I have no answer."

Surprised at Daniel's refusal to answer his question, the captain decided not to press him. He'd wait until Daniel's treatments made him more cooperative. "Thank you, Daniel. You are dismissed. The MP will escort you to the test lab where they are waiting to do the TA. I'm sorry...the thought analyzer."

Captain Taylor watched the athletic young Guardian leave his office. He liked what he saw. He even liked his refusal to accuse anyone else—loyalty. *How do we convert your loyalty to Omega I and the Guardians, Daniel?* On the other hand, where had Daniel taken the van? If answering endangered another cadet, he doubted Daniel would confide. Perhaps, he was taking a weekend jaunt with friends into Mexico.

Daniel entered the sterile environment of the lab where he was told to undress and put on a white cotton jumpsuit. The attendant taped electrodes to each side of his head and to the base of his skull. Terror swept over him. He'd always kept his thoughts to himself. It was a safety mechanism. What was a thought analyzer? The technician sat down across from him twisting dials that lit up a machine. Daniel didn't speak but watched as the electric wave darted across the screen and converted his thoughts into words. *This machine could tell what he was thinking.* He was doomed.

The technician cleared her throat, "I'll ask a question... say a certain word...the machine will record your thoughts."

"Ascension..."

Before Daniel could restrain himself, the word *death* appeared.

"Ascension," she repeated.

"Grandpa George"

"Grandpa George"

"Murdered"

"Guardian"

"The President's arms and legs"

"Initiatives"

Daniel fought to block his thoughts. How could he keep the machine from reading his mind? Then he had an idea. He'd concentrate on the yoga mantras as soon as the question was asked.

"Initiatives"

"Better minds than mine"

He read the analyzer. So far so good.

"Rick"

"My partner"

"Rick"

"Don't trust him"...Be careful, Daniel.

By the end of the session, Daniel was drained. Had he beaten the machine? Not at first. What registered before he began the yoga mantras? He thought it was just the Ascension which the captain already knew about and maybe, something about his partnership with Rick.

Captain Taylor studied the TA results on Daniel. So the Ascension was at the heart of Daniel's problems. Looking further, he laughed, recognizing the Guardian mantras being repeated time after time. So... Daniel *was* a thinker. *Well, Daniel, you'll not outthink me.*

The captain designed a strenuous program. He ordered magnetic laser treatments for the morning. They would knock Daniel out for a few hours and be followed in the afternoon by electroconvulsive therapy (ECT) which would produce electrical seizures in Daniel's brain. He hoped by bombarding the frontal lobe he could quickly erase memories of the Ascension. True, it would also erase memories of Daniel's grandparents but if the captain watched carefully, Daniel should be helped without the insertion of a Vagus Nerve Stimulator.

In 2005 the FDA ruled that in cases of severe depression an implant could be placed in the brain. Little research had been done yet on the Vagus Nerve Stimulator but it seemed like a good option for depressed people. Later, as with most attempts to overcome depression, patients helped for a while regressed, some becoming suicidal.

The captain's only other option for treatment was an old one. You overdosed the patient with glucose causing a convulsion and then a coma. By monitoring the coma time, the doctor could alleviate the depression. Memory loss followed and ability to learn new things was difficult. *Don't make me use this treatment, soldier.* After a few weeks, he'd retest Daniel when he had less ability to resist.

The captain hoped Daniel realized this was not a game. And if it was mind chess, the captain had a doctorate in treatment of the psyche. His goal was to obliterate Daniel's short term memory—to erase all memory of his grandparents' death. By the end of the treatments, the captain would *know* Daniel Jordan.

Daniel returned to his quarters. He was hungry but there was no food in the room. He tried to analyze the situation. No physical force had been used yet. He suspected the room was bugged, but who did he have to talk to? A voice from the communication center interrupted Daniel's thoughts, instructing him to dress in a scrub suit and be prepared for therapy in thirty minutes.

Daniel obeyed. Thirty minutes later, an attendant also dressed in blue scrubs came to get him. He had no choice but to follow the attendant. They entered a room filled with machinery and Daniel was told to sit in a padded chair in the middle of the room. The attendant placed a metal helmet on his head. Daniel closed his eyes feeling helpless. The first blasts of laser sent a searing pain through his head. The second left him unconscious.

Captain Taylor watched Daniel from the viewing window. He intended to monitor Daniel closely. He saw potential in the young cadet and didn't want the technicians to turn him into a mindless robot like they had the Alaskan cadet from Daniel's Guardian class.

Daniel awoke unsure where he was. Then he remembered—the laser and the pain. How long had he been unconscious? A soothing voice droned on. . . *"You are privileged to be chosen as a Guardian...A Guardian is trustworthy... a Guardian obeys orders without question...a Guardian upholds the truths of Omega I. Omega I is all knowing. You do not have to question Omega I."*

Vulnerable in his semiconscious state, Daniel resented the voice planting suggestions in his subconscious. But he had no control and no choice except to listen.

A Guardian appeared, with a lunch tray. "Hey buddy, try to eat." The soldier looked uncomfortable. He hated to see a fellow Guardian in this place. He cleared his throat speaking quietly. "If you want to get out of here, don't fight the system. Understand?"

Daniel understood. The food was all right but it was tasteless. He forced himself to eat, wondering what was next. The laser treatments were brutal. Had the captain said he'd be getting electric shock treatments? At two p.m. the medical assistant returned with a syringe full of medication. Daniel's instincts were to knock the syringe out of his hand. He hated drugs. He was an athlete. Athletes did not put drugs in their body. But it wasn't his body any longer. His body belonged to the government. The Guardian's words came back to him, "Don't fight the system." Daniel stumbled along behind the attendant, the medication making him drowsy. He vaguely remembered climbing onto a gurney. The overhead clock registered three p.m.

Daniel opened his eyes. His arms and legs were in leather restraints. Every muscle in his body twitched. He felt sick. Really sick. He hoped the attendant monitoring his treatment knew he was awake. In a few minutes, the attendant returned and unsnapped the restraints. He handed Daniel a towel and told him to sit up carefully. Daniel wiped his face with the cool wet towel. The attendant led him back to his room where he collapsed in the leather chair. The ECT treatments wiped him out. He had no energy. He stared at the blank white walls. This was only day one. What would his body and mind be like in a few weeks? The MP brought him a salad, steak, and baked potato. He had no desire to eat.

"Listen soldier, eat. You're gonna need your strength."

Daniel looked up. "Thanks."

"Don't thank me, kid, just do what they tell you. Hear me?"

He nodded. The steak tasted like cardboard and he found it hard to swallow. He choked the last bites down. When he finished, he sat in his chair, the sultry voice sedating him. The MP picked up his food tray. "Just so you know, kid, you'll be swimming laps every night. Helps wear off the treatments. I'll be back for you at 1900."

Daniel struggled out of his scrubs and into the swim trunks. How much swimming would they expect him to do in this condition? He learned the answer five minutes later —fifty laps.

The cool water slowly revitalized him. The sluggishness departed. With each stroke, his mind said, "Stay in the game, Daniel, just stay in the game."

Chapter Forty-six

What happened to Daniel Jordan? Alarmed when Daniel didn't report for duty, Dr. Hart scheduled a meeting with his partner Rick Hathaway. Daniel's disappearance meant trouble for Daniel and possible danger for Dr. Hart. Unaware that Dr. Hart used him to rescue patients from certain death by driving them to Rancho Christo, Daniel might reveal his secret missions to the authorities giving them the directions to the ranch. Dr. Hart leafed through the memos on his desk finding a memo from Daniel's partner. Rick was requesting a new assignment which could mean only one thing—Daniel wasn't coming back. Rick would be in the office at 0900.

"Nan…"

"Yes, Doctor."

"Call the Command Center. See what you can find out about Daniel Jordan."

"Yes, sir. Anything else?"

"Send Rick Hathaway in as soon as he gets here."

Nan was worried. The doctor was taking too many risks—the surgeries on the senior citizens, rescuing Maria Sanchez and her Down syndrome baby and sending Daniel to Rancho Christo with patients and supplies. The other doctors in the clinic were suspicious. They watched his operating room. And now Daniel Jordan was missing. She'd tried to warn Greg, but the doctor was obsessed, focused only on what good he could do in his position at the Center for New Age Medicine. It was getting dangerous.

She dialed the Command Center.

"Sergeant Olson."

"Sergeant Olson, this is Nancy Coleman at CNAM. One of our Guardians has disappeared—Daniel Jordan. Can you check to see if he's been reassigned?"

"One moment, Ma'am. He's been reassigned to Fort Thompson."

"Thank you, Sergeant."

"You're welcome, Ma'am."

Nan stuck her head into Dr. Hart's office. "He's been reassigned to Fort Thompson."

Dr. Hart signaled her to join him. What happened? Fort Thompson was a state-of-the-art mind retraining center. He shuddered to think what they would do to the young cadet. Even worse, since Daniel held the secret of Rancho Christo, many lives were in the hands of the young Guardian. "It's a mind retraining center, Nan."

"What does that mean, Doctor?"

"It means they have access to everything in Daniel's mind."

"Rancho Christo?"

" I'm afraid so."

Nan sat down. The transfer of Daniel Jordan would endanger them all—her included. "What can we do?"

"I think we need to pray."

Nan lowered her head. "Doc, I have an intense feeling that you are in danger."

"We're all in danger, Nan." The doctor opened a locked drawer, pulled out an envelope and gave it to her. "You need to read these."

Nan read the first document. It was a deed to Rancho Christo. The second document was a handwritten will conveying the ranch to her. "But Doc, I can't accept this."

"If anything happens to me, Nan, take this deed and get out. Go to Rancho Christo and take care of the people as well as you can. Work with your pastor. I had Daniel take medicines, supplies and food there. Elena takes care of everyone but she will need someone to manage it and administer the medical clinic. We can only hope the government doesn't discover the connection. If we only knew what they know..."

The Prophet looked at the document before him. Three doctors from the Center for New Age Medicine reported violations on Dr. Hart, the president's friend. All pointed to surgeries performed on the elderly and chronically ill. He picked up the hot line to the president.

"Omega I."

"Sir, I have a report here on your friend, Greg Hart."

"Go on."

"Seems he's running his own 'save-the-elderly program,' performing surgeries and medicating the chronically ill."

"I was afraid of that. Well, he did set up CNAM for us... but perhaps his usefulness is over. Eliminate him before there's trouble."

"An accident?"

"Whatever is the most useful."

Nan slipped the file drawer key under the lining of her shoe. The doctor had also given her a map to Rancho Christo. At least they had a plan. Now if she could just get him to go there himself. She looked up to see Rick watching her.

"The doctor said to bring you right in when you came. Follow me." She knocked, opening the door slowly.

"Rick, come in and sit down," called the doctor.

Rick obliged the doctor. He looked up, "What are you gonna do with me, Doc?"

"What do you want me to do with you, Rick?"

"I'd like a transfer to the Guardian Police, if that's possible."

"I'll see what I can do. Tell me, what have you heard about your partner's disappearance?"

"The MPs picked him up Saturday night at home. He's at Fort Thompson getting his brain fried, I guess."

"Do you have any idea what the problem was?" Dr. Hart watched Rick closely.

"Yeah, I gotta good idea. He wasn't in tune with Guardian work. He was real upset having to work the Ascension."

"How did the authorities know this, Rick?"

"It was my duty to report it, sir. That is our instruction."

Dr. Hart turned his back, "You'll receive new orders in a few days. Check your communication system. You may have to take a couple of days off. Dismissed."

The telephone rang making Judith jump. Her nerves were terrible.

"Mrs. Jordan?"

It was a strange voice. "Yes."

"Captain Taylor, Fort Thompson Retraining Center. I've interviewed Daniel and I'm sure we'll be able to help him."

Judith sighed. "Oh, I'm so glad, Captain. I was worried. The MPs were so rough."

"I'm sorry about that. I can assure you Daniel's already started treatment."

"Do you know how long he'll be there?"

"Not yet, but I'll keep an eye on him and be in touch. These things can take a while."

Judith closed the communicator feeling Harry's eyes on her back.

"Who was it, Judith?"

"Captain Taylor, from Fort Thompson Retraining Center. He said Daniel has started treatment. He assured me they could help him but he didn't know how long it would take."

"Do you have any idea how they help him, Judith?"

Waves of ice traveled down her spine. "No, I suppose... counseling."

Harry laughed. "I really can't believe you, Judith. It's a military retraining center. The least they will do is give him mind drugs, probably electroconvulsive therapy or worse."

Pale, Judith set her jaw. "No matter what you think, Harry, I did it for his own good."

"Did it occur to you that this might end his career in the Guardians?"

Judith's eyes opened wide. "You don't think they'd take him out of the Guardians, Harry? I never thought...I just knew he was unhappy. I heard..."

"You eavesdropped. You overheard him confide in me. Why didn't you just talk to us?"

"I knew neither one of you would listen to me. You act like I'm the enemy. "

Harry was dumfounded. Was his wife really that naïve? He took a deep breath. "Daniel is in danger at Fort Thompson and if you weren't an atheist, I'd ask you to pray for him, but that's only something my parents would do, and they're dead now."

Judith turned and walked away. She'd never seen Harry so angry. He acted like she'd done something wrong when all she'd done was try to get some professional help for Daniel. She was not the villain. She'd acted like a good mother. She wouldn't believe Captain Taylor would do anything to hurt Daniel.

Chapter Forty-seven

*W*as it night or day? Daniel was losing track of time. Why was he locked up in this prison? It was hard to remember. So many treatments. He was losing it. A wave of nausea and diarrhea hit him forcing him into the bathroom. Finished, he leaned on the sink and examined his reflection in the mirror. A stranger returned his gaze...vacant eyes... pasty skin. *Who are you, Daniel?* he thought. For the first time in his life, he was really scared. The door opened and the MP entered with his dinner.

"Do you know how long I've been here?"

The MP set the food down. "Kid, deal with one day at a time. Eat. You need to eat."

Worse even than the treatments was the isolation. He was a team player, a family member, a friend. Soon he'd be talking to himself just to hear a voice. He threw up. The treatments had taken a debilitating turn and Daniel realized from the image in the mirror that he was going downhill fast.

The soldier turned toward him. "You've been here five weeks."

Five weeks. Everything was foggy. Macaroni and cheese...he picked up his fork shoveling the tasteless pasta into his mouth. Everything tasted metallic. The only thing he looked forward to in this place was his evening swim. It felt normal. He'd swum fifty laps all through high school.

Pushing the tray away, he hobbled back into the bathroom and reached for his swim trunks. At the pool he noticed he wasn't alone. Someone was swimming laps in the pool. He studied the boy's face. It was the Alaskan Guardian. Had he been here for a year? Deciding to risk an encounter, Daniel swam across the lane. "Ted? Is that you?"

The Alaskan Guardian stared at him.

"Ted, it's Arizona, don't you recognize me?"

Vacant eyes returned the stare. There was no recognition. Ted swam off repeating the statements of the anonymous voice on the intercom. "I'm a Guardian...I don't ask questions. I swim laps."

Daniel's heart stopped. There was no one there anymore. Horror hit him. The vacant eyes were the same eyes that looked back at him from his own mirror. The treatments would turn him into a walking zombie, too. He pounded the water swimming furiously. What could he do? How could he resist? He flipped over on his back and with each stroke felt more desperate. Tears ran freely down his face. *Oh, Grandpa,* he thought, *what can I do?* What a terrible nightmare...he was going to lose his mind...he'd never be home again. By the time they finished his treatments, he wouldn't even know his own family.

He closed his eyes and prayed to his grandpa's God, the one who created the stars, "Oh, God, if you can hear me, I need your help." A soft yellow light began to fill his inner vision. The strange light dissolved his pain and anxiety, leaving him calm. Words drifted into his mind: "*I am the light. The light shines in the darkness and the darkness cannot overcome it.*"

Daniel knew these words. They were the beautiful poetry he'd read in Grandpa's Bible. The face of Grandpa George formed. He was saying something, "Search for the light." Then the vision faded. Daniel finished his laps drying his hair on a towel. Was it a hallucination?

The next day the laser attendant placed the helmet on Daniel. *"Help me, God, please...help me."* The gentle yellow light blanketed his mind just as the laser was beamed. This time Daniel felt no pain although the second blast still knocked him out. When he awoke, his mind wasn't foggy.

The electroshock treatments were only three times a week or so he thought. Physically, Daniel was still losing ground because he couldn't keep any food down.

Captain Taylor scolded himself. He'd intended to keep a close eye on Daniel Jordan but he'd been called into Phoenix for meetings with the Prophet. He stared at the young Guardian who stumbled into his office. "Daniel?"

Was someone speaking to him? Or was this another delusion?

"Daniel, do you know who I am?"

"Yes, sir."

"Who am I, Daniel?"

"You're the captain, aren't you?"

We're losing him, the captain thought. "Daniel, I'm taking you off the ECT treatments. Do you still want to swim laps?"

"Yes, sir."

"Fine." The captain stroked his beard. He must do something to reactivate Daniel's mind or what was left of it. "I want you to begin some computer work—situations where you must choose the appropriate course for a Guardian. Are you up for this, Daniel?"

"Yes, sir, I'll try, sir. But sir, could we stop the laser treatments, too? They make everything so foggy."

The captain tapped his pen on the desk. "I'll stop them for a while, Daniel. Do you remember why we started the laser treatments?"

"To erase my memories of the Ascension."

"You still have them?"

"I see my grandpa's face sometimes, but I think it's the drugs. I think I'm hallucinating." Daniel paused as if trying to think what he wanted to say. "It doesn't hurt to think of him anymore."

The captain wished he could believe this but he had his doubts. At any rate the boy needed to eat and get his health back. Perhaps the mental exercises on the computer would salvage some of his brain cells. *What a waste*, he thought. Well, time would tell. "Try to eat, Daniel. I think your appetite will return. Send the lessons to me over the computer and we'll go from there."

"Yes, sir. Thank you, sir."

The captain had no children. He admired the young soldier struggling to obey his command. Had Daniel's memory been altered? He didn't trust the TA tests to discern Daniel's mental condition. When Daniel was better, the captain would send Ariel to ascertain Daniel's state of mind. Ariel had never failed him.

Chapter Forty-eight

Harry hadn't spoken to Judith for days. He couldn't believe her naiveté. Anger smoldered in his heart ready to burst into flame at the least provocation. He didn't trust himself and, evidently, neither did Judith. She used Penny as a conduit for anything she wanted to say to Harry. And he was tired of Penny saying, "Dad, Mom wants you to know," but he guessed they needed a buffer.

One night Harry turned on the World News Network trying to relax and catch the day's news. A car bomb explosion in the parking lot of the Center for New Age Medicine caught his attention. Harry leaned forward The newscaster continued…

"Dr. Gregory Hart fell victim tonight to a terrorist bomb. Witnesses in the underground parking lot said when Hart stepped on the accelerator, his black SUV exploded in flames. The fire authority put out the fire but was unable to resuscitate the doctor. President Blackstone had this to say, 'Dr. Hart served his country well. He designed the Center for New Age Medicine and organized the first two Ascensions. He will be missed.'"

Harry turned off the satellite. A car bomb meant only one thing: Someone had assassinated Dr. Hart.

Spellbound, Pastor Neal Matthews watched the eleven o'clock news as the SUV exploded and burned. He spoke quietly into his wrist phone. "Nan, call me. It's urgent."

Nan Coleman saw her digital phone blinking. Showered and ready for bed, she hesitated, but checked her message — Pastor Matthews. She voice dialed his number.

"Pastor, Nan Coleman here. You said urgent. I hope—"

"Nan, did you watch the eleven o'clock news?"

"No, it's such a downer I've given up watching."

The pastor hesitated. "Dr. Hart was killed tonight by a car bomb. They're saying terrorists and the president has already made a statement to the media."

Nan sat up in bed all thought of sleep gone. "You're sure?"

"I have Channel 12 on now. The fire authority was unable to resuscitate him."

Stunned Nan whispered, "I can't believe it, pastor. I just saw him a few hours ago. We even made a plan in case of trouble."

"What trouble? Did he have enemies at CNAM?"

"I think several of the other doctors objected to the surgeries he did to help the chronically ill and old people."

"Enough to kill him?"

"No, enough to report him."

"To?"

"To the vice president...you don't think the president..."

"It was the president who gave him the job, wasn't it? Nan, this puts you in grave danger."

Nan was crying. She could hardly hear the pastor. Dr. Hart was her best friend. *Could he have suspected something?* "Should I go to work tomorrow?"

The pastor had no answer. Would they interrogate Nan as his assistant? He was afraid for her. Yet, if she didn't go, her superiors would immediately suspect her. "Go in, Nan. I'll pray for you. But get a plan, your time at CNAM is over."

Nan hung up the phone. Taking the key from her shoe, she dressed and left for the office, afraid by morning it would be locked down and under heavy surveillance. Staying away from the underground garage, she parked on the street, slipping through a side door with her magnetic pass.

She avoided the elevator climbing the stairs slowly to the twenty-third floor. Winded she paused to catch her breath. Was she too late? Would the police be in control of the office? She pushed open the glass door. The office was dark—a good sign. Not wanting to be seen through the windows, she resisted the urge to turn on the lights and moved stealthily into the doctor's office. So far, so good. She unlocked the drawer, removed the will and deed but as she turned to crawl out, she heard footsteps on the stairs.

She crouched under the desk as the office door opened. *"Oh, Lord, keep me as the pupil of Your eye,"* she whispered. The footsteps stopped. She held her breath afraid that her breathing would be heard. *Leave, leave. Everything's okay.* The footsteps walked into the surgery. Lights blazed, ricocheting into the outer office area where Nan crouched hidden. What would they think if they found her hiding under the desk? Was it the night security guard? Shaking, she stayed in the shadows of the desk. All she could see were the heavy brown shoes of a man. In what seemed like hours, the lights went out and she heard the door lock.

Paralyzed, she sat still listening as the footsteps entered other rooms of the complex followed by the slam of a door. Fifteen minutes passed. Her knees ached from being doubled up. Slowly, she moved out from behind the desk and crawled to the door. The hallway was dark. She crept down the stairs, anxiety causing her heart to beat irregularly. At the bottom of the stairway, she heard voices and a siren. She tried to pull herself together. *Be a nurse. If you're stopped, identify yourself as a nurse there to help.* She stood up, pushed the heavy door open and walked into the night. She'd return at 7:30 a.m.

Judith kept reapplying her lipstick. She dried her eyes but a steady stream of tears smudged her makeup. Unable to concentrate on playing bridge, she'd left her bridge club meeting. She thought things at home couldn't get any worse, but the car bombing of Dr. Hart had really upset Harry. *You'd think he thought the government had something to do with it rather than terrorists,* Judith thought. The president's words for the doctor were full of appreciation. It was a dangerous world. Who'd ever think terrorists would blow up someone in Phoenix? Well, at least Daniel was safe at Fort Thompson. Did he know that his doctor had been killed in an explosion?

Captain Taylor sent for Daniel. He wished to verify his physical condition and ask him a few more questions before assigning him to new duty. Was he still Guardian material?

Watching Daniel enter the office. Captain Taylor thought his color looked less yellow. He'd put on a few pounds and, thankfully, his eyes were clearer. "Daniel, there's been an accident at CNAM. A car bomb explosion killed Dr. Hart last night." He watched Daniel's reaction. Daniel appeared startled.

"Dr. Hart? Dead?"

"Yes, he's dead. The administration of CNAM will be turned over to one of the other doctors. Is it possible that Dr. Hart had anything to do with the five hundred miles a month you put on the vans, Daniel?"

Daniel lied. "No, sir, he had nothing to do with the miles on the van." Daniel had never told such a blatant lie before but if there ever was a time for one, he knew it was now.

"You're sure?"

"Yes, sir."

"And you still can't tell me where you were going?"

"No, sir. I'm sorry, sir."

The captain was frustrated. He needed to understand Daniel in order to assign him duty. He had only one hope... Ariel.

"You are dismissed, Daniel. You're looking much better."

"Thank you, sir."

Daniel finished his computer simulations, forwarding his answers to the captain. While doing the exercises, he asked himself only one question. What was the Guardian response? But he had many questions, one especially bothered him. What had really happened to Dr. Hart?

A timid tap on the door surprised him. His watch said 2200. The door slid open and the most beautiful girl-woman Daniel had ever seen stood before him.

"May I come in, Daniel?"

Daniel longed to talk to anyone. Isolation was against his friendly nature. Strangely, an alarm went off inside him and his heart beat uncontrollably. Was something inside him trying to warn him of danger with this girl?

"Sure, come in. Who are you and what's your name?"

"Ariel," answered the violet-eyed, black-haired girl. "My name is Ariel."

Daniel stepped back into the room. Ariel was dressed in filmy layers that reached the floor.

"I'd like to be your friend, Daniel. Would you like that?"

Daniel felt like a wounded animal. He longed for the lovely girl to touch him, to comfort him, to caress him. As soon as he formed those thoughts, the beautiful creature seemed to understand. She crossed the room leading Daniel to his bed. Lying down, she motioned Daniel to lie beside her.

Ariel began to stroke his face. She ran her fingers down his arms drawing her body close to him. Weeks of loneliness and isolation melted under her touch. Even though alarm bells had gone off again, he couldn't resist the invitation.

Daniel felt dizzy. He had to get a grip. Instinctively, he knew if he gave in to the passion soaring through his body, the sensitive young woman would know his innermost thoughts. Daniel pulled away from her. He needed space between himself and the girl. She was, after all, sent by the administration.

"Ariel," he stuttered, "tell me about yourself. Have you been assigned here long?"

Ariel's eyes clouded. She withdrew her gentle stroking. Her face hardened and she seemed to change before Daniel's eyes, no longer appearing young but old and ageless. She didn't answer Daniel but left the bed and vanished as strangely as she'd come.

Captain Taylor played the video tape of Ariel and Daniel on the monitor. At first all seemed to go well. Ariel never failed her mission, able to transform herself into the male's ideal woman. What had gone wrong? Unknown to Daniel, she was a clairvoyant, a psychic who could easily ascertain Daniel's inner emotional state.

The captain was disappointed. He thought all young men sowed a few wild oats. Daniel was too smart or he had a kind of ethics which belonged in another century.

Either way, Daniel Jordan was still a puzzle.

The captain did not want to risk sending Daniel back to the Center for New Age Medicine. He still had no answers to the mystery of the van and he knew he would get none from Daniel. Daniel was protecting someone. And although the captain knew he could break Daniel, he also sensed Daniel would never betray a friend.

Chapter Forty-nine

Nurse Nan Coleman's hands trembled as she dressed for work. Even though she and Pastor Neal decided that it would arouse suspicion if she didn't go to work, she stalled, remembering last night when she'd almost been discovered by security. She choked back tears. *Why Greg? Had the president ordered his death?*

Nan parked in the underground garage far away from the car bombing. She forced herself to get out of the car, walk to the bank of elevators, place her thumb on the elevator security pad and wait while the doors slid open. Without looking, she pushed the twenty-third floor keypad. At 7:30 a.m. the elevator was empty. Her heart raced; fear surged to a state of panic. Then the door opened and she saw World Federation agents combing Dr. Hart's office. One of the agents stopped her.

"I'm sorry, Ma'am. You can't come in."

Speechless, Nan controlled her emotions. "Sir, I work here. I'm Dr. Hart's nurse."

"Not today, Ma'am. Maybe you should go home. We'll want to talk to you, later, ask you a few questions."

Relieved, Nan noticed the other doctors in the clinic already seeing patients. She felt out-of-place...unneeded. She typed a short note of resignation on her smartphone stating that because of Dr. Hart's death, she was accepting a new position. As an afterthought, she opened the hall closet and removed her coffeemaker, remembering the daily forbidden coffee. *I'm so sad to lose you, Doc. We had fourteen good years.*

She drove to Pastor Neal's house unaware of stoplights or streets. The door opened before she could ring the bell and she found herself embraced by the pastor's sister.

"He's waiting for you in the den," Nellie said. "I'm so sorry, Nan."

Nan nodded, following Nellie to the den.

Pastor Neal put his arms around her. "How did it go?"

"Fine, no one recognized me or seemed to care. The Feds were going over his office and I'm so glad I went in last night..."

"Last night? You went into the office after I spoke to you?"

"Yes, it was scary...but I had to get the will and deed to Rancho Christo before the police and federal agents closed the office. I was afraid to wait until morning and I'm glad I followed my instincts. I didn't turn on any lights but almost got caught by security."

"You got the deed?"

"Yes, and Pastor, Dr. Hart asked me if you could add Rancho Christo to the safe houses list. He wanted you to be able to send people in danger or come yourself. It's about four hundred and thirty miles from Phoenix in the Lordsburg, New Mexico, area on Highway 10. He used one of our Guardians to take people he wanted to save and to stock it with food and medical supplies. If anything went wrong, he wanted me to go there, manage it and run the little hospital infirmary on the property." She stopped to catch her breath, revealing the will and deed.

"Did he take the number, Nan?"

"Not to my knowledge, I think he planned to go there himself but he waited too long."

"You're leaving soon?"

"Yes, if anyone from the church needs a place to stay, I paid my rent ahead. There's six months left in my lease. I'll go back and pack up a few things, then I'll be off."

Pastor Neal took her hands, "*Lord,*" he prayed, "*You've told us You'll never leave us or forsake us. I know You'll bless Nan in her new work at Rancho Christo. Let her feel Your guidance and presence every hour of the day. Keep her safe till Your coming. In Jesus' name. Amen.*" Then he added, "Let's stay in touch, Nan."

Nan left the pastor's home relieved to have a plan. It wouldn't be long before the federal agents searched for her. She'd leave today. Her answers to their questions would put her in danger, if not in prison.

As she prepared to leave, she looked around her apartment spotting the little rocking chair that had gone through four generations of her family. She would have to leave it behind. Swallowing a lump in her throat she spoke to the Lord. "*It's only a thing, Lord, I'll be all right.*" She packed her car with a suit-case of clothes, a bag of shoes, her coffeemaker, Bible, hymnal, a special afghan her mother had made her, some photos, and her laptop. She had room for one other object and decided to take her two yellow canaries, Chip and Chirp. She set their cage on the backseat with a bag of bird seed and looked around the apartment. Had she forgotten anything? She wrote a quick note to the landlord saying she would be taking a new job and a friend or two might stay in her apartment while she was gone.

Trying to leave behind her anxiety and grief, she jumped into her VW hatchback. Thankful for the hybrid car, she turned on the GPS—Highway 10 all the way. The GPS showed Lordsburg in Hidalgo County in an area of ghost towns. Its population was under 6,000. The ranch was about ten miles south of Lordsburg. She concentrated on her driving, at least comforted that she had a place to go and people to care for—a new beginning.

Chapter Fifty

C aptain Taylor rarely got personally involved with the soldiers sent for retraining but Daniel Jordan intrigued him. His gut told him Daniel wasn't Guardian material—too inquisitive. He'd done as much for Daniel as he could with Fort Thompson's retraining methods and thought Daniel's emotional pain about his grandparents' death in the Ascension had decreased. It was decision time. What assignment could he give Daniel?

Perhaps, if he looked through Daniel's original records from high school he'd get some insight. The Captain pulled up his complete record on the computer and leafed through it. Good student...recommended for the College of Professional Athletes in San Diego. The captain paused. Daniel had given up a career as a professional athlete with all its glamour and money to become a Guardian. What motivated this decision? He made a note to ask Daniel. He scrolled through the other reports stopping to read the comments of teachers, coaches and his principal.

Physics teacher, John Frye: "Daniel has a fine mind, eager to learn, full of questions, a real researcher."

Coach Tillman: "An outstanding athlete and leader, often sacrificing personal glory for team work."

Principal Jacobs: "A well rounded, individual, dependable, loyal—an excellent scholar and athlete."

The captain reread the entries. So he was right. Daniel was a thinker…a deadly quality for a Guardian. Even assigning him to the Guardian Training School would really not utilize his best qualities, though it would use his athletic skills. He buzzed Daniel's room signaling the guards to escort Daniel to his office. There were a few questions Daniel should be able to answer.

Captain Taylor stood facing the desert garden. He allowed Daniel to wait on him. Suddenly he turned and confronted Daniel. "Daniel, let's lay our cards on the table. I'm going to be candid with you. It is my duty to choose your next assignment. I'm finding that difficult. I suspect your unhappiness with the Guardians goes deeper than the Ascension. I'm satisfied that you have less pain in thinking about your grandparents, but is that really the problem? Can you tell me that you would be able to assist in further Ascensions? Or is it the Ascension itself you have a problem with?"

Daniel remained silent.

"I need an answer."

"I would be more comfortable as a Guardian trainer, sir."

The captain paced behind his desk. "That might be a possibility, Daniel. I've thought about sending you back to the school. You could also continue here at Fort Thompson assisting other soldiers in treatment. How would you feel about that?"

What could Daniel say? Sir, I don't want to be part of turning bright young men into vegetables…

"Tell me what you are thinking, soldier."

"I would be happier at the training school, sir."

"And why is that, Daniel?"

"I'm an excellent marksman. I work well in a group situation and could encourage team play. I'm a leader. I could use that to help train new Guardians."

The captain listened with interest. The young man knew his assets. He was careful, correct but... "Daniel, do you really want to be a Guardian?"

"Sir, I have three more years of duty."

"One more question, I've reviewed your high school records. You are to be commended. I am perplexed as to why you would give up an opportunity to attend the College of Professional Athletes with so promising a career ahead of you in world soccer.

Why did you make this choice?"

"Sir, I want to be honest with you. I love my country and being a Guardian seemed like a wonderful way to serve her. On the practical side, only two of us got the opportunity to apply from our school—I didn't want to let the school down. And lastly, I figured with fifty guys trying out, the odds were fifty-to-one that someone else would be chosen."

The last comment made the captain smile. It was the first nineteen-year-old statement he'd heard from Daniel and it rang true. "By the way... Ariel...why didn't you take advantage of her?"

Daniel hesitated. "My parents and grandparents had one great love for their lives. I want to wait for mine." Daniel continued, "She worked for you, sir."

"Thank you, Daniel, you are dismissed. You will continue your retraining until such time as I've made a decision."

Daniel left the office.

Captain Taylor still had reservations about Daniel serving as a Guardian. He shuffled through the stack of paperwork that littered his desk, picking up a high profile sheet from Omega I's office. A youth council...could this be the answer? He wasn't sure he understood the purpose of the youth council being solicited by the advisory council to Omega I. He read the profile...creative...original thinking... team player...a perfect description of Daniel Jordan, if he sent only the reports from his high school and the Guardian

Training School. *Well, there should be some perks to being a captain.*

Normally, he would leave this kind of nomination to others but ....perhaps, this was the wastebasket into which he could deposit Daniel. The Guardian training and the weeks of retraining were a financial investment. Daniel was only nineteen. The risk might be worth taking. Captain Taylor relaxed. He liked the idea of saving someone. He erased all record of Daniel's time at Fort Thompson and forwarded an application on Daniel's behalf.

Daniel was still uneasy in the captain's presence. It wasn't like the authorities to overlook something like putting five hundred miles a month on a government van. What was Rancho Christo? Could Dr. Hart have risked his life to rescue people from their fates? Daniel made up his mind not to expose Rancho Christo, whatever the cost. A knock on the door interrupted his thoughts.

"Daniel, the captain wishes to see you."

Would this be the final confrontation? If he didn't answer the captain's questions, would he be subjected to more brainwashing techniques? Beads of sweat broke out on his forehead.

"Captain."

"Daniel, sit down. I'm recommending you for a new youth council being formed to act as consultants for Omega I. It's a very select group. I don't know if you'll be accepted." He studied Daniel noting relief in his eyes. "You will under no circumstances be sent back to Phoenix to the Center for New Age Medicine. If you are not accepted, I'll try to put in a word for you at the Guardian School." He paused, "Would you like to call your parents? I think they would like to hear your voice."

Why wasn't the captain pursuing the van question? Why would he recommend Daniel for this special council? "Yes,

Captain, I'm sure my parents are worried. Will I be going home before my new assignment?"

"I am undecided at this point. You'll wait for the Council of Twelve's decision here, however. I want you to continue the retraining program until that time."

The captain dialed the long distance number for Daniel, pointing him to the communication screen. Then the captain did an amazing thing. He left the room.

Penny answered the video phone. "Jordans'. This is Penny."

"Hey, kid."

"Danny is that really you? Where are you?"

"Here at Fort Thompson."

"Are you all right, we've been so worried."

"Yes, I'm all right. Are the folks home?"

"Just a minute, Danny. Mom, Mom, it's Daniel and he's all right."

Daniel saw his mother's face on the communication's screen.

"Daniel, is it really you?"

"In the flesh, Mom."

Judith smiled. Whatever they'd put Daniel through he could still make his corny jokes. "Are you coming home soon?"

"I haven't been given my assignment yet, Mom. I'd like to but I'm not sure. Is Dad home?"

"Penny went to get him. Dad, it's... Daniel!"

"Son, it's good to hear from you."

"It's good to hear your voice, too, Dad."

"Everything okay?" Harry realized Daniel had no way to tell them of his ordeal. It was a miracle just to hear his voice and know he was all right.

"Dad, I may not be coming back to Phoenix. I think I'll be given a new assignment."

Harry was afraid this might be the case. "Let us know what your assignment is when you can."

"All right, Dad. Don't worry about me. I'm okay. Tell everyone good-bye, okay?"

"Okay, Danny, remember we love you."

Daniel closed down the communication center just as the captain returned.

"Your parents well? Glad to hear from you?"

"Yes, sir. Thank you, Captain." Returning to his cell, Daniel was overwhelmed that his worst nightmare, returning to CNAM, would not happen but instead he would be given another opportunity. He held little hope that he would be accepted for the youth council with his time at the Fort Thompson Retraining Center on his record, but he hoped that he would not be assigned to the Retraining Center—home of the walking dead.

Chapter Fifty-one

His hands shaking, Daniel flushed the two small white antidepressant tablets down the toilet. No more drugs! He wanted his life back which meant he had to control his body—not rely on drugs or doctors. But the ECT treatments had really done a job on him and his brain was not reacting well to cold turkey withdrawal. Sunlight hurt his eyes. And for once Daniel was glad he lived alone. Talking wore him out. He looked down at his hands which continued to shake. If life was like a merry-go-round, Daniel was standing outside watching it spin, unable to get on.

He continued his retraining program even though the Guardian scenarios seemed unreal. Trying to get his strength back, he worked out twice a day in the gym avoiding the Guardians who used the facility for their own exercise. He trusted no one. Days grew into weeks. With the drugs gone, his appetite returned and Daniel could finally taste food. The best part of the day continued to be the evenings when he swam his fifty laps. The cool water relaxed him, taking away the sluggish pain and fog that surrounded his brain.

A Guardian buzzed his door. Daniel stood up.

"The captain wants to see you, Daniel."

Daniel's heart froze. In a few minutes he would hear his assignment. His life was so screwed up. *Please don't assign me to Fort Thompson.* He shuffled down the hall behind the

Guardian, dragging his left leg—a nerve evidently injured during one of the ECT treatments. A picture formed in Daniel's mind of running down the soccer field deftly kicking a goal. He turned off the hurtful memory and concentrated on his meeting with the captain. He longed to be home with his family at the ranch and out of this hospital prison.

The captain stood facing the desert rock garden. Daniel waited. Abruptly, the captain turned, his eyes surveying Daniel. The cadet's skin no longer appeared pasty, and his weight appeared better even though Daniel's clothes still hung on him. "Daniel, sit down." The captain fingered the papers in his hand. "You have been accepted as the Arizona representative for the President's Youth Council."

Daniel couldn't believe his ears. *What did this appointment mean?* "But sir, how could they with my time here at the retraining center?"

The Captain looked grim. "I only sent your high school records and certificate of graduation from the Guardians, Daniel."

The captain did what? He didn't tell them Daniel had spent a year in the retraining center or that he'd been court-martialed? "Sir...I don't know what to say."

"It gives you a new beginning—a 'do-over' so to speak. Are you up for the challenge?"

Daniel looked down at his feet. "I hope so, sir." Tears of unbelief smarted in his eyes. He brushed them away, ashamed of his emotions.

"Just do your best, son. You're made of good stuff. Make the most of this opportunity."

"Thank you, sir."

"I'll contact your family with the news. I'm afraid you won't be able to visit them. I have an osprey leaving Luke day after tomorrow with a delivery for the capitol. You'll be the only passenger."

Daniel saluted the captain and followed the Guardian back to his cell.

The Guardian shoved Daniel good-naturedly, "You did it, buddy! You did it!"

Daniel grinned. The merry-go-round was slowing down so he could get on. A new life. He was the newly appointed Arizona representative for the President's Youth Council. Unbelievable. Would he be stationed in Washington D.C?

Captain Taylor relaxed. Daniel Jordan was no longer a problem to be solved. But, he wondered, what would the young man think when he stepped off the plane and saw the nation's highly secret new capitol nicknamed, The City of Gold?

Book Two

2025

City of Gold

S.D.Burke

Chapter One

"Hey, buddy, you my cargo to the Capitol?"

Daniel gazed into the weary eyes of a sixty-year-old man dressed in faded jeans and a Harley T-shirt, surprised the pilot wasn't military and that his plane was a vintage Boeing chopper.

"Yeah…I guess I am," Daniel said.

Seeing the kid look him over, the pilot said, "Expecting a military escort? Well, this is your lucky day; you get to ride in Old Flo, named her after my mom."

"What kind of plane is this?" Daniel asked.

"Not a plane, Son, a cargo helicopter. She's carried Marines and supplies all over the world, even in Iraq. Flo's a faithful bird, a Boeing CH 46 Sea Knight, 1960 vintage, to be exact."

Daniel smiled as Jerry patted the belly of the old helicopter, finished his last minute checks and turned to Daniel.

"Shove your backpack in between those exotics and climb in."

"What's with the plants?" Daniel yelled as he eyed the cargo of prickly pear, bird of paradise, orchids, bougainvillea, and flowering trees.

"Getting ready for some big TV presentation in the Capitol. These boys are the finishing touch. The one good thing is they give off oxygen, lots of oxygen."

Jerry watched the young Guardian sink down into his seat and try to buckle his seatbelt. Daniel's hands shook with the effort. "You all right, kid? You aren't going to heave on me are you?"

Daniel stopped, unable to slide the seatbelt together. "No...I don't think so."

Jerry leaned over grasped the seatbelt and shoved it together until it clicked. He felt sorry for the kid and wondered what the wackos had done to him in the funny farm. He pushed the engine starter button and the helicopter blades began to whirr.

So ... you ready for the big adventure?"

"Yeah, I could stand the change."

Jerry frowned. How could he warn this kid that all would not be roses in the new Capitol? How could he tell him that he wouldn't be the pilot lackey for the administration if they hadn't blackmailed him into service by agreeing to keep his mother off the Ascension rolls—payment for his secret service to the Prophet? Whatever the kid had experienced at Fort Thompson would not compare to what lie ahead, if Daniel got off on the wrong foot with the administration.

After take-off, Daniel's head fell forward and the young Guardian drifted into a deep sleep. For two hours, Jerry fought increasing turbulence. A sudden jerk jarred Daniel awake. He heard the pilot curse sharply under his breath A whiteout. A wall of snow. The helicopter was caught in a blizzard. Suddenly, Daniel saw an iridescent dome open before them. Jerry set the copter down on a landing pad on the roof of one of the buildings.

"Go ahead, son," the pilot instructed, "this is where you get out."

Daniel jumped down from the cockpit of the helicopter and stood transfixed by the golden city sprawled below him. His first impression was that someone tried to create their idea of heaven. It was breathtaking.

Jerry got to work unloading the exotic plants. Daniel watched, then, started to help Jerry unload the plants.

"No, kid, I got it covered. That's why they pay me the big bucks. Save your energy."

Jerry stopped and looked out over the city, "Well, what do you think?" he said. "Doesn't look much like DC does it?

Daniel stood gaping at the city before him. Light danced off blue glass buildings, each with its unique design. Some had gardens and pools on the roofs. The giant overhead dome provided a natural greenhouse even in winter for palm trees, bougainvillea, bird of paradise, orchids and lilies.

Strange metallic vehicles glided soundlessly along the golden streets pulled by solar rays ricocheting off a forty-foot golden sculpture. A stream wound its way under footbridges and streets that appeared to be glass block with threads of gold. Daniel whistled low under his breath.

Outside the city, but still under the dome, Daniel saw vineyards, orchards, wheat fields and herds of cattle. The Capitol appeared self-sustaining. From his military training, he realized that a capitol located inland would be easier to protect from nuclear missiles. The city took his breath away. Its beauty shocked him more than the ECT treatments ever had.

Maybe his mother was right. This president was creative. He was taking America into a new era. The pain of his early Guardian years and the deaths of his grandparents were in the past. A great weight lifted off Daniel. He remembered Captain Taylor's words as he left Fort Thompson, "It's up to you now, Daniel."

"I'll do my best Captain. Thanks for giving me another chance."

S. D. Burke is the author of *Putting Humpty Dumpty Together Again.* She has published articles in HomeLife magazine, The Christian Communicator, and The Secret Place. She and her husband George split their time between Michigan and Arizona. *2025* is her first work of fiction. She invites questions or comments on her website www.2025sdburke.com.

CPSIA information can be obtained at www.ICGtesting.com
Printed in the USA
BVOW071108100612

292170BV00001B/33/P